BEOWOLF

CERTIFIED CERBERUS TACTICAL K9

FIONA QUINN

THE WORLD OF INIQUUS

Ubicumque, Quoties. Quidquid

Iniquus - /i'ni/kwus/ our strength is unequalled, our tactics unfair – we stretch the law to its breaking point. We do whatever is necessary to bring the enemy down.

THE LYNX SERIES
Weakest Lynx

Missing Lynx

Chain Lynx

Cuff Lynx

Gulf Lynx

Hyper Lynx

Marriage Lynx

STRIKE FORCE
In Too DEEP

JACK Be Quick

InstiGATOR

Fear The REAPER

Striker

UNCOMMON ENEMIES
Wasp

Relic

Deadlock

Thorn

FBI JOINT TASK FORCE
Open Secret

Cold Red

Even Odds

KATE HAMILTON MYSTERIES
Mine

Yours

Ours

CERBERUS TACTICAL K9 TEAM ALPHA
Survival Instinct

Protective Instinct

Defender's Instinct

DELTA FORCE ECHO

Danger Signs

Danger Zone

Danger Close

CERBERUS TACTICAL K9 TEAM BRAVO

Warrior's Instinct

Rescue Instinct

Hero's Instinct

CERBERUS TACTICAL K9 TEAM CHARLIE

Guardian's Instinct

CERTIFIED CERBERUS TACTICAL K9

Beowulf

This list was created in 2024. For an up-to-date list, please visit www.FionaQuinn-Books.com

If you prefer to read the Iniquus World in chronological order you will find a full list at the end of this book.

BEOWOLF

CERTIFIED

Cerberus Tactical K9

BY

FIONA QUINN

The Players

Eastern District of Virginia

- **Olivia Gladstone, U.S. prosecutor**
- Jaylen, best friend (and her baby Matilda/Tilly)
- Henrietta, Olivia's Cockapoo
- Mickey Pauley soon-to-be ex-husband
- Steph Abner, United States attorney
- Gail, paralegal
- Kyle Offsed, defendant
- Candace Hockman, witness

Cerberus Tactical K9

- Bob Palindrome, commander Cerberus Tactical K9 – Team Alpha
- **Beowolf, Certified Court Facility Dog**

Panther Force

- **Thadeus (Tad) Crushed (callsign Nutsbe), tactical operations coordinator**
- Sy Covington, Iniquus lawyer
- Titus Kane, tactical force commander
- Thorn, operator
- Gage, operator
- Margot, operator

The Players Continued

Strike Force

- Gator, operator
- Deep, tactical operations commander

FBI Joint Task Force

- Steve Finley, special agent, terror
- Rowan Kennedy, special agent, Eastern Europe

1

Nutsbe

Sitting in his wheelchair, facing the sunlit window, Nutsbe knew what was coming.

His brain clanged with warning bells, his nerve endings sizzled and sparked. Nutsbe was fighting himself even before he had to fight the guy grabbing the back of his chair.

Nutsbe struggled to keep his muscles loose.

It took a concentrated effort not to clench his abs, not to grip the arms of his chair, not to turn his head and look. But Nutsbe knew that any reflexive motion could take him out of the fight before the fight even began.

He was going to ignore his impulses.

Breathe, he reminded himself. *Relax*.

Planting a foot on Nutsbe's chair stabilizer to use it as a fulcrum, the backward lurch that followed was always a roller-coaster-belly flight.

As the front wheels lifted from the ground, it was a given that the attacker would jump to the side and out of the way, protecting his knees and shins from the unwieldy metal tumbling toward him. He'd take an extra step back to keep from getting pinned under the flailing weight of a hundred and eighty pounds of gym-hardened muscles sitting in the chair.

When Nutsbe first tried fighting from his wheelchair, he thought the best self-defense move in this circumstance would be to reach over his head and grab his opponent. Using a tight grip to soften the drop, maybe his weight and momentum would drag the attacker down to the ground, where surprise would allow him to get some kind of lock on the guy.

But a human was a human; a brain was a brain.

Few people trained on how to attack someone in a wheelchair. So they jumped back. And that overhead reach always left Nutsbe grabbing at thin air.

With a little practice, Nutsbe figured out how to take advantage of the aggressor's jump. He learned not to fight on the way down. He spent that moment of disequilibrium tucking his chin to protect his head from taking that initial hit, preventing a cracked skull, the concussive effects of a sloshing brain, and whiplash. Spreading his arms wide, hands facing backward, Nutsbe waited for the jolting stop when he smacked the ground, dispersing most of the energy from his fall. The rest of that energy became the momentum he needed to throw his legs toward his head, rolling over his shoulder, bringing himself upright, hands lifted and battle-ready.

That Nutsbe was suddenly sitting up and reaching offensively for the attacker was unexpected.

Surprises were good in a fight. The brain stuttered as it realigned with the new information. It put the other guy back on his heels.

It was only a split second, but sometimes that made all the

difference. It would be Nutsbe's best shot at subduing an attack.

Nutsbe grabbed his opponent's pant leg. Curling his fingers into the fabric, he trapped the cloth in his balled fist, preventing the guy's escape. Then, Nutsbe jerked his elbow along his ribcage, dropping the man backward onto the mat. With his opponent's leg tethered, Nutsbe's sparring partner, Chuck, couldn't do his own rolling energy dispersal. He took the full brunt of the hit.

There was no time for self-satisfaction. In a real-world fight, Nutsbe's task was to pay attention to how the assailant reacted to the fall. That initial muscle-memory response to a fight could tell Nutsbe the level of his opponent's combat skills.

Chuck threw his arms wide, curving his head as he tipped over, a trained fighter, not a street rumble junky.

There was good and bad in that. Newbie fighters, with their flailing kicks and wild haymakers, were dangerous in their unpredictability. Knowing that his opponent would be precise and strategic had to come into Nutsbe's calculations as he moved to stop the attack before the stutter of surprise passed and his opponent recalibrated.

Nutsbe grabbed Chuck's foot, twisting the heel, forcing the man onto his stomach. Like with the head, the person who controls the foot controls the opponent's body. As soon as Nutsbe had Chuck on his stomach, he pressed the guy's heel toward his thigh, depriving his opponent of a quick-release tactic. With a hurried shuffle over the pebbled red mat, Nutsbe positioned himself between Chuck's knees to keep him from successfully twisting free.

Chuck's nimbleness and athleticism allowed him to crawl forward when Nutsbe's stress hold would trap most people.

Instead, Chuck was able to flip onto his back, putting Nutsbe at a severe disadvantage.

In a split second, Nutsbe had shoved himself into position, sliding either leg around Chuck's thigh and gripping him tightly in place.

As Nutsbe rolled onto his elbow, he rammed Chuck's foot under his armpit, trapping Chuck's ankle. From there, Nutsbe sucked in his stomach, curving forward to make a small space between his chest and Chuck's leg. That was the magic of this move. Once Nutsbe got Chuck's calf fully wrapped into a nice tight hug with his left arm, he could grab that wrist with his right hand. In a street fight, Nutsbe would continue his roll forward. Adding his weight to that joint lock would destroy his opponent's ankle.

Chuck patted Nutsbe twice on the shoulder while saying, "Tap. Tap." A sign that Nutsbe should immediately stop and release.

Boundaries were about safety.

No means no in all civil society.

Billy raced his wheelchair forward, stretching out his hand to make a slashing motion through the air.

The fight was over.

Spinning in his wheelchair, Billy faced the dozen or so students ranging in front of them and said, "From here, class, the only help for Chuck is from a friend. Hopefully, Chuck came to this fight alone. If the aggressor had buddies around the corner, the violence and destruction would notch up considerably. Knock him out, break his ankle, anything it takes to keep it from being a pile-on." Billy turned his head toward Nutsbe. "Over before you even got started." He shook Nutsbe's hand. "Well done."

Nutsbe sat on the mat, his thighs wide for stability. He

had detached his below-knee prostheses for this demonstration, and they were across the room, leaning against the wall.

Silicone cups covered Nutsbe's implanted metal bone anchors that held his prostheses on with a quick-latch system, thanks to osseointegration—a way to implant hardware into the bone so an amputee can easily attach their prosthetic legs. Using the silicone covers was a safety step Nutsbe took to protect his sparring partners should he kick out and accidentally make contact.

Chuck popped up to stand and took a few bounces to reset his system. He caught Nutsbe's gaze. "New move."

"You have to stay fresh." Nutsbe grinned up at him. "Stale fighting leads to apathy. That's never good."

"Never." Chuck reached out to shake Nutsbe's hand and then plopped down so they sat side by side.

Looking over the beginner-class students, sitting absolutely still, with their eyes wide and their brows up around the hairline, Nutsbe thought they looked spooked.

Billy must have thought the same because he started with, "No one's going to dump you on the ground today." He maneuvered his chair around to face the class square on. He sat there, gently smiling, giving them a moment to process what had just happened.

Watching someone getting tipped in a chair hit a nerve.

Even knowing it was coming, even having the mats beneath him, even having explicitly asked his fighting partners to push him hard for his own benefit, Nutsbe found that backward drag terrifying.

After a moment, the anxiety settled.

"Since this is your first class, we thought a demonstration was important. My name is Billy. I'm paralyzed from the waist down from a car accident when I was in my teens.

That's Chuck." He extended his hand Chuck's way. "We're instructors here. For well over a decade, we've worked with people with disabilities using all manners of assistive apparatus, tools, and weapons. By weapons, I mean both dedicated weapons that you've prepositioned on your body or on your assistive technology but also weapons of convenience—pens, phones, lamps, anything within reach—for self-defense. As you train, we'll keep you as safe as possible but challenge you too." He stopped and turned to Chuck, tag team.

"Billy and I have each been martial arts trainers for around fifteen years. We started training in various martial arts forms when we were kids. We also both have doctorates in physical therapy. Your own medical team will be directing your work with us. So you come as you are. You show up. We figure out your strengths and how to overcome your weaknesses together. You do you. No comparing allowed. Focus on you and your own self-defense and sense of security."

There were head nods and murmurs.

Chuck reached out his hand to indicate Nutsbe. "Our guest playing an attack victim slash guest speaker today is Tad Crushed with Iniquus Security, otherwise known as Nutsbe Crushed." As usual, there was a beat while people put his name together in their minds, and a titter swept over the group. "You want to say something to start us off, Nutsbe?"

Nutsbe gave a wave. "Yeah, Tad or Nutsbe, it's your choice. I go by either one. As you can see, like many of you, I have below-the-knee amputations." He lifted one leg, then the other. "When it comes to self-defense, using my wheelchair has some unique challenges." He laid his hand over his heart. "One of the things that made me feel the most vulnerable when I was first going out in public with my new body structure was the idea that I was an easy target. I've adjusted my thinking. *Anyone* can be a target." He rocked from hip to hip to find a more comfortable position. "At Iniquus, I work with a team of retired tier-one operators. It seems every Tom, Dick, and Harry wants to throw down with them to see how well they'd fare against a Delta or a SEAL. One-on-one?" Nutsbe pulled his chin back and shook his head. "Not well, I promise you. But anyone can get a lucky punch. You lose a tooth, break a jaw, get shoved into a sharp corner, and split open your head. Anyone can find themselves in a tight spot. Even my teammates—some of the most effective hand-to-hand fighters in the world. My best advice? Vigorously avoid a fight. You're here to build some skills in case avoidance becomes impossible one day." Nutsbe signaled Chuck to come around. "Chuck and Billy asked me to go over some basic fighting concepts with you."

Nutsbe laid back down and signaled Chuck to climb on top of him.

"Let's start here with three psychological factors you'll lean on as you train: resilience, perseverance, mental toughness. Those are three attributes that all of you have been developing." Nutsbe added, "Qualities you already have. Now, you can learn to apply them to another skill set."

Chuck settled his hips above Nutsbe's. Immediately, Nutsbe brought his forearms into play, guarding his neck and face.

"Controlling your mind is paramount. When you're flat on the ground with someone on top of you, panic sets in. It's natural. Even after all my training, I feel it. I want to push him off or struggle to get away from him. But what would that serve? I'd only be exhausting myself and benefiting the attacker." He cranked his head around to see the class. "*Don't help your attacker.*" He turned back and gave Chuck a nod to let him know to engage. "Let's see what could happen if I flailed. First, if I take my guard away to push or pull at him or try to get leverage—"

Chuck's fists came in with slow-motion punches to show the holes that Nutsbe was creating as he floundered around. Chuck's fists made light contact with Nutsbe's nose, eyes, throat, and jaw.

"Do you see that?" Nutsbe brought his arms back into guard position. "Now try it."

As Chuck threw a punch, Nutsbe pressed it away and returned to his guard. "If you flail, not only can he get his punches to land, but he can use your momentum to get you to roll."

Chuck lifted up enough so that Nutsbe could turn over.

"Face down on your stomach is a dangerous place to be," Nutsbe said breathlessly as his lungs compressed with Chuck sitting on his back. "A few punches to the head or neck, and you're unconscious or worse."

When Chuck shifted around as he feigned those strikes, Nutsbe had to battle-breathe through the welling panic. After years of training, he still had trouble detaching from the sensation of drowning. "They can wrap your neck and squeeze your carotid. Eleven pounds of pressure, ten seconds, and you'll go night-night."

Chuck moved to put Nutsbe in a sleeper, sending off do-or-die signals in Nutsbe's brain. With adrenaline coursing through his veins, as soon as he felt Chuck's pressure, Nutsbe tapped out. No reason to torture himself for a demo.

Instantly, Chuck flung himself off. And with relief, Nutsbe turned to the side to address the class. They looked every bit as horrified as they had when he was dumped from the chair. Nutsbe thought these demos might be seeding new anxieties. It wouldn't be his tactic for a new class, but he'd trust his friends' years of experience. They had planned things this way on purpose.

Nutsbe pushed himself to a seated position and tapped his hand on his chest. "Fear tightens the lungs, making breathing hard. No air, no good ideas. Fighting without a plan, without training, without a next move increases anxiety—the sense of claustrophobia. It leads to panic." He pointed at the mat where he'd just laid. "I was feeling panic creep up when Chuck got a lock on my throat. For real, here, we're humans. And that's a biological system that's part of our survival DNA. But panic is your enemy. It's exhausting. You make erratic choices. Remember, a fight is a game of strategy. You move, they move. The best moves win. And by win, I mean you get out of the situation. Two points here, TV and movie fights are bunk. The bad news: The human body can't withstand what the script writers put on paper. The good news: Fights in the street last mere seconds, even with trained martial artists, possibly a minute or so. It's fast. And then it's over. Okay? We just need you on the winning end of the whistle. You can do that."

"To be extra clear," Chuck said, coming to his feet and planting his hands on his hips. "You only have one goal in a fight. Survive and move away. Fighting back is about getting free. You're not an avenging angel. You're not trying to punish anyone. You're not showing them a thing or two."

Nutsbe nodded. "Cool, and precise, and in your rearview. Justice happens in court, with a prosecutor managing the battle. Okay?" He glanced up at the clock. "All right then. That's my time. I'm going to leave it to your instructors— also my instructors, so I'm sure I'll see you on the mats." He sent them a grin to show them that this was fun and he hadn't been hurt.

Chuck went to the side of the room to retrieve Nutsbe's prosthetic legs.

"How many fights have you been in, Nutsbe?" a student asked.

"Real-world?" Nutsbe reached for his legs, then focused on clasping them into place. "Zero."

"But you were in the military. Iniquus Security, right?" He pointed toward the logo on Nutsbe's compression shirt. "They only hire ex-deployed military. So before you lost your legs, how many fights?"

"I was in the Air Force. I dropped cruise missiles on the enemy. Personally, I hope and pray I never have to fight. Property? Take it." He stood up and moved back to his wheelchair, setting it upright and sitting down. Nutsbe found it was easier to roll out to his car rather than push his chair along. "The only reason I would fight is to protect my own body or that of someone who needed my help. I've never found myself in either circumstance."

Chuck brought Nutsbe's gym bag over.

"What does this tell me?" Nutsbe balanced it on his lap, pushing the silicon covers into a pocket, then pulling out his gloves to keep his hands clean from wheel filth as he headed back to Headquarters and his meeting with the FBI Joint Task Force. "Two things. One, chances are good you'll never need these skills. Attacks aren't inevitable."

"But you train," the man insisted. "You *do* expect it."

"Point two, I have found that when I carry a first aid kit in my car, I never need it. It's at the times when I leave the damned kit on the kitchen table to re-stock the bandages that melted from the heat in my trunk that I come across an accident or what have you. Put another way," Nutsbe moved a hand to his chest, "in my life, I've found that being prepared is its own kind of insurance policy against the event ever taking place."

The guy tipped his chin up a little higher.

"Personal observation," Nutsbe said. "My philosophy both at work and in my personal life is prepare and hope like hell you're *never* put to the test."

2

Olivia

Bursting through the side door of the courthouse, the glare of the midday sun momentarily disoriented Olivia. She lifted her hand to shield her eyes, scanning the parking lot for a gaggle of reporters who might be staking out this exit. Finding it clear, Olivia mapped a beeline to her car.

Dressed in her professional uniform of a straight skirt and high-heeled shoes, Olivia didn't want to take a single step more than absolutely necessary.

The nose of her car peeked out enough for identification, and Olivia started toward the adjacent public parking lot. She would leave home extra early on court days to ensure having one of the few coveted spaces here. She loved how the summer-thick trees cast a shadow of privacy over her vehicle. After being the focus of the jury's eyes for hours as she methodically walked the coroner through the prosecutorial line of questioning, Olivia was looking forward to a moment of respite, a picnic in the back seat, and the counterweight wholesomeness of a chat with her best friend, Jaylen.

Today, Olivia had the rare chance to simply fish her phone from her purse instead of waiting to get to her car's glove compartment.

The defendant's brothers had made threats. Not specific enough threats to bring charges, but they'd pushed their toes right up to the line. So much so that Judge Madison issued prior approval allowing Olivia to have her phone on her person while in the courthouse.

It wasn't often that a federal judge would approve a phone in the courtroom—even on airplane mode—but in this instance, there was a genuine fear that if Olivia left her phone in her car per the courthouse rules, she wouldn't be able to call the police for help as she left the building.

Threats to federal prosecutors weren't the norm.

They also weren't that infrequent.

Olivia appreciated the judge's concern.

While she was prosecuting a single monster doing the unimaginable, Olivia believed that the defendant's two brothers were in on the crimes. Her team didn't have the solid evidence that a federal case required to initiate a trial.

They had Kyle Offsed dead to rights, though. He was going to trial, trying to avoid the life sentence he so richly deserved.

Kyle hadn't left jail since his arrest for the murders. That was to protect the public. There was also the benefit—whether Kyle agreed or not—of protecting him from his partners in crime. If his brothers thought Kyle would bring lynchpin evidence against them or testify to their shared culpability, it was possible they'd try to silence him—blood was not thicker than jail time.

When presented with the mountain of evidence against

him, Olivia's team had hoped that Kyle would take a plea deal to a lesser charge and name his brothers.

But that hadn't happened. *Yet.*

Once the jury found Kyle guilty, and he faced a life-without-parole future, there was always the possibility that he would ask for sentencing leniency. He might even get it if he offered up some useful information that would scrape his brothers' scum from out of the societal pot. Olivia was sure that the Offsed brothers would go a far piece to make sure that never happened.

With Kyle tucked out of their reach, Olivia knew that one way the whole vile Offsed brotherhood might try to slide free of repercussions was to get a mistrial. And it occurred to her that if she, the lead prosecutor, were to suddenly vanish, the Offseds might think that the trial would vanish, too.

That's not how things worked.

But was Olivia willing to risk her safety on the assumption that the Offseds were interested in doing an Internet search?

No.

As Olivia sent another glance around the parking lot for any possible listeners, she pressed the quick dial for her boss's paralegal, Gail.

"Hi, Olivia. Do you need Steph?" Gail's voice was a chipper mismatch to Olivia's exhaustion.

"Is she free?" Olivia lifted her fob and beeped her car open.

"Beeping, you must be on lunch break. She's right beside me but on another call if you want to hold."

"I can do that."

"How's the trial going?" Gail asked.

"The jury seems bored," Olivia admitted as she opened the back passenger side door and climbed in. With the sunscreen blocking out the windshield and the trees protecting from the side, Olivia felt she had a good amount of privacy. "I think they watch too much TV and came to the trial believing it would have a stronger entertainment value. I bet they'd give this a one—maybe a two-star review. One lady keeps nodding off and waking up with a snort. The judge gave her a warning." Olivia dragged the door to her, shutting it with a bang and a quick flick of the locks.

"I need the jury to focus. I'm trying to build enough of a knowledge base that they don't let Kyle off because they believed some bizarre plot twist they watched on some CSI show."

Pleased that she had pre-positioned the front seat as far forward as it would go before going into court that morning, Olivia had plenty of room to maneuver as she dragged the top off her cooler. She set the lid on her lap upside down, with the edges making a catch-all system for her food. Any crumbs or spills needed to stay trapped and off her clothes.

"So, what's going on with the jury?"

"Right now," Olivia said, "my witness is factually correct, but his presentation is dry as toast."

"This morning was the coroner, right?" Gail asked. "I mean, science isn't for everyone."

"At this point in the trial, all they've heard was a lot of circumstantial evidence, and I need the jury to buy into my legal theory as we move forward."

"You've got this." Gail's Gen Z supportiveness made Olivia smile. "Tomorrow, you're calling your witness. She survived it. She'll be compelling."

Olivia unwrapped her sandwich and took a bite, setting it on the tray. "Only one eyewitness. You know? Five victims and only one survived," Olivia said, looking at her sandwich, stomach churning. She had to eat. But for now, she'd set the sandwich down to give her stomach a second to settle. "Though, I've been—" Her phone rang with a second caller. Olivia looked down at her screen, saw Mickey's name, and swiped to cut the connection. "I've been getting weird vibes from my witness."

"Weird like you think she was making things up?"

Olivia forced herself to take a bite of sandwich as the phone rang again—Mickey. She swiped it off. "No. She most certainly isn't making things up," she said, talking past the food. "Witnesses get cold feet, sometimes. They don't want to come in and relive."

"I can understand. Ah, Olivia, Steph says she'll call you back as soon as she gets off the phone. I need to go grab something for her."

"Yup. Thanks." As the connection ended, Olivia looked at the green leaves dancing in the breeze. It was soothing.

"You know what I need right now?" she asked her cheese sandwich. "A bit of wholesomeness." She tapped her quick dial for Jaylen and was immediately greeted with a shriek from the receiver.

"Hey," Olivia said, pulling her water bottle from the cooler. "Was that a cry of pain or delight?"

"Delight. Miss Tilly-Matilda is full of herself this morning." Jaylen offered up an exasperated sigh. "I swear I don't know what this child thinks she's up to, but I just picked her up from her highchair. And now I know how she ate her spaghetti all-gone so quickly. She just dumped it into her diaper. It's dripping down her legs. It's only noon, and somehow, I smell like a pig farm. Do you think I'll get into a shower at some point? Are you on lunch break? Wait, it's one o'clock? No wonder my stomach is gurgling."

As Jaylen rattled through jars in search of food, Olivia tapped the speaker on her phone then dropped her cell into the cup holder. Sliding her high heels off to give her feet a break, she spread her toes and rubbed her soles on the carpet. It was an enormous relief after a morning on her feet.

"Okay, I've got the makings of a PB and J and some baby carrots. I'm set."

The phone rang a third time—Mickey.

"Do you need to take that?" Jaylen asked. "Who's calling?"

"The shithead."

Jaylen's next sentence had the gummy sound of words spoken through a mouth full of peanut butter. "In the middle of the day?"

"Yeah." Olivia took a swig of water. "Well, next Tuesday is divorce court. That Wednesday, I wake up a free woman."

"Why is he calling you, though?"

"I don't care. Listen, I need to eat, so you're on speaker. Tell me about your day."

"Lonnie is out of town until Friday, of course. Other than that it's been just normal mommy stuff. Oh, here's a story for you. I told you I got Tilly a big-girl toddler bed?"

"Yup, she like it?" Olivia unscrewed her container of day-old roasted broccoli, settling in to listen to the sheer banality of her best friend's life. Jaylen was a touchstone of normalcy, leading a life messy with vegetable gardens, dogs, a bearded goat, and a dimpled dumpling baby. Olivia needed that steady dose of ordinariness, so she didn't think that all of humanity was as depraved as the violent criminals she prosecuted.

And Jaylen, in turn, needed someone with an adult brain to talk to throughout her day. They kept each other sane.

"I dressed Tilly like a princess, and she laid down under her glitter blanket and fell right to sleep for her morning nap."

"Aww."

"You're a prosecutor," Jaylen said. "You know better than to jump to conclusions like, aww."

Olivia chuckled as she took a bite of sandwich.

"I had trouble sleeping last night, so I thought I'd take advantage of Matilda's nap and get one in for myself. I slept hard, only waking up to Tilly singing to herself."

"Cute," she said, past the food in her mouth.

"Objection. Not cute. While I was sleeping, Tilly took a red magic marker and colored my comforter."

Olivia swallowed and coughed. "The white one?" Olivia's phone rang. "Jaylen, it's my office. I have to take this, don't go away." She tapped the button. "Hey, Steph. What's up?"

"Three fires I thought you should hear about ASAP. And Gail said you were on lunch break."

"Yup,"

"I asked you if you could sit in on Malik's deposition for the grand jury after you're done with court tonight. I know you're swamped with your current trial, but since this new case is your bailiwick, I want to lean on you a bit as the Offsed case resolves. It's a lot. I understand that. I'm sorry."

"It's okay, Steph, I asked to be involved. I'm good to go for tonight."

"Keep in touch. I think that deposition is going to be postponed."

Olivia's lips sank into a frown. "This doesn't sound good."

"Malik was supposed to come in this morning to talk with me," Steph said, "but he was a no-show."

"He's one of the coffin nails you need to bang into place. You called him to check in? Could he have gotten the date mixed up?"

"I called his cell," Steph said, "his office, his home line. I reached out to his emergency contact number—his girlfriend

—she's pretty frantic because she hasn't seen or heard from him in a few days."

"Do you think something happened? Something beyond cold feet?" Olivia pursed her lips hard with concentration. This was a national security case, and a lot was riding on this grand jury outcome.

"I don't know, but he's risking his cooperation status. Speaking of cold feet—"

"Uh oh." Olivia put her hand on her forehead, feeling a wash of dread flood her system.

"The Offsed case. I got a call from Candace. That's actually what spurred this phone call. She says she's very ill and won't make it to the witness stand tomorrow. She wants to know how to tell the judge she's down for the count with an aggressive, debilitating flu. She's in bed and doesn't think that she's going to be up again for weeks."

Olivia's sole surviving witness. "I can ask for a continuance. Judge Madison will want documentation from a doctor, of course. How did she sound to you?"

"Like she was laying it on thick," Steph said. "But I'm a cynic. Maybe she was talking to me while she was clinging to her toilet bowl, getting ready to spew."

"She's been so brave. Really an amazing young woman after all she went through. And here we are *so* close." Olivia stared out the side window, focusing on a squirrel clinging to the tree trunk. "I'm not buying the timing of this illness. Did she say anything else?" Olivia drummed nervous fingers on the cooler lid.

"Yeah, that the last few days she thinks she keeps catching glimpses of Kyle's brothers."

"We have protective orders in place. Did Candace call the police?" Olivia asked.

"The men are on motorcycles with helmets on, so right

now, she's not a hundred percent sure. She's guessing from the shapes of their bodies. But I think that's what's got her terrified. She's moved to a temporary place—a friend's empty rental. I have the address. I'll text it to you as soon as we hang up."

Olivia's lungs caught. "Motorcycles?"

"Another reason I'm calling. You told me you haven't been able to sleep this last week because of the motorcycles revving in your neighborhood. If you think that the Offsed brothers are harassing you, maybe you should consider staying at a hotel until sentencing."

Well, that would make all the sense in the world that the sudden late-night intrusion of motorcycles roaring up and down the neighborhood roads was the Offseds trying to rattle her in court. But how would they have found out where she was living?

"Olivia?"

"Do you know how many people in Northern Virginia have motorcycles? The chance of me being a target is slim to none. Candace, maybe. But she's moved. She happened to get sick the day before her testimony? I'm a cynic, too. We need to focus on getting Candace in tomorrow, even if she's clinging to a puke bucket."

"How do you want to handle this?" Steph asked.

"Okay, new plan. I'm going to assume she's terrified and doesn't want to be retraumatized by being in the same court with Kyle, dredging up the story, and getting cross-examined. So she needs support." Olivia shifted her hips farther back in the seat and sat up straight. "I'm going to call Bob Palindrome."

"Cerberus's court support pooches? Good idea if Candace will go for it. And if the judge signs off. Short notice, though."

"Very short. Before I reach out to Candace with the offer, I'll see if it's even a possibility with Iniquus and the judge."

Her phone buzzed—Mickey. She tapped him silent.

"Defense might hate the idea," Steph said.

"Defense won't have much of an argument," Olivia leaned back until she felt the cool leather through her silk blouse. "Look, I only have a few minutes until I need to be back in court."

Her phone buzzed—Mickey.

"Who is that?" Steph asked. "Do you need to take it?"

"Robo call. I'm on this Candace debacle. I'll keep you abreast."

Olivia ended the office call, then typed a message for Mickey: **Call me again, and I'll file for a restraining order.** She looked it over and erased it before she pressed send. The last thing she needed with less than a week until divorce court was something that might make her look paranoid or aggressive to the judge.

She pressed the button. "Jaylen?"

"I'm still here."

"Sorry. Work. Okay, you were telling me that Tilly colored your white comforter?"

"And the walls in red magic marker. I didn't even know we owned a red magic marker."

"Water soluble?" Olivia shoved her last bite of sandwich into her mouth and reached for her celery sticks.

"Nope. Permanent."

"Ouch."

"I have to get some stain-covering paint at the hardware and repaint the wall," Jaylen's voice muffled as she called out. "Hey! Don't pull the dog's ears, Tilly. He doesn't like that." Olivia waited as Jaylen handled the situation, then returned to the call. "I'm going to bleach the heck out of the comforter and see if I can salvage it."

"Did you get mad at her?"

"How could I?" Jaylen asked, her voice warmed with a smile. "Tilly was delighted. She told me it was pretty. I imagine she was doing it as a gift, a nice surprise for when I woke up. So what could I do? She's two. I got her a pad and told her we only make art on paper."

"I hope it works. Still, you need to hunt around and see if this pen has a twin."

"I can hear you chewing," Jalen said. "Is that celery?"

"With peanut butter and raisins." Olivia shoved the rest of the food into the cooler with their wrappings.

"Harkening back to your youth?"

"It's what I had in the fridge." Olivia wiped her fingers on her napkin and opened her phone contacts. "I'm down to an inch in the milk carton and an array of condiments. I'm eating chef's surprise–basically what I could piece together until I can get to the grocery store."

"When will that be?"

"The grocery? Hard to say. Hey Jaylen, I've got to go." Olivia scrolled until she got to Bob's number. "Thank you for being so normal. Truly, you're my fulcrum."

"Fulcrum? Okay, I've been called worse things. Phone me later."

"Yeah, once I'm out of court for the day. Love you. Kisses for Tilly." With a frown, Olivia pushed the cooler cover to the side while she called Bob. She listened to the ringer: once, twice.

"Bob Palindrome."

"Bob, it's Olivia Gladstone from the U.S. Attorney's office. I'll cut to the chase. I need a last-minute dog."

"Olivia from the Eastern District office, good to hear

from you. I, uhm, could you tell me a little more? What's a last-minute dog?"

With a quick explanation of her situation, Bob said, "Okay, I have a court-certified dog available. The problem is that he needs a court-certified handler. Both Cerberus Tactical K9 teams are in the field along with their support personnel."

"Well, that's disappointing," Olivia said quietly.

"Don't despair. I have one other certified handler I can ask. Tomorrow, you said?"

"Yes." Olivia glanced at her watch and slid her feet back into her shoes.

"Do you know what time?"

"My witness will be called after the lunch break, say around one o'clock or so." Olivia scraped her teeth over her lip. "Would it be okay with you if I act as if things will work out? I haven't broached this with the judge yet, and I also need to ask the witness if this will help. I can call you back once I have my ducks in a row and confirm. I'm doing this a little bit backward."

"Just tomorrow afternoon?" Bob asked.

"The witness will be testifying tomorrow. And she mentioned that she'd like to be present when the jury reads their verdict." Olivia looked toward the building, thinking it would save her walking time and foot pain if there was a closer parking spot. She didn't see anything open along the road. "No telling when that would be. I think let's concentrate on one thing at a time."

"If I can get the handler's schedule cleared, we need to get everyone in a room tonight—you, me, the witness, the handler, and the dog."

"You're bringing in Valor, aren't you?" She opened her door, stepped out, and swept a hand over her clothes. "I know her pretty well already."

"Valor is out on a mission. The K9 I have available is Beowolf."

"Beowolf?" Reaching for her purse, Olivia slammed the door and lifted her fob to engage the locks. "Sounds monstrous. Has Beowolf been in court before?" She turned and started back toward the courthouse.

"Yeah, he's been a court-certified support K9 for the last two years in both D.C. and Northern Virginia. I'm not sending you some mutt we just picked up at the pound."

"I'm sorry." She stepped out of the way of the pickup truck, speeding toward the exit. "Sorry. I just had Valor in mind."

"Beowolf's actually the reason Cerberus got involved with doing this kind of community service. But hey, just so the judge doesn't think you pulled a fast one, you should let them know that Beowolf—that's with an O as in wolf and not a U—"

"Oh, it would have been so much funnier if it were two Os like Beo-woof." She woofed the last sound.

"Ha! And so obvious when you say that. Too late now. Beowolf with just the one O is a bullmastiff."

"Mastiff?" She was breathless from her quick pace. "How big are we talking about here, Bob?"

"Three feet at the shoulder. Two hundred pounds, give or take. No take, just give—two

hundred pounds plus some."

"So, like a pony?"

"That's about the right image." Bob chuckled.

Olivia stepped onto the sidewalk. "Does he fit on the witness stand? We have to keep him out of line of sight with the jury."

"He can be surprisingly compact when he needs to be."

"Okay, well," Olivia smiled at the image in her head, "I'll say mastiff and see if any questions follow."

"Gentle giant." Bob's voice sounded amused.

"Yeah, okay. I'll keep that descriptor in my pocket." Olivia grabbed at the door as a man moved in ahead of her. "I'll pursue it with the judge and the witness. I'll call you back with an update. Thanks, Bob."

She pressed the red dot to end the call. Resting the edge of her phone on her chin, Olivia tried to imagine the tiny box available for witnesses, the size of the chair, the size of Candace, and now add to that a two-hundred-pound dog. *This'll be interesting.* She tapped her screen and scrolled through her contacts until she came to Candace's number.

Standing away from the line moving through the metal detection machine, Olivia made her last phone call before she needed to be back in the courtroom. "Candace? Olivia Gladstone, here." She painted her voice with concern. "Hey, I heard you weren't feeling well."

3

Nutsbe

With a thumbs up from the guard station, Nutsbe pulled through the massive metal gates that protected the Iniquus compound. He liked this drive, the quiet of the green expanding out in all directions, the woods off to the side, and today—with his windows down to enjoy the first crisp day since the heat wave—the rushing waters of the Potomac making the white noise that filled his ears.

There was peace in the drive.

It was a chance to gain focus, a time to let go of personal distractions as he headed to work.

Nutsbe assumed that Command intentionally designed the entry for that very reason.

Everything they did was with great purpose.

Up ahead, the Headquarters building looked a lot like a stately country club. It was the Mata Hari of buildings—in a good way. Beauty on the outside, cunning strategy on the inside. The exterior evoked thoughts of elegance and low-voiced conversations. Yet, walking through the doors, the interior was modern, with machine-like efficiency. There, a hive of men and women joined forces to keep Iniquus's clients safe.

The people signing contracts with Iniquus ranged from the private to the corporate to the institutional. Iniquus was Uncle Sam's favorite nephew when he needed to keep a diplomatic arm's length from history-changing world events.

And it seemed, this week, that Nutsbe was playing a starring role in one of those events. *Sucks to be me,* Nutsbe thought, drumming his thumbs on the steering wheel.

His stomach was making ugly gurgling noises as his body dealt with the stress.

Driving past the guest and executive parking area, Nutsbe locked eyes with Bob Palindrome. Bob was leaning against one of the pillars outside the front entrance to the atrium. His phone was to his ear, but his gaze followed Nutsbe's car. Nutsbe pulled into his dedicated space in the Panther Force section of Parking A. The proximity to the main door was a perk necessitated by being part of a tactical force, where the members might be racing into action—jumping on a plane, roaring down Dolley Madison toward Langley, or Pennsylvania toward the FBI. And it was a definite time advantage not to have to take a shuttle from the barracks or the satellite parking areas.

Today, Nutsbe wasn't going to the FBI. The FBI was coming to him. *Joy.*

Still in his gym clothes from his lunchbreak fight demonstration with Chuck and Billy, Nutsbe would grab a quick shower and change into his uniform before the big meeting got underway.

Exiting his vehicle, Nutsbe reached for the hook in the back. Snagging the hanger with his uniform, he noticed that

Bob had swiveled and still held a straight line of sight, obviously waiting for him. Nutsbe wondered what was up.

Later today, Panther Force would be in the air, heading back from Estonia. Bob might just want a report on how the newest Cerberus Tactical K9, Take It to the Max, did on the flight since Nutsbe had been his temporary handler. But that didn't make much sense. That was a phone call from their respective Headquarters. Bob wouldn't have left Cerberus on the east side of the Iniquus Campus for something like that.

As Nutsbe strode closer, Bob raised a hand, ensuring that Nutsbe knew he needed a word and that Nutsbe wouldn't turn toward the cafeteria entrance.

Nutsbe was hungry. The cafeteria would be good, but with a packed schedule, he'd pull something from the Panther Force War Room fridge, where the concierge unit always kept things stocked. Not just a perk but often a necessity when a tactical force was ramped up, and there was no downtime to play with.

Nutsbe raised his hand in response.

"Good timing that I'm running into you," Bob said.

"Feels like this is on-purpose good timing that you coordinated with overwatch."

Bob grinned. "You have a finely tuned understanding of how things work around here."

Reaching the main entry together, Bob pulled the door wide. "Mind if I walk with you? I know you're about to have a meeting."

Nutsbe checked his watch. He should still have time to get himself showered and ready. Tipping his ear toward the elevator bank, he kept moving. He had a lot to get done in the next twenty minutes.

"I just need a quick yay or nay," Bob said. "I have a prosecutor who reached out to me just now. She's in the middle of a trial, and her witness is either extremely sick with a mega case of the flu—"

"Or terrified of taking the stand." Nutsbe pressed the up button.

"Everyone's money is on the terrified part." Bob slid his hands into his pockets.

"Okay." Nutsbe stepped onto the elevator. "What do you need from me?"

The command structure over at Cerberus was slightly different from the force operations on the main campus. Bob was a commander but also took on a share of the tactical operations tasks. Under the direct command of Titus Kane, Nutsbe was solely focused on supporting his team as the head of their TOC—Tactical Operations Center (pronounced *talk*.) Pretty much any capability Nutsbe had, Bob had it, too. So the ask here wasn't obvious.

The elevator doors slid wide, and Bob followed Nutsbe on, then pressed the button for the tactical force level. "Olivia wants to offer her witness a court support dog."

"We have one of those?" Nutsbe draped his uniform over his shoulder, curling his finger into the hanger wire to keep it in place.

"We have four of those as part of our community support work. Didit started the initiative, and Iniquus embraced it as another way to provide community service. Of those four, we only have one available right now, Beowolf. The others deployed."

"Okay." The car bounced to a stop, and the doors slid open.

"And along with all my dogs out on missions, so are all the folks I normally have that go to the court." Bob stepped into the hall, turning to wait for Nutsbe.

Nutsbe's brow drew in tight. "You need a K9 and a handler."

"Right. And since you went through the K9 handler training and certification, you're on my roster. I checked your file, and you don't need to re-certify for the courts for another eight months."

Nutsbe was getting a sick sensation in his stomach—could be the stress about his meeting, could be that his intuition was suddenly sparking about this case. Hell, it could be that sewage water they called coffee over at Chuck's place. "You would think there was special protocol and training for going into the courts."

"It's all wrapped into our Iniquus training program." Bob opened the file he'd been carrying under his arm, holding it wide.

Nutsbe glanced down. "Sure enough, I'm certified to go to court. Okay, I'm remembering that now." He braced. "It's a female, right? What did she witness?"

"Olivia, the federal prosecutor, didn't go into it. I could hear in her voice that she was worried about losing the witness's cooperation. She only does big cases with violent offenders or cases that have to do with national security. It would be bad if this guy was back out on the streets because the witness wasn't willing to witness."

"When is the trial?" Nutsbe was stalling, looking for an excuse to professionally decline.

"It's going on now, but they don't need the K9 in place until tomorrow. Possibly on another day when the jury is reading their verdict."

"All right." Nutsbe dragged his index finger under his lower lip. "That's going to have to be a no from me."

"Yeah, I was afraid you'd have your calendar filled already. Olivia was throwing a last-minute hail Mary. You know how that goes." Bob paused with a tip of his head and a furrowed brow. "Your calendar isn't filled, is it? You're just a flat-out no."

"I am. You'll have to pull from someone who already does this."

Bob drew his brow in with confusion. "Do you mind if I ask why?"

"A woman's going to be on the stand."

"That's right." Bob posted his hands on his hips.

"And the person on trial did something terrible to her."

"He did."

"And the entire time she's in there," Nutsbe said, "she's going to be sobbing. Rightfully so."

"That's why she needs Beowolf to hug. To give her some support."

"Yeah, man," Nutsbe shook his head, "it's like this, I would take that piece of shit out into the alley and beat the living crap out of him. I would dive through fire to get to her while she was being hurt and pull her to safety while my skin melted. I would do a lot of hero shit, willingly. But there is one thing I *cannot* stomach, a woman in tears. I *cannot*. Just can't. It just kills me. It's kryptonite."

"Okay, I hear you. I feel the same. Except—"

"Shit," Nutsbe said on the exhale.

"You're the only one that's certified to go. If it's not you, that poor woman's going to go alone. She'll maybe have a bailiff in the room to make her feel a little safer from this devil."

"Guilt trip much? What about Didit? You said this was her outreach baby."

"Didit is in the field. All of Cerberus is in the field except for the kennel hands and me. I can't leave the K9s."

"Lynx would do it." Nutsbe swiped his hand along his jaw. "Yeah, but she's on her honeymoon."

"On Panther Force, Margot is certified. Is she coming in with the rest of the team?" Bob asked.

"She's still testing positive for Covid. She's in Helsinki."

"Okay." Bob held out his hand. "Thank you for considering."

Nutsbe took Bob's hand and held the shake. Looking down at his sneakers, he frowned. "She'll face that guy all alone?"

"All alone."

"Yeah, I can't have that." Nutsbe shook, then slowly nodded his head. "I guess I'll have to do it." He looked up and caught Bob's eye. "What time is this?"

"The witness is scheduled to testify in the afternoon session tomorrow. You'd probably need to be at the witness's house around noon. You'll escort her to the courthouse."

"And you'll bring me up to speed before that?"

"We can talk about it in the car this evening. If you're going to court, you need to hang out with Beowolf a bit, so you get to be buds. We also need to go over and introduce you and Beowolf to the witness and the prosecutor."

"Olivia."

"Right. Olivia Gladstone."

Nutsbe let out a whistle. "I know her by reputation. She's no wilting flower. This is her case, huh? And she doesn't know Beowolf yet?"

"I looked it up. Beowolf has been working in the courts for about two years. But Olivia's witnesses usually end up with Valor."

Nutsbe smiled. "Such a sweet mama. I bet she's great at giving support in the courtroom. I can see her doing that job."

"Yeah, well, Beowolf isn't really the sweet mama type. He's more of a blob of protective honey."

"Interesting." Nutsbe quirked a single brow. "Not sure what to do with that picture you just painted."

"So you can get away from whatever you've got on your plate this evening and also do the trial support duties tomorrow?"

"I'll figure it out." Nutsbe glanced down at his watch. He had ten minutes to make himself look professional. He turned and started down the hall. "Text me the times. I'll do what I have to to make it a go. But right now," he reached out for the door handle on Panther Force War Room, "I understand that I might have inadvertently sparked World War III. So I need to go in and figure that out."

4

Nutsbe

Showered and dressed in his Iniquus uniform of gunmetal gray compression shirt and gray camo tactical pants, Nutsbe shook hands with FBI Joint Task Force members Kennedy and Finley as they came through the door, taking their usual seats at the conference table.

Those two had been both Iniquus adversaries and close partners on a number of cases over the years.

Nutsbe wondered which side of the coin they landed on with this case.

The only other guy in the room was Sy Covington, one of Iniquus's top lawyers, so either way, Nutsbe knew this was bad.

"Let's dive straight in," Kennedy said. "I was working at an FBI station in Eastern Europe. Your name is lighting up communications between Russia and Albania."

"Oh." Yup. This was what Nutsbe had been afraid of.

"It's hard to tell what's going on from the context of the

conversations," Kennedy said, a worry line formed between his brows.

"It's my name explicitly?" Nutsbe's heart thumped hard against his breastbone. *They had his name. Shit.* "Nutsbe Crushed?"

"Thaddeus Crushed," Kennedy said, "explicitly. Looks like you've ruffled some feathers."

Nutsbe laced his fingers, planted his forearms on the table, and leaned forward. "So you didn't hear my name in your New York office?"

Finley and Kennedy turned to each other, checking to see if their partner had that information.

Finally, Kennedy turned back with his lips pursed. "Is New York working with you on a case? We aren't here to step on toes."

"If they were working with me, they'd say Nutsbe, not Thaddeus." He unraveled his fingers and knocked on the table. "Thaddeus is my legal name." Nutsbe swallowed hard and focused on Kennedy since he worked internationally. Finley worked out of D.C., where he worked on terror threats, and he was probably here as a backup of some kind. "Did Russia mention that I was targeted for a hit?"

Again, the two looked at each other before turning back to Nutsbe. "A hit?" Kennedy asked.

"Plutonium tea?" Nutsbe asked. "Nerve agent on my doorknob? A quick trip down a long flight of stairs?"

"Why would they care about you?" Finley asked.

"No one in your chatter is talking about specifics?" Covington sat to Nutsbe's right, pressed back in the captain's chair with his ankle comfortably on his knee. His elbows relaxed on the armrests while his hands perched on his stomach. Zero tension. But then again, he was legal counsel, and no one was potentially putting him in the crosshairs.

"From what we've picked up, it seems that Nutsbe—Thaddeus—created a problem that they hadn't considered." Kennedy looked directly at Nutsbe. "My sense is that you opened a can of worms. We wondered if it was an Iniquus mission. Yours was the only name we picked up."

"But you knew it was *my* name. Not some rando Thaddeus Crushed from elsewhere."

"Thaddeus Crushed, working in Washington D.C., connected to the FBI," Finley said. "We did a public search of the area, and there are no other Thaddeus Crusheds on the East Coast. Closest one is in Ohio, and he's in his mid-seventies. We could have done a deeper dive into government records, but our team member, Prescott, remembered being on a mission to save DARPA scientist Zoe Kealoha when you mentioned that name to the good doctor."

"Yeah, she wasn't keen on calling me Nutsbe. Small world. And damned good memory on Prescott's part." Nutsbe slid his palms down his thighs to his knees and left them there. "Well, Russia and Albania are chatting about me. Listen, I need a heads-up if they decide to kill me. If you hear anything, I'm an immediate call."

Kennedy's brow drew in a little tighter. "Of course we would."

Nutsbe jutted forward. "There's no, *of course,* about it. That's not how these things work. What you'd do is weigh me and my life against whatever was going on, and you'd figure out what outcome was the most advantageous to you."

Covington shifted in his chair.

"Respectfully," Nutsbe added.

"So you know what this is about, the whys of your name on the channels." Finley's even tone was a counterpoint to the agitation that Nutsbe was feeling. "We're hoping you can share the information with us. That way, we can do our due diligence and keep you safe if things go from a simmer to a rolling boil."

Nutsbe turned to Covington. "What do I do here?" His lips were buzzing. That had only happened to him on a few occasions in his life: his first jump out of a plane, his F16's engines dying in the sandstorm, waking up to find that he'd had both of his legs amputated.

"Command prefers that you cooperate with the D.C. Joint Task Force once they've assured you that they'll protect your confidence," Covington said with carefully chosen words.

"How do you see that playing out?" Kennedy asked.

"Simple." Covington offered an easygoing smile. "You didn't get the information from Thaddeus Crushed. You *came across* the information. I know your protocols will create chain of command and process issues." He opened his palms upward. "But this is a choice you need to make." He laced his fingers again and gave a nod as if the decision was a done deal.

Nutsbe thought Covington was working the special agents. There was a men's club chumminess to all this. A brotherly pact he was articulating.

"You assure us that this is a protected conversation, knowing the full strength of Iniquus stands behind Mr. Crushed." Covington smiled a slow smile. "Or we shake hands, and I will escort you to your car," Covington spoke with a monied southern drawl. It put people at ease.

Nutsbe's mom loved that kind of voice. She said it was "solace." Nutsbe always knew when he found his mom curled on the couch, knitting and watching *To Kill a Mockingbird*, that she was emotionally wrung out and needed a dose of Atticus Finch to make her feel safe and calm.

I should call Mom. As soon as the words formed in his brain, he jerked that thought to a stop. Nutsbe needed to stay away from his family unless and until he figured out how Russia discovered his name and what that would mean in the shakeout.

This was why Iniquus employees went dark once they signed their contracts. They worked to have a zero footprint, especially the members of the operational teams. Nutsbe even paid for his house in full with his cash signing bonus. His trust held the title. It would be nigh on impossible to trace his personal address back to his name.

Nutsbe scanned through the normal modes of tracking someone down. Yeah, all his official papers—driver's license, voter registration, income tax forms—all listed his barracks apartment on Iniquus's high-security campus as his address. And like Finley said, there was nothing beyond the absolute necessity in terms of his name in the public sphere.

Who had a reach that could touch Nutsbe's info?

Banks had his voice for phone recognition. That technology certainly existed. If someone had recorded his voice along the way, they'd have to put it together with Thaddeus. That was the confounding part. The planes of his face were mapped, and his fingerprints were taken as part of his security clearance. The FBI had access to that.

The FBI's reach and capabilities were the problem here.

As Nutsbe thought through the possibilities, Kennedy and Finley had taken a moment to discuss Covington's proposal. And though they didn't look thrilled about it, Kennedy said, "You've got a deal."

"Not quite," Nutsbe said. "More. I need updates on what's going on. You don't keep me in the dark when it comes to the *me* part of the case."

"We've got you," Finley said.

It wasn't an official "We've got you" it was a verbal handshake kind of deal. That Covington had put the weight of

Iniquus into play was an incentive. Nutsbe knew these men, and they had always been forthright and dependable. He just hoped that when he was talking about their counterintelligence chief, the one that might have a trickledown effect on their career trajectories, they could hold onto their ethics.

"This touches close to home for you. So, here we go," Nutsbe said as he splayed his fingers wide on the dark mahogany of the conference table. "Panther Force was working with a longtime client out of New Jersey. A couple of years ago, they approached us because they had an executive that they were concerned about."

"Who was the client?" Kennedy asked.

"Confidential," Covington said.

"What was the concern?" Kennedy asked. "Just in general."

"At the time they came to Iniquus, their in-house security detected emails and phone calls going to Albania," Nutsbe replied. "At first, they thought that their guy—" Nutsbe looked at Covington. "Can I say that name?"

Covington gave him a nod.

"First name Blerim. Last name: Hotel. Oscar. X-Ray. Hotel. Alpha. He pronounces it *Ho-JAH,* just like the former Prime Minister of Albania Hoxha, but there's no familial connection. I checked." Nutsbe bit at the inside of his cheek. "At first, the company thought Hoxha might be concerned about his family and that he was reaching out to relatives."

"They brought it up with him?" Kennedy asked. "That he shouldn't be making international calls of a personal nature from the company line?"

"Right," Nutsbe said. "He reassured them that this was about business. The CEO wasn't satisfied with his answers, so he quietly got Iniquus involved. It was handed to our team because this was right before Panther Force provided a close protection detail for their execs heading over to Montenegro for a retreat near the Albanian border a couple of years ago."

"So you started looking into this guy's background to see if he presented a threat to his coworkers while they were abroad," Kennedy said.

"Exactly," Nutsbe said. "Hoxha had ties to Albanian intelligence."

"Recently?" Kennedy asked.

"No. Decades ago. Hoxha would be sixty-four-ish," Nutsbe said. "He came to the U.S. when he married in his early thirties and became an American citizen. But since he raised a bunch of red flags for the company's president, we were allowed to make audio recordings of Hoxha's phone lines."

Covington leaned forward. "That's his work number that goes through their switchboard, but it's also the company-owned cellphone that is issued and is supposed to be dedicated to work calls only. This is a precaution to keep any spyware, malware or tracking from attaching to the company, and also so the company can legally monitor their workforce. New Jersey has a one-party consent law. And whether Hoxha remembered or not, when he was hired, he gave written consent to record all calls made on company phones."

"What industry?" Finley asked.

Covington steepled his fingers under his chin. "Confidential."

"But we can look up Hoxha's name and find that out," Finley pointed out.

"You could," Covington agreed. "But you didn't get that information from us. We can give you Hoxha's name because he is no longer with the company. He's dead."

Finley leaned forward. "Dead, how?"

"Hard to say." Nutsbe raked a hand through his hair. "I

have had my finger on that pulse since the company pulled us in two years ago. About six weeks ago, at the beginning of August, Hoxha didn't show up for work. Hoxha had access to the company's highly confidential and possibly highly lucrative data. They were very concerned with the how and why of his and his wife's sudden disappearance. The company started looking for him."

"You all went looking?" Finley asked.

"We don't operate such cases out of state," Covington said. "Our client did, however, inform us that their local PI discovered the bodies of husband and wife at their beachfront property. In the heat of the summer without the air conditioning on, the bodies had advanced to a point where evidence was scarce. The coroner listed it as a murder-suicide."

"The police are investigating it further?" Kennedy asked.

"I couldn't tell you." Nutsbe frowned. "And that's not why you're here. You're here to know why Russia and Albania have my name in their mouths."

5

Nutsbe

Here we go. "I had my AI system find and flag all calls from Hoxha's line related to Albania. And in that way, I discovered that Hoxha was in communications with FBI's Leonard McMahan."

Finley pressed his hands onto his knees with a startled look on his face. "Wait. FBI Counterintelligence Chief McMahan?"

"That was my reaction," Nutsbe said. "When I heard McMahan's name, he was only involved in phone calls and never emails. When I heard the context of their conversations, I hoped I was mistaken, that I wasn't investigating an FBI head honcho. So, I checked McMahan's voice with our AI's library of known voice samples. It was a match. Too close of a match-percentage to think that nefarious AI software was manipulating the voice. It was him."

Finley turned to Kennedy. "Does that make sense? I mean, as counterintelligence chief, he wouldn't be running a case or even making any ground-level case decisions." He swiveled back to Nutsbe. "Do you know why Hoxha was talking to McMahan?"

"Yeah, I do. First, Hoxha introduced McMahan to an Albanian official. McMahan was trying to get help with getting a business deal to go through, mostly around oil. Oil is *not* one of the main focuses of our client's business. So this jumped out at me." He shot a glance toward Covington, who sat stoically while he listened.

"McMahan was doing this as part of an FBI operation, and you stumbled on it, putting the two together?" Finley asked.

Nutsbe shook his head.

"The oil business, did it sound like it had to do with an FBI investigation, or was it personal business?" Kennedy asked as he crossed his arms over his chest, his lips slightly curled with disdain.

"All I can say is that things evolved." Nutsbe squared his shoulders. "In my mind, it sounded like a private deal. However, it could have been a well-designed, ongoing FBI operation. The FBI connection only made sense in that if this were an ongoing FBI operation, they had to get McMahan involved because they were interfacing with a high-ranking government official. It couldn't be John Q. Special Agent from New Jersey on the phone line. They needed someone of high stature in there doing what they were doing." Nutsbe bladed a hand toward Kennedy. "And I know that's the kind of work you do—develop relationships and steer people with power toward benefiting the U.S. —no insult intended, this guy was pretty high up there. Like at the top of the food chain."

"None taken. Keep going."

"During these calls, Hoxha acted like an interpreter.

Seeing nothing new in the interactions that involved our client's business, I was about to close out and hand the information over to Command to decide what needed to go in the report to our client, but things changed." Nutsbe looked toward Covington who gave him a nod to proceed.

"Note here that when Russia attacked Ukraine, Hoxha and McMahan seemed to change sides, becoming pro-Russia. They started working with a shipping guy—his Americanized name is Victor Popyrin. Not an oligarch—but oligarch-adjacent, who is very friendly with the Kremlin. Popyrin runs ships to New York, among other ports, or did. It seemed that Hoxha and McMahan really ramped up their work of favors benefitting various Eastern European businesses—the businesses that Popyrin and others were using to thwart the world sanctions placed on Russia as a punishment when they invaded. As an aside, Hoxha and his wife's disappearance happened just a couple of months after Popyrin was abducted on his yacht off the coast of the Seychelles. That attempt was thwarted." Nutsbe didn't add that Iniquus had inadvertently saved the man.

"Again, I need to know if McMahan was doing this as an FBI operation," Finley said.

"I heard—" Nutsbe cleared his throat. "What I heard on the last set of phone call exchanges before Hoxha died—this would have been the end of July—was that Hoxha and the execs were going on another retreat to Montenegro. Panther Force is the close protection on that company retreat. It's scheduled for end of September. But add in there that I learned McMahan was offered a cash payout."

"Cash," Kennedy said. He'd stopped blinking.

"They talked about two-hundred-and-fifty-thousand dollars. And it seemed that Hoxha had a way to smuggle that money back to the United States from his trip to Montenegro and would personally hand it to McMahan. Hoxha said there was plenty more where that came from for the right information."

"Information," Kennedy whispered under his breath, then turned to Finley. "McMahan worked in New York City. Much of his focus was on finding and shutting down foreign intelligence that wanted to operate near the United Nations. He'd have all the recent information in his mind. He'd know what everyone was working on and the details of the how and why. He'd decide what operations took precedence and where to place our assets. He could steer eyes toward or away from anything—shipping, for example."

"Can you imagine the amount of damage McMahan could do to U.S. security?" Finley asked. "The practices and names of the people in the field that could be exposed?" He turned back to Nutsbe. "This is mind-boggling in its capacity to harm."

"Yah think?" Nutsbe pressed his hands against his knees.

"I have to commend you, Nutsbe," Kennedy said. "A man could keep that to himself and be able to sleep better at night."

"Only if sleeping better meant not fearing for my life. That was every day when I deployed to the sandbox. I'm used to it." He skated a hand out. "I don't like it. Don't want to live that way. But I know how to deal with that part. The part where I would choose to ignore my oath and fail to defend my country? That's what would keep me up at night. So here we are."

"I'm caught on the two-hundred-and-fifty thousand." Kennedy focused on Finley. "At retirement, McMahon would have a cushy pension and would be paid high dollar to give speeches and advice. Does just over a quarter million sound like a reasonable amount to risk a soft retirement versus the potential for a hard cot in a supermax cell?"

"It sounds like the amount of money you offer someone as a carrot," Finley said. "And the stick is exposure. The timing for the ask makes sense. McMahan's last polygraph test would be in his rearview. They only do a thorough security check every five years, so he was cleared through retirement. He wouldn't have to lie, and he wouldn't have to thwart the technology."

Kennedy turned to Finley. "This hasn't been in the papers. There haven't been any arrests." He wiped a hand over his mouth, then turned to catch Nutsbe's gaze. "You didn't tell the FBI?"

Covington leaned forward. "We handed it off to the DOJ. They're investigating."

Kennedy's voice was painted with sympathy. "Brother, the communications we intercepted make all the sense in the world. Russia knows we—the US government—know about their McMahan asset. And Russia knows we know because of you. So it looks like you're the key that might end up locking out at least some of Russia's ability to bring in revenue to fund their war effort against Ukraine."

"Lucky me." Nutsbe felt his face blanche as his blood pooled in his stomach. It was a body's technique to send all the nutrients to the vital organs in a survival crisis. Obviously, he felt exposed and vulnerable.

"I'm sure you understand," Kennedy said quietly. "That there's no quick fix here. Investigations take time. Then there's the possible trial where you're called to testify against McMahan." Kennedy paused, seeming to choose his words carefully. "I want you to know this *isn't* going away. You'll be dealing with the ramifications for years to come. It's going to be a low hum in your world for the foreseeable future. Of course, with Hoxha dead, you'll be okay once McMahan's behind bars and out of the picture. Time."

"How did Russia and Albania land on his name?" Covington asked.

Nutsbe nodded. "I need to know if they just have the name or if they have more. Can they find me and trace that back to my family?"

"When did you hand this information to your commanders?" Finley asked.

"First week of August after they found the Hoxhas's bodies. Why?"

"There was an email that McMahan retired." Finley glanced at Kennedy. "August, right?"

"That sounds right. Let me—" Kennedy pulled out his phone and did an Internet search. "August first." He looked up as he slid his phone back into his suit pocket. "McMahan no longer has access to our data banks and can't do a search of our security clearance files. Even if Russia asked McMahan to reach out to a colleague to do it for him, I'd find out who used their login code. There's no way to hide that. I have your file tagged looking for just that. I did that search as soon as Prescott mentioned your name. So far, there's nada from the FBI's direction."

"Good timing with this coming to a head after that retirement, I guess," Nutsbe said.

"Small favors, right?" Finley asked. "In fact, Kennedy and I are here asking you questions because nothing is popping up with your name on it from any direction other than Russia. I'm glad, for your sake, that Iniquus runs a tight ship and keeps everyone's personal information undiscoverable." Finley stood. "Kennedy and I will keep looking into this thing with Russia." Seeing Nutsbe's startled reaction, he added, "We'll do it quietly." He reached out a hand to Nutsbe. "In the meantime, stay frosty."

Kennedy stood. "We'll keep close tabs on the players in the Eastern Europe station. We'll keep you and Covington advised if there's any chatter about you going forward." He shook hands first with Covington and then with Nutsbe, holding it just a moment longer. At the same time, he said, "Just keep an awareness for anything out of the ordinary and report it to Finley immediately—anything at all that makes you think that you've been lined up in their crosshairs."

6

Nutsbe

Nutsbe strolled into the Team Alpha wing of Cerberus Headquarters to find it empty. Sticking his head into the locker room, he called out, "You there, Bob?"

"On my way," echoed from the shower room shared by both the K9s and their handlers.

Nutsbe wandered over to the conference table, pulled out a captain's chair, and took a seat. *Here we go. The first step on a painful Achilles heel.*

There was a clatter of nails against the tile, and a beast of a dog stopped in the doorframe. His broad chest puffed out, a challenge in his eyes. The draping jowls surely hid sharp teeth along his powerful jaw. The image of a circus performer sticking his head in a lion's mouth came to mind. "You just gonna stand there, buddy?" Nutsbe asked with a friendly, easy-going tone. "Or do you want to come over and give me a sniff?"

The stranger-danger posture shifted, and Beowolf trotted

forward with Bob trailing behind him, drying his hands on a white terrycloth towel.

Nutsbe slowly stretched curved fingers toward the K9's scruff and scratched. "Beowulf, huh? I guess that makes sense now. Epic and monstrous." Since Beowolf accepted his scritches, Nutsbe felt safe to bend and put his forehead against the velveteen folds of the dog's forehead.

"O, as in wolf, not U. He's a big boy, all right," Bob said. "But he's not hurting anything."

Beowolf took a step forward, shoving himself between Nutsbe's legs and giving him a thorough sniff from belt to chin. Nutsbe tipped his head back to receive the doggo kisses on his neck rather than his lips. "This guy looks like he could eat an entire village."

"Yeah, well, never say never." Bob moved away from them and sat behind his computer at the top of the table. "Though it would be uncharacteristic. It's not what they're bred for. Their job was to thwart poachers. If the poacher got hurt or even killed, that could cause big problems for the landowner. So they developed a dog that could knock someone down and trap them."

"Yup. If he leans on me any harder, I'm going to tip over."

"Nah, you're not the enemy. While trapping was their job, they're also bred to be docile around a family—a manor dog. They're especially good around kids. Hence their reputation for being gentle giants."

"Such a sweet guy, aren't you?" Nutsbe rubbed Beowolf's sides, feeling the soft caramel fur and thinking this was exactly what it would feel like to pet a lion. "Okay, he's not a biter. How about the risk of getting dragged when I walk with him? These muscles are no joke," Nutsbe said, patting along Beowolf's sides. "How much does he weigh?"

"I bet you'll never have met a more docile walking companion." Bob slid down in his chair, lacing his hands behind his head and looking comfortably at ease. "He was only two-forty last time I had him on the scales."

"Only." Nutsbe laughed. "Yeah, he definitely outweighs me." He sent a glance toward Bob. "And I haven't put my prostheses to the test getting pulled forward with that kind of power."

"I've never seen Beowolf drag a handler. Though, I'd go ahead and introduce him to the idea of your limbs."

This wasn't new for Nutsbe. He did this with the K9s that he occasionally handled.

Nutsbe pressed Beowolf back to give himself room to maneuver. Leaning over, he grabbed the laces on each boot, untied them, and loosened the tongues.

The last time he did this was for the new dog Max before a very long—and frequently odiferous—trek delivering the Malinois to his handler in Estonia.

The Cerberus trainer, Reaper, had been around for that introduction and suggested the approach Nutsbe was now taking as he pulled off his boots and set them aside.

"Take It to the Max" was a tactically trained, high-energy, adolescent Malinois; those descriptors presented their own challenges beyond the gas on that flight.

That Max was the second Iniquus Max. The first one, a German shepherd named Maxamillion, had recently retired. Out on a deployment, he tore his ACL and was no longer mission-ready. Now, he lived with Reaper and his family. Reaper's service dog Houston and Maxamillion were besties. As far as Reaper was concerned, there couldn't be enough tactically trained K9s around to guard his family, especially with a new baby in the house.

He had a point.

It wouldn't be a bad idea for Nutsbe to have another set of protective eyes and ears at his place since he preferred living in his own house off campus when his team wasn't rolling out on a mission.

Dragging off his socks, Nutsbe decided he should probably give that some more thought. Especially now that his name was riding the airwaves between Albania and Russia.

Beowolf shuffled back so he could lie down, look at, and then sniff Nutsbe's robotic feet. His massive face tipped up until intelligent eyes caught Nutsbe's gaze. He raised his right eyebrow, then his left, then his right again. It was an almost comical inquiry. "Hey, dude, what've you got going on down here?"

When Nutsbe reached for his Iniquus tactical pants cuff, Beowolf lumbered up to all fours. The effort reminded Nutsbe of camels on the dunes, pushing their bulk forward and backward as they rocked and unfolded to get on their feet.

Working his pants legs over the prostheses, one then the other, Nutsbe gathered the fabric up until he exposed his knees and thighs dotted by sensor pads on their mapped and tattoo-marked positions, the end of his residual limbs, the bone anchors, then the metallic robotics prostheses below.

Beowolf padded back a step. His massive square head with the black mask tipped this way and that. His eyes were curious.

Nutsbe smiled down as the moist nose tickled his knee and chuffed warm air over his skin.

As Beowolf inspected, every once in a while he'd look up to check on Nutsbe. With that connection, a strange feeling passed between them. Something tightened deep down in Nutsbe's abdomen. The sensation moved up into his chest and across his shoulders as Beowolf continued his assessment.

A dog sitting shotgun to keep him company as he drove through packed gridlock traffic would be nice, Nutsbe thought. And yeah, there was also the idea that on days when Nutsbe used his wheelchair, no one would dare come close, let alone tip him over backward.

Besides the safety factor, a dog like Beowolf might be nice to have around for companionship, especially one with a temperament like Bob described. It would be good if Nutsbe could find a dog that could also do an Iniquus job, so the doggo could go in for training and socialize at the Cerberus Kennels during the day or hang out in the fields so he wouldn't get lonely and mischievous at home alone. Especially when a mission meant round-the-clock focus in the Panther Force War Room.

Nutsbe decided to give that some thought, maybe have a talk with Bob about any holes Iniquus needed filling and see if that was something the Kennel Master could take on.

The next time Beowolf caught his eyes, Nutsbe thought things had clicked into place, and Beowolf understood the situation. Beowolf turned in a wide circle and backed himself up like a semi, stepping into the space between Nutsbe's knees. Plopping into a sit, Beowolf scanned the room and settled his gaze on Bob.

"I think he's okay with the hardware," Nutsbe said as he pushed Beowolf forward to get himself put back together—pulling on his socks and boots, adjusting his pants legs.

"Okay, next step is for you to take him for a walk." Bob stood and twisted toward the door where leather leashes hung from a hook.

"Can he run? I guess gallop would be the better term." Nutsbe reached for the lead that Bob extended toward him. It was important that he was the one who attached it to the collar so Beowolf wasn't confused about who was in control. "Could he jog with me?"

Bob stood back as Nutsbe moved past him through the door to the hall and across the entryway. "Bullmastiffs are more of a walking companion. I'd say no to being a jogging partner, especially at the distances you run." He swiveled to tap the automatic door button. "They like to go outside and meander around."

With the heat wave blown out to sea by the rainstorm the other day, they stepped out into one of the more pleasant late afternoons Nutsbe could remember.

"Your backyard with lots of space and plenty of trees," Bob said, trotting down the step, "that's the kind of thing mastiffs would like—someplace to prowl around and smell the flowers." He stopped on the sidewalk. "How about you take the river path. It's a twenty-minute circuit. Make sure you're very comfortable with each other, so there are no issues this evening."

"You're going to be there, aren't you?" Nutsbe asked. "I thought you were driving."

"I'm going to make the introduction and answer your questions in the car. But I won't go in with you. Bullmastiffs like things the way they like them. You, the witness, and Olivia will be teammates with Beowolf. If I'm there at the meeting but not there as part of the team in the courtroom, he might be agitated that everyone isn't accounted for."

"Interesting." Beowolf lumbered beside him as Nutsbe moved down the steps to stand beside Bob.

"One thing with the bullmastiff, though, Nutsbe, is they're super smart. What I want you to do when you're working with Beowolf is not to tell him 'no.' Only tell him what you want him to do. It's not 'Don't bark.' It's, 'Quiet.'

It's not, 'Don't jump'—not that he would but as an example —it's, "Sit.' Otherwise, with Beowolf, he'll think, 'Well, you took that off the table, but look at all these other choices I have.' And Beowolf is clever."

"And slobbery."

"That goes without saying with these dogs." Bob handed out the terrycloth hand towel he had tucked into his belt. "Just keep the slobber off the judge's robes, and you'll make a great team."

"Hear that Beowolf? No slavering on the judge."

Beowolf raised his brow and gave him a look that Nutsbe read as, are you kidding me right now? Nutsbe chuckled and turned back to Bob. "How long are we going to be at this meet and greet?"

"Half-hour, forty-five minutes. We're not settling in for the evening." Bob checked his watch. "You'll be back at Iniquus before nineteen hundred hours."

"And you don't know anything about this case?"

"What I know is that it's an Olivia Gladstone case— which means that it involves the worst of society's worst— that you are providing a 'last-minute dog,' as she calls it, and that I'm grateful that you're willing to pit yourself against your kryptonite."

7

Nutsbe

With Beowolf loaded in the back of the vehicle, the two men seatbelted in, and the motor purring, Bob handed Nutsbe a small binder. "Here, refresh your memory on the protocols." Bob backed them out of their space. "You'll keep it with you tomorrow in your EDC pack in case you need to reference our decision-making policies." Bob referred to the Everyday Carry pack, a small one-armed backpack with the things normally stored in the pockets of the operator's tactical pants —pockets missing from the Iniquus suits. Though, every set of clothing issued by Iniquus was tactically structured. If things got wild and hairy, the operators could move with ease.

Of course, from his EDC pack tomorrow, Nutsbe would have to leave his multi-tool and cell phone in the car along with anything else that wouldn't get through the metal detector and security check at the federal courthouse. And there would be the addition of slobber rags.

"Is the judge going to quiz me on this stuff?"

"There haven't been any challenges to our presence so far. We go in before the jury, get in place where the dog is out of the jury's view, offer unintrusive support, and walk out with the witness. Typically, the judge will call a recess so that the jury exits and never sees that a dog is there." Bob flipped the cover open. "Better to be prepared and not need it than to need it but be unprepared." He tapped an envelope in the jacket pocket, shifted to drive, and started out of the parking area. "I've put your certification and Beowolf's certification here. Again, you have it if anyone asks. That might happen as you go through security. Most importantly, that's got the judge's order that Olivia obtained last night."

Nutsbe slid the envelope out and opened the papers to get eyes on. It was an Iniquus mantra that you never trusted a weapon, whether it was a gun or a paper shield, until you tested it yourself.

"Tomorrow," Bob said, "Beowolf will wear an Iniquus K9 work vest. That should preempt some questions, and it should keep most people from running up for a snuggle." Bob shot Nutsbe a glance before he turned onto the main drive, taking a left toward the exit.

"This beast?" Nutsbe threw an arm over the seat to rub behind Beowolf's ears. "His size will deter that, wouldn't you say?" he asked as Bob's phone rang, and Bob snapped it up.

Nutsbe turned to find himself face to face with Beowolf and the warmth coming from the doggo's liquid brown eyes. "Are people going to run up on you, buddy? Are they going to try to give you some lovin'?"

Thinking back to his arrival at the airport in Estonia, Nutsbe remembered walking Max toward his handler, Halo, when a stranger crouched with her hand out, looking wistfully like there was nothing she would like better than to get over to Max and pet him. Max sure did want to comply. That woman ended up working with the Panther Force team in an emergency. Her showing up turned out to be one of those magical encounters that could make even the biggest atheist believe that there was a hand that directed the universe. But surely, the story of Max, Flagpole Mary, and Halo was an aberration.

Nutsbe assumed that everyone got at least one miracle handed to them at birth.

It was Nutsbe's portion to get a double dip. He survived the Afghanistan convoy explosion. Then, when the PJs flew him to the field hospital, there was a group of researchers there taking a tour. They got Nutsbe involved in their robotic prosthetics research project, which Nutsbe found fascinating.

While he didn't have a Mary—or a Max, for that matter—he lived a satisfying life. Well, a gratifying life with a side order of loneliness if he were being honest.

Nutsbe was happy for Halo and all his brothers, who had found love over the years.

But now that forty was on the horizon—distant horizon—at his age, Nutsbe figured that just wasn't for him. He dated. He had some good fun. He might even have felt enough of a connection to call it love a time or two. But eventually, as a couple, they'd come to the conclusion that it wasn't a good fit for the long haul, and they'd moved on.

Not a good fit, Nutsbe mused.

That happened with people as well as dogs. How many times had he seen that with the K9 handlers? A good handler could work with any old pooch. But for them to make a great team, things had to click. It had to be the *right* one.

"Sorry about that." Bob set his phone in the holder. "You were asking about Beowolf's size being a deterrent. You can't count on that. Some people just like big dogs." Bob swiveled to smile at Beowolf, then back to look out the front window.

"The bigger, the better. You need to keep an awareness." Bob slowed to salute the guard at his guard station as they lifted the exit arm. "It's easiest if you can get your body between Beowolf's and theirs before they're on the ground and wrapped around his ribs." Bob turned right out of the Iniquus campus. "Once they're locked into place, if you stop them, the public will look at you like you're snatching candy from a baby. And in my experience, it is a long-winded explanation that sometimes needs some physical action. Your job is to keep the public safe from any mishaps and to keep Beowolf safe from the public. It's usually good to just block, smile, and say, 'Sorry, working dog.' And if they press with word or action, don't respond. Start walking. The speed of the walk is directly correlated to their frustration that they didn't get a hug."

Beowolf shook his head, and a string of slobber flew over the seat and wrapped Nutsbe's arm.

Bob lifted a cloth from the pile, resting between the two men, and handed it to him. "Slobber rags—you'll want to keep them handy."

The rest of the way to the witness's house flew by.

Dread will do that to a clock.

"Here we are," Bob said as he pulled into a drive. "No other cars. Let's wait here until Olivia pulls up so she can make the introduction."

"I'm surprised that the prosecutor's showing up for this," Nutsbe said. "What's that about?"

"She likes to see the dog and witness together." Bob put the vehicle into park and turned off the engine. "She doesn't want any chaos in the courts." He let his seat belt go, then swiveled around to face Nutsbe. "She needs to know that the support will be provided seamlessly. And I guess she wants to make sure that the dog, especially a dog Beowolf's size, isn't going to make the witness even more anxious."

"The judge knows Beowolf is a bullmastiff, right?" Nutsbe turned in the direction of an approaching car, but it drove on by. "And they were okay with it?"

"Olivia said the judge mentioned having had facility dogs in his courtroom before. Seemed like he was pretty jazzed to have Beowolf there."

"Which is great. It'll be interesting to see this go down— just as long as there are no women crying." Nutsbe could feel the aversion growing in his shoulders and buttocks—like he was priming himself to run and fight.

"So I should send a support dog along with you, too?" Bob chuckled. "You know, I think my wife would let you take Jingles. Granted, he's a teacup chihuahua. But he'd fit in your suit coat pocket. And you know it's the little dogs that are the fiercest. Jingles could protect you from the tears." Bob sent Nutsbe a grin. "Say the word, man, and I've got you covered."

"Yeah, I hear you." Nutsbe turned his head to the passenger window. "Here she comes."

The car was far off, but this one felt right.

"I don't think there will be crying tonight," Bob said. "Possibly at court, but you may dodge the bullet altogether. Some people just don't cry."

When Bob popped his door open, Beowolf gave another shake of his head.

"Put it this way, crying or no crying, with Beowolf, I can guarantee you're gonna get damp."

Nutsbe wiped himself off, stuck a clean cloth into his belt, and then climbed from the car.

Bob stood at the back hatch. "Hey, Nutsbe, you need to

command Beowolf so he knows who's in charge of this excursion."

Nutsbe felt sweat form on his lip and swiped at it with the clean edge of the beast cloth. "You sure you don't want to go in?"

Bob fobbed the hatch open. "It's more than just Beowolf's confusion at the courthouse that keeps me from holding your hand, sunshine. In a group, we tend to gravitate to the people who make us most comfortable. I don't want the witness to gravitate to me, and then I'm not able to show up for her."

"Are you taking a jab?" Nutsbe reached into the back and picked up the lead. "Come on, Beowolf. Get dressed." It was the Iniquus command for stand still while I put something on you—anything from a leash to a vest to doggy goggles for a parachute jump.

The blue sedan pulled into the driveway. The woman driving was younger and smaller than Nutsbe had anticipated. He caught a brief glance of long blonde hair.

"Just saying you're a bit stiff. I get it. This isn't your natural habitat. But you might want to do a Beowolf and shake some of that off before you look the witness in the eyes. You're here for *her* support." He sent out a backhanded slap across Nutsbe's chest. "Cowboy up."

"Message received. Wilco." Nutsbe let go of Beowolf's lead to wipe the double line of slobber from his doggy chin.

"Come on, let me introduce you."

8

Nutsbe

Olivia opened her door, swiveled her gym-toned legs, and set her high heels onto the drive. Leaning out, her attention was fixed on Beowolf. "Oh!" she called. "You're more beautiful than I could ever have imagined!" Her arms opened wide, and with a happy rumble, Beowolf took off, galumphing his way to Olivia, dragging his lead, tongue dangling, slobber helicoptering his head like a damp halo.

Pressing up from his crouch, Nutsbe now understood the problem with strangers in public. Though, in Nutsbe's experience, once the Iniquus K9 had their vest on, they knew they were on the job and maintained a good work ethic. Obviously, that wasn't the situation today.

Beowolf came to a muscle-twitching stop and buried his head in Olivia's lap to receive his hug.

Her blonde curls draped over Beowolf's back. Her eyes closed tightly as she absorbed the moment. "You're so, so beautiful," she whispered into his scruff.

Yes, she was, Nutsbe thought. And not *at all* what he was expecting. In person, Olivia Gladstone didn't look like the battle maiden he'd seen in the grainy black and white photos in the D.C. newspapers. She looked sunny, approachable, like a friend. *Friendly,* Nutsbe corrected himself. Those thoughts flashed through one part of his brain; the other part was processing the outcome of hugging the droolminator.

"Hello, precious! What a nice welcome." She patted the K9's sides. "You are amazing. Look at you." Her voice bubbled with delight. "There is so much of you." She bent over to kiss Beowolf as Nutsbe took long strides toward her, the drool rag draped over his palm.

When she turned her head to see Nutsbe, she startled, then blinked. But that might have little to do with Nutsbe himself and more to do with Beowolf's draping his copious jowls across her lap as he sat, looking up at her with his big doe eyes.

She could probably feel the slobber absorbing into her suit skirt.

"Ma'am," Nutsbe started, and Olivia sat up. "I'm Nutsbe, your handler. Uhm, the dog handler for your case. I apologize. Beowolf's a drooler." He held out the rag he knew she'd need.

"Oh," she said, accepting it with a smile, switched it from one hand to the other then held out her freed right hand for a shake. "Olivia Gladstone."

Her fingers were cool, her skin soft. Her clasp was fine-boned and small, and he felt like he had bear paws in comparison. Nutsbe had no idea what he said or if he said anything. He was held in place by her smile and the sensation of warmth radiating from her hand to his.

He didn't want to let go.

Might not have let go.

Might have just stood there looking like a fool. But thankfully, Beowolf broke the spell by pressing his head against Nutsbe's thigh, giving him a nudge as if to say, "Yeah, that's enough. I'm the only one with a license to drool." As soon as Nutsbe moved, Beowolf shifted his head back into the petting zone.

Reluctantly, Nutsbe released her hand and turned to give Bob space to join the conversation.

"Hey, there, Liv. How was court today?" Bob asked, coming to stand next to Nutsbe.

"I thought that tonight I might practice some kind of song and dance routine for the morning to keep my jury focused. That way, I can use lunch as a change of scenery and come back with this guy for the afternoon." Olivia stroked a thumb over Beowolf's wrinkled forehead.

Bob looked at Nutsbe. "She's kidding, you're going to try very hard not to let the jury know there's a dog in the courtroom."

"Got it."

Turning back to Olivia, Bob said, "You know, a lot of lawyers I've talked to say that crime shows on TV are making the actual work of prosecuting that much harder," Bob said.

"Exactly. I was just saying this to our paralegal this morning. The jury expects entertainment. And I'm just not the kind of prosecutor that makes a rabbit appear with the tap of a wand."

When Olivia looked down, Beowolf lifted both his brows, waiting for a directive but not moving until absolutely necessary. Nutsbe could understand that. It looked like a nice place to be. As soon as the thought popped up, Nutsbe pushed it aside. He was here as an Iniquus representative and not some guy looking to buy a girl a drink at the bar.

"Beowolf," she said with a smile. "Can you back it up, sweetheart? I need to get out now."

Nutsbe stepped to the side and tapped his thigh. "Beowolf, flank." For a moment, he was afraid that Beowolf would ignore him for Olivia's exuberant attention. But Beowolf swung his head around, then trotted over to stand on Nutsbe's left. "Good boy."

Olivia stood.

"Uhm." Nutsbe wiggled a finger at her skirt. There was a poorly positioned wet splotch. "Again, my apologies, ma'am."

He couldn't really read the mix of emotions on her face. "Not ma'am, just Olivia, thanks." She swiped the rag down her skirt, but the liquid had already been absorbed. It didn't seem to bother her much. Olivia had focused on the house. "Come on, I can see Candace watching us from behind the curtains. Let's go in and see how she does."

"Olivia, I'm staying out here to make some calls," Bob said. "Nutsbe's got you."

Olivia shifted her gaze to Nutsbe. "Right, Nutsbe, you said?" She stepped onto the sidewalk. "But Thaddeus Crushed on your court papers."

"That's right. People call me Tad or Nutsbe. Your choice." Nutsbe felt ice wash over him. His name was going to be in the court's public documentation. If anyone knew how to look, he'd be exposed. Nutsbe would have to tell Sy Covington what was going on.

He thought certain leaders in the FBI might be interested in making the McMahan debacle go away by alleviating the friction point, him. If his testimony were interrupted, the whole "counterintelligence chief as Russian asset" might never find the light of public awareness. And the FBI might never be exposed to scrutiny or embarrassment. And though

Nutsbe held the FBI in high esteem, it was a broad organization with a variety of personalities and personal goals. Yeah, Russia and Albania weren't the only ones with skin in this game.

With Thaddeus Crushed transcribed into the court records, that could very well be the way to draw a bead on him.

Olivia led the way to the front door.

While she rang the bell, Nutsbe waited on the sidewalk with Beowolf in a down-stay. He wanted the witness to have a bit of distance to see Beowolf's size and come to some conclusion about how she felt.

"Nutsbe, this is Candace," Olivia said. "And that beast there, Candace, is Beowolf. He's your personal knight in shining armor. His job is to gallantly sit with you and support you the entire time you're in the courtroom."

"Big," she said, hugging herself.

Candace presented as an oxymoron. Her face was soft and pale with a splatter of fat freckles that, for some reason, made Nutsbe think of Huckleberry Finn. Spikes jutted through six different holes in each of her ears. With her orange-auburn hair clipped into barrettes, her natural curls draped over the chunky, grey wool sweater hanging loose from her slight frame. Around her neck was a thick dog collar-styled choker. The spikes on that made Nutsbe nervous that if she nodded her head, she'd impale herself.

His gaze traveled to her shoes. Nutsbe found that a person's shoes said a lot about the role they were playing at that moment. Here, black work boots peeked out from her wide-legged jeans. From the shape, he knew they would have steel toes that would set off the metal detector if she wore them tomorrow. He'd never faced that before. It could be that the officers would consider them a weapon—the footwear version of brass knuckles—in a fight. They were deadly if you knew what you were doing.

Candace nodded and retreated into the house. She sat on an overstuffed chair in the corner. It was the position someone with a great deal of situational awareness would choose.

With Beowolf at his side, Nutsbe walked over to Candace. "Why don't you spend some time with Beowolf and become friends?"

She looked up at Nutsbe. "Can I get down on the floor with him?"

"Yeah, sure. This is your time." Nutsbe smiled woodenly. "I want you to be comfortable."

When Candace got down, Beowolf lay beside her, sniffing at her clothes and hair, making her laugh.

That was a sound he hadn't expected. Maybe he could relax a little.

Nutsbe put a knee on the ground so he wasn't looming over her. He didn't want Candace to feel vulnerable. "Tomorrow in court, Beowolf will be right at your feet. You can pet him. Slide your feet out of your shoes and put your feet on him. He's there for you."

"Okay," she said, then laid down next to Beowolf and wrapped herself around him. When she tipped her head in, she started whispering.

Since Beowolf looked relaxed with no whale eyes or signs of stress, Nutsbe climbed back to his feet.

Olivia had found a place on the couch, and Nutsbe went to sit near her. The room was silent except for the tick, tick, tick of the hall clock and the *swhss-swhss* of Candace's secret conversation with Beowolf.

Nutsbe thought this was going pretty well and that he'd

probably stressed out for no reason. But that thought formed on the cusp of a sob.

It started with a choking noise, a kind of hiccough, and then Candace was like a volcano letting off hot lava emotions.

A sheen of sweat glistened Nutsbe's skin. His lungs constricted, and he wanted one of two things to happen—a dragon to slay or an exit route. He pulled at his collar, feeling his face grow red, and he turned to Olivia to see if she was watching the panic rise in his system.

"This is good," Olivia pronounced. Her focus was on Candace. "She needed to let some of her pent-up emotions go." Olivia slowly turned concerned eyes on him.

Desperate for a distraction, he blurted out. "I've read about you in the paper. Seen your photo. You look different in person, less like someone who could get dangerous people thrown in prison for life." She was just so familiar. The where of it, though …

"More approachable without my game face?" She smiled.

"Were you ever in the military?"

"No." She shook her head, but the smile didn't fall off and Nutsbe found himself smiling back despite his churning stomach and nerves lit on fire.

He didn't know her from the war. Nutsbe tried to focus on the puzzle of this sensation. How did he know her? The answer was like a word sitting on the tip of his tongue that his brain simply wouldn't retrieve. "Have you ever been to North Carolina?"

"No. I haven't. Is that where you're from?"

"Until I graduated from high school, and then I went to the Air Force Academy in Colorado. Have you been out that way, Colorado?"

"I haven't. I'm told it's beautiful." She tipped her head,

and her eyes crinkled at the corners. Her smile seemed to ask, what's this about?

"I'm trying to place how I might know you beyond your newspaper photo, that is. So far, in my timeline, we haven't been in the same state. I was stationed in Maryland and quickly deployed, so that's not it. Do you happen to know anyone at the VA?"

"I think we're neighbors." Her smile widened. "I'm almost a hundred percent certain that you live in my neighborhood or not too far. Isn't that you who jogs by my house most mornings? I'm on Millrace."

"Oh?" Millrace was the road that ran behind his.

"I have the charcoal gray house, white trim, and an obnoxiously bright raspberry-pink door."

"I know the one. There's a sweet little cockapoo that likes to look out the window." He felt the fizz of excitement bubble across his skin. "That one?"

"I prefer my best friend's term, cockapoodle-do." Her smile turned into a bashful laugh. "Her name is Henrietta."

Nutsbe turned his attention to the picture window and looked out front toward her car. He had never seen Olivia at that house; he'd remember. And the car didn't seem familiar either, though she could keep it in her garage. That the car didn't ring a bell wasn't that unusual; Nutsbe didn't normally memorize cars in driveways along his run. The bright raspberry door, though, stood out against the reliably neutral colors in his mid-century neighborhood.

"That's a brightly colored door," he said.

"When I left my soon-to-be ex-husband. I moved into my rental property and never got around to repainting that door. It's not my style, but it's also a low priority. It was the real estate lady's idea for curb appeal, making the house stand out as memorable."

"She was right," Nutsbe agreed. "I knew exactly the door you were talking about. Big fence at the back of your backyard?"

"Very big. Poor Henrietta has a serious case of fence envy."

"Why's that?" Nutsbe was relaxing into the warmth of Olivia's smile, and after the sound of female sobs jangling his nerves, this felt like a refreshing dip in the pool on a blistering day.

"My marital house has a fenced-in yard. She used to like to hang out in the back, make friends with the butterflies, and sleep in the sun rays."

"Ah, well, that's my fence," Nutsbe said. "So not just neighbors but we abut."

"Seriously?" She tipped her head back and looked at him as if she didn't believe it.

"You have a back patio with blue urns. They're empty, though. I can see them from my bedroom window."

She laughed nervously. "So that's right. Huh." She paused. "They say it's a small world. I shouldn't be shocked at all that you're my behind-me neighbor. At least for the moment, anyway. Divorce court is Tuesday. It all depends on what the judge says. I'm hoping—since my husband left me for another woman, then got mad that I wouldn't take him back—that things will go pleasantly in my direction."

The grandfather clock in the entry chimed.

Olivia leaned toward Candace, who was now quietly curled against Beowolf's stomach with her eyes closed. She looked like she was asleep. "Six o'clock, Candace," Olivia sing-songed.

Candace blinked her eyes open as if she was surprised and momentarily disoriented.

"How are you feeling down there?" Olivia asked. "Will

going to court tomorrow with Beowolf at your side gives you a little more confidence? Make you feel safe?"

Candace shifted around until she was sitting up with crossed legs. "Yeah. How does all that work?"

"Would you like me to pick you up?" Nutsbe asked.

"I'd prefer to drive by myself." Candace hugged herself tightly.

"Okay, I'm going to meet you here, then," Nutsbe said. "And follow you to the courthouse. Once we're there, we'll park side by side. We'll go through security together." He pointed at her boots. "Steel toes?"

Her blush was made more vivid, surrounded by carrot-orange hair.

"They may set the metal detector off. I'm not sure of the rules at the federal court." He turned to Olivia.

"I've never had it come up." She faced Candace. "Do you have another pair of shoes you could wear? Something comfortable? But also, the judge is a little old-fashioned. And under such circumstances, every little strategic move can be important."

"You're saying I should dress like a demure lady?" She touched the spiked collar at her neck.

Olivia looked decidedly ill at ease with that characterization. "Do you want to go up and get something you think might be court-appropriate and bring it down? Maybe I can help you choose something, and then I have to get going." She leaned forward. "Listen, Candace, I want you to be you. I want you to be comfortable."

"But you also want us to win." She pushed herself to stand. "Right. Me too." Candace started out of the room, then turned. "Can I take Beowolf up with me?"

"Sure," Nutsbe said. "Beowolf follow." He pointed.

Beowolf shambled to his feet. He gave a whole-body shake, then the two trudged up the stairs.

Olivia leaned his way. "Do you have any questions about tomorrow?"

"I'd like to be near Candace the whole time," Nutsbe said.

"She'll be in a side room until the bailiff calls her. You can be in there with her."

"And once she's called to go in," Nutsbe asked, "I'm allowed to follow her to the witness stand and make sure that Beowolf gets settled?"

"That's correct. We want that to be as quiet a process as possible so the defense attorney can't make it an issue."

"I think we've got that handled." Nutsbe laced his fingers and lowered his elbows to his knees. "But once he's sitting with her. I want to be as close as possible. I can't imagine anything going wrong. But I don't want to be in the back should I need to intervene."

"Yes, absolutely. So the way I've done this before, and the way I had planned to handle it tomorrow—since this is a public trial—is to have one of our paralegals go with me to court and sit in the spot directly in front of the witness. She'll get up when you walk in."

"Good." He glanced around at the sound of footsteps on the stairs.

Candace walked into the room. The change was a shock to the system. She was wearing a cream-colored, short-sleeved dress made of the kind of floaty material that women wore when they took social media pictures in flowering meadows. Her hair was in a loose bun at the back of her nape, with a few whisps framing her face. The juxtaposition of sweetness and the fire of the slash mark scars on her neck and arms was startling. "I thought something like this," she stammered. "This is how I used to dress. And they would probably understand better if they saw who I used to be."

Olivia walked over and took Candace's hands. "You will get to a point in your life when you can be anyone you want. Dress however you like. That's going to take time. And therapy. But I believe in you, Candace. I believe that you'll get those choices. And I completely agree. We need the jury to see who you were when Kyle Offsed shifted your world. Very well done. I'm proud of you. Dressing like this took bravery."

Nutsbe shifted uncomfortably. Even without tears, here was the kryptonite—the sense of powerlessness when he wanted desperately to erase the pain.

"I have to get going." Olivia looked over her shoulder at Nutsbe. "What time tomorrow?"

"I thought eleven would give us plenty of time," he said, his voice gruff with emotion. "There's going to be traffic."

Olivia, still holding Candace's hands, turned back to her. "Eleven, Candace?"

"Yeah, sure." Her lips pulled into a deep frown.

Olivia ran her hands up and down Candace's arms. "Try to keep yourself distracted this evening, okay? Call a friend. Put on a good movie."

"Yeah, okay." The words caught in her throat and were barely audible.

When Nutsbe and Olivia walked outside, with Beowolf trailing behind, Candace shut the door quietly behind them.

Nutsbe had a bad feeling that that didn't go as well as Olivia might have thought. He was getting the vibe that Candace might just jump in her car and drive through the night.

Of course, if she did that, Offsed might win his case and be back out in society, free.

And then, would she ever be safe?

9

OLIVIA

BEOWOLF WALKED on one side of Nutsbe and Olivia on the other. Nutsbe was a head taller than Olivia, and that was while wearing heels. Up close, his shoulders were as broad, and he was as solid as he looked when he ran past her house, athletic.

For some reason, seemingly outside her control, her fingers twitched against her thigh, wishing she could slide her hand into Nutsbe's where it belonged. It didn't belong there; she'd just met the guy. He was just familiar, familial even, because he regularly jogged by her house.

And to be honest, after seeing Candace's distress, Olivia's emotions were barbed. She could use the comfort of human touch.

Bob stood at the end of the sidewalk. He held up his phone. "If I don't move more than three inches, I can get a signal here. Strange." Bob tipped his head. "Are you okay, Olivia? You look tired."

"Oh, yeah, fine." She combed her fingers over her scalp so her hair fell down her back and out of her eyes. "Motorcycles have been roving around the neighborhood, keeping me up with their noise."

"They have earplugs for that," Bob said kindly.

"Situational awareness." Olivia gave a half smile. "There aren't usually motorcycles in our neighborhood. And not that loud. And not making a circuit." She did a half turn to face Nutsbe. "Have you heard them?"

"I have." He gestured a sit command, and Beowolf plopped his butt onto the cement. "Turns out Olivia and I live in the same neighborhood," he explained to Bob, then focused back on her. "They were an annoying buzz, but I slept through them just fine. I got used to the constant activity of a military base. But now that you say that, it does stand out as strange."

"You need a dog to take over the situational awareness and let you get some sleep." Bob shoved his phone back in his pocket.

"I have Henrietta," Olivia said with a sigh. "She likes her beauty sleep too much to be bothered with alerting me." She paused and focused into the distance. "You know, I'm not sure what Hen would do if a bad guy showed up at my house. I have a terrible feeling that she might try to lick the guy to death." Olivia flicked a smile toward Bob, then checked her watch. "Speaking of Hen, I need to run by the house and get her fed, then it's back to the office. I've got some work to do for a grand jury that was just seated." Olivia stepped forward and bent to give Beowolf a kiss. "I'm so glad to have met you." When she stood, she handed Nutsbe the terrycloth slobber rag from their greeting. "Thank you for this."

Shoving the cloth into his pocket, Nutsbe asked, "Do you usually do two high-dollar trials at the same time?"

"This one happened to land in my area of expertise, and I wanted to be involved. I'll be burning the midnight oil for the next week or so. I have a long night ahead of me, so I better get going." She extended her hand. "Bob, I can't tell you how much I appreciate your coming to the rescue with Nutsbe and Beowolf. I promise not to make this short-notice thing a habit."

"Don't let that stop you if you find yourself in another bind, Olivia. It doesn't hurt to ask. We'll step up when we can."

"Nutsbe, so glad to finally put a name with a jogger. It's nice to know you're on the other side of the fence." She offered a finger wave as she walked to her car and climbed in.

"Nice to know you're on the other side of the fence?" Olivia muttered to herself after she shut her door. It sounded like she was glad there was a fence between them, and she was not.

She pinched the top of her nose and closed her eyes as she filled her lungs with air.

Okay, today had been a long day, and she had used a lot of words. Right now, she was going to give herself a bit of grace.

Olivia reached forward and pressed the engine on as she reviewed her conversation in the house.

There was something about Nutsbe's eyes—the way he looked at her—that seemed to tug at her secrets. Well, not secrets per se—just not conversational fodder with a stranger that was so incredibly personal. Only Jaylen and her attorney knew Mickey had left her for someone else. Not even her siblings knew about the tawdry end of her marriage.

And then there was the fact that—even though there was a sobbing woman rolling on the carpet with a dog—this had still been a professional meeting, not a social call.

Okay. No more of that. Move your thoughts elsewhere.

She let her motor idle while Nutsbe and Bob loaded Beowolf into the Iniquus vehicle.

Beowolf was exactly the dog Bob had described over the phone as a gentle giant. Just looking at him had a calming effect.

He was lion-sized, though. And it would be a trick for him to go unnoticed when he went into court with Candace, the way Valor might have done.

With the Iniquus team driving off and her seat belt in place, Olivia put her car in gear. Twisting to look over her shoulder as she backed down the drive, she caught a glance of herself in the rearview mirror—face flushed, eyes bright. The grin painting across her face was too big and toothy. She didn't remember smiling. Had she been smiling like this the whole time?

Olivia shifted into drive, started down the road, and at the stop sign, looked at herself again. Still smiling, still pink-faced, she put her hand to her forehead to see if she was feverish, but her skin was cool. She tried to drop the smile, but it popped right back into place.

That was how she had looked in there?

That was how Nutsbe had seen her?

The car behind her tapped its horn in a friendly, "Could you move it along?" beep. She raised her hand by way of apology and turned the corner.

To think, Nutsbe had been living behind her, possibly for the entire two years since she'd moved in. *Years.* Of course, with that fence, it wasn't like she could have wandered up to his kitchen door and asked to borrow a cup of sugar. But no doubt, had she known he lived there, she would have found some excuse to go over and introduce herself. After all, she had figured out what time he jogged, the mornings when he ran.

Tumbling that through her mind now made Olivia feel uncomfortable. Sure, he was cute and built, and she had thought of him as an innocent bit of eye candy while she drank her coffee. No, not even that. That wasn't a good characterization. There was something safe about his jogging by. Something comforting about knowing he was in the area.

Stop smiling.

He knew Henrietta from his jogs.

Yeah, Henrietta liked him, too, and always went over to stand in the window or the opened door to watch him. Henrietta was actually the reason Olivia spotted Nutsbe in the first place, and Henrietta was the reason why Olivia knew when Nutsbe was coming up the road.

Yeah, she wasn't the stalker. Her dog was.

Olivia understood why; Nutsbe just had "good guy" written all over him. And speaking to him didn't diminish that image in Olivia's mind.

Although, that look of utter helplessness on his face when Candace started crying, had been comical.

It was endearing to watch a tough guy go all mush.

Other than that, he was as she had seen him on his runs.

And what might he think of me? Olivia wondered. She peeked over at the mirror again. If I was grinning like this, he would have thought I was high on something.

And there was that whole thing about Mickey.

The more Olivia went back sentence by sentence through their discussion, the more uncomfortable she became with her behavior. If that were a movie scene, it would depend entirely on the background music to define the genre of the film. Put a little horror music on, and her "Hey, I live behind you. I'm getting divorced, I watch you run" conversation would make most audiences call out, "Boy, you're in danger."

Olivia reached for her phone. "Hey, Jaylen, I'm driving with you on speaker. Whatchya doing?"

"Tilly is fresh from her bath and is reading to her dolls. I am picking rice out of the carpet from her dinner. I forgot to lay the plastic down under her seat. Are you heading home?"

"Home to feed Henrietta and let her take a quick pee. I give her ten, fifteen minutes tops. I need to text her pet sitter and ask for some extra snuggle time tomorrow. I think Henrietta needs me to get another dog so she can have a companion. She used to have Mickey's cats, and she did fine, but she's been mopey lately. She has to be lonely."

"Another Cockapoodle-do?" Jaylen asked.

"Maybe? I don't think it would be fair to get a puppy. I just don't have the time right now. Maybe a rescue that's about Henny's age. It's something on my list of things to figure out. First, I want to get the divorce finished up." Olivia looked in the mirror, and her expression had returned to normal. Jaylen was a dependable, stabilizing influence, and Olivia was grateful for that.

"So why fifteen minutes tops?"

"Looming deadlines. I'm going back to the office to get some paperwork done. Later this evening, I have a meeting with Steph."

"Did you eat?"

"No. I plan to go through a drive-through or something on the way home from the office later." Olivia reassured her. "My day's just been slammed."

"Hey, wasn't this afternoon the meet and greet with the court dog? How did that go? Was she sweet?"

"Beowolf? Boy dog. He was like hot chocolate on a snow day. I don't know any other way to describe him."

"So he and the handler person got along well with your witness?"

"Yeah, it's usually a woman. But this time …" Olivia felt herself blush. "Jaylen, it was ridiculous. My mouth opened, and it was like I just decided to get fully naked in front of this guy."

"What are you saying? Like you lost your mind and ripped off your clothes? This guy must be *sexy* as hell."

Olivia wiped a hand over her forehead, into her hair, and scratched her scalp. "Yeah, he is. But that was a sad attempt at a simile." She checked her side mirrors and switched to the fast lane. "And get this, turns out that he's my behind-the-house neighbor."

"The one with the great fence?"

"That one. Also, the one that I told you about, the guy that jogs by most mornings, the one that Henrietta drools over in the front window? Yeah, he noticed her. He knew the house when I told him. Though, fortunately, when I told him about seeing him jogging, I left out any mention of drooling."

"The neighborhood Adonis? Are you kidding me right now? Great fence *and* killer bod?"

"He's better close up. He's got hazel eyes that are smart, engaged, emotional, thinking. Yeah, good eyes. And I liked the amusement crinkles at the corners. Like he sees life for all of its absurdities. Mmm, it wasn't like he thought what was happening was some kind of joke. It was that he seemed nice. Genuine."

"Genuine crows' feet," Jaylen deadpanned.

Olivia ignored that. "And he had this rich brown colored hair with bronze highlights, and it looked clean."

"Clean hair, huh? Well, that's a positive."

"I mean, it looked—" Olivia searched for a good descriptor. "Yeah, clean and soft."

Jaylen snorted. "So you pet him like the dog?"

Olivia caught herself grinning again. "Maybe I wanted to. But I was able to restrain myself."

"So a chiseled jawline, an athletic bod, and amusement crinkles. No wonder you were ripping off your clothes."

"Cut it out. I didn't rip off my—okay, not literally. In my mind? Possibly. Probably. We sat off to the side while my witness sobbed against the dog. Beowolf, by the way, is *the most* loveable carnival first-prize-sized teddy bear of a dog I have *ever* seen. Do you know who he reminded me of? Nana from Peter Pan." Olivia answered herself without giving Jaylen a guess.

"St. Bernard?" Jaylen asked. "For court?"

"Bullmastiff," Olivia corrected. "Two hundred pounds. But he was gentle and nurturing."

"Okay. And you were imagining yourself naked in this scene? Look, Olivia." Jaylen's voice turned exasperated. "I'm tired, and I have my attention on you, the rice mess, and Tilly all at the same time. Stop talking in circles. Cut to the chase."

"I told Nutsbe about Mickey leaving me, then the woman dumping Mickey, then Mickey wanting me to take him back."

"Did you also tell him that Mickey thought the other woman's money bags were present-day, and your money bags were years in the future?" Jaylen's voice ratcheted up with indignation like it always did whenever they were talking about Mickey. "That the shithead would rather be a millionaire present tense, than wait for your aunt to pass. A bird in the hand kind of disgusting thought process? You told him that?"

"I didn't say that, no. Just that my divorce is the reason I have a raspberry door with an extra splash of TMI." Olivia rubbed her thumb between her brows, hoping the throb wouldn't become a full-blown headache.

"Yeah, I guess that's a lot to take in with a greeting handshake."

Olivia's phone rang.

"Let me guess, Mickey."

"Yup."

"Take it," Jaylen said. "At least tell him that you want this to stop. It's harassment, isn't it?"

"I'll do that. Tell him I'm blocking the number. Look, I'll call you back when I get home, so you don't worry. Love you!"

On the third ring, Olivia swiped the call open. "What?" she barked.

"Thank god. Olivia, listen. This is an emergency. I need to talk to you *now*. In person."

"Your lawyer can talk to my lawyer in court."

"*Please*, Olivia. I'm begging you. I have something to tell you, and not over the phone. Are you at your place? I'm heading that way now."

Fear sizzled up her spine.

Olivia had had enough court cases where the victim said, "I should have trusted my instincts. I knew that something bad was waiting for me if I walked past that car. But—" There was always a "but," which usually involved expense or inconvenience. "But I didn't have money for a cab." "But it was raining, and I was tired."

Not wanting to fall into that category, Olivia lied. "I am not. And I won't be heading home in the foreseeable future. I'm not staying at the Millrace house right now. So you're heading in the wrong direction." She pulled to a stop at the light. "I'm hanging up and blocking your number. Don't you *dare* reach out to me in any way *ever* again."

A veil of perspiration left her damp and cold. She reached

out a shaking hand to cut off the vents, then gripped the steering wheel.

Olivia had been in the courtroom facing down violent predators for over a decade. Was her job frightening at times? Absolutely.

But in all of her years dealing with objectively dangerous criminals, Olivia had never experienced this wash of absolute primal terror lighting her nerves like this. She was heading toward a full-blown panic attack.

Flipping her blinker on, Olivia pulled to the side of the road, hoping her heart would stop thundering in her chest. She rested her head between her hands on the steering wheel and tried to find some space for air around the edges of her terror.

10

NUTSBE

BOB DROVE SILENTLY, taking sideroads to stay off the highway and out of the post-workday snarl. It was a perk to have navigation from Iniquus. The computer system could develop the most strategic path from Point A to Point B in real time. It lowered stress and increased the operators' time efficiency.

Nutsbe draped an arm over the back of the seat, rubbing Beowolf's head.

The whole way back to the campus, Nutsbe held on to the picture of Olivia smiling at him. She'd not only told him where she lived, but she was candid about her personal situation and the upcoming divorce. Did she say all that to let him know she was almost free? That she might be interested in him? Kind of sounded that way to Nutsbe.

"Home again, home again," Bob said, pulling into a spot by Cerberus Headquarters' front door. "How about you get

Beowolf and hand the lead to me so Beowolf has a clear understanding of who's in charge now." Bob reached up to press the automatic button to raise the hatch.

As the lift gate pinged a warning to stand clear, Beowolf crouched in the back, waiting for Nutsbe to round the vehicle and give him an unload command.

After giving Beowolf a final scrub and a promise to pick him up early the next day so they could have a walk together before court duty, Nutsbe said good night to Bob.

Once in the Panther Force War Room, Nutsbe sent an encrypted heads-up message to Sy Covington, letting him know that his legal name—the one that Russia knew—was in the federal court documents. Granted, it wasn't the first time his name had been listed in various courtrooms across the United States. Nutsbe was often called as a witness. But this was the freshest iteration.

Yeah, this one felt bad to him.

Usually with his job, Nutsbe was danger-adjacent. The field operators were the ones fast roping into the fray.

The FBI, Russia, Albania—Nutsbe didn't love that his name was part of the chatter that U.S. intelligence was picking up.

Nothing to be done, Nutsbe concluded as he headed home for the day.

The operators liked to talk about the three-foot square around them. Deal with what's in front of you.

What was in front of him was a day in court with a scared young woman who had obviously walked into hell and somehow survived. He didn't know the how or the why, but he'd hear her story tomorrow. And he needed to get his mind right. He needed to show up as strength and protection, no matter his personal shortcomings.

It was about his ego; Nutsbe fully recognized that.

When anguish came up, Nutsbe wanted to fix it. He wanted to relieve the burden, to cool the burn, to assuage the pain.

If there was no physical action he could take to make it better, his whole system went haywire.

It sucked.

This deficit on his part had interfered in all his relationships with women. They needed an ear to listen to them when he'd rather have a hammer in his hand fixing the damned thing.

Nutsbe was aware of his hypocrisy. He had down days, bad days—physically and psychologically. When he'd left the military, going to therapy had helped—talking it out, and yeah, emoting—whether it be to rage or cry. He did that, especially in the beginning with survivor's guilt and acute traumatic stress. Nutsbe wanted to tell his story. But he certainly didn't want anyone to tell him what to think or feel or, worse, to try to fix him and say that he was emotionally better.

Better was a journey, and it was *his* alone to travel.

After a while, his feelings evened out. He got used to his new life, and things improved.

They were good.

His life was really good.

For him, therapy was ongoing, as it was for everyone in field positions at Iniquus. You'd think he would have gotten better at being around women crying after all these years. But so far, he had not.

Nutsbe could use some tips, maybe some mentorship from Beowolf. Beowolf had moved calmly through that whole scene. Having Beowolf in the room had been interesting. He was like an emotional sponge, seeming to sop it all up. But when the front door shut, he trotted away from the group to the middle of the lawn, looked around, and shook his coat like he'd just come out of the lake. He shook it long and hard. And Nutsbe thought that was how Beowolf was able to do what he did. He took it on, then shook it off.

Skills. Man, Nutsbe would love to learn that trick.

With that thought, he concluded that with Beowolf in the courtroom doing his Beowolf support duties, Candace would get what she needed, and Nutsbe would be off the hook, searching for a way to pressure wash that woman's pain away.

To get off the gerbil wheel and clear his head, the whole way home, Nutsbe sang along to the music blasting from his radio. Pulling into his drive, he thought it would be cool to see Olivia in action tomorrow—watch her shift from a friendly neighbor into a cut-throat prosecutor.

With his motor idling, Nutsbe looked past his fence to see Olivia's roofline. She'd been living *right* there all this time. He'd run by her house day after day, waving at her pooch—Henrietta, the cockapoodle-do. He grinned. It was all so bizarrely normal that she had lived a sedate suburban life, then went to work, facing down vicious criminals. "Poor Henrietta has fence envy," he said, putting his car in reverse.

Sunset turned the clouds tangerine and purple. There was still daylight left to burn, enough time for a quick fix, he thought. Nutsbe motored back up the street and hung a left. Within ten minutes, he was at the hardware shop. Thirty minutes later, he tied an exterior door frame to the roof of his vehicle.

A quick run of the circular saw. The wizz of his drill. The cool metallic taste of screws held between his lips. And the *piece de resistance*, a coded door lock so Olivia could access the yard any time she wanted, and the job was complete.

Nutsbe stood back and admired his work. The wood would take a little time to weather and blend in. But all in all, it looked professional. Nutsbe whistled as he cleaned his tools and returned them to the garage.

Coming back around for a second load, he thought that a dog lying on the porch, keeping him company, would make this scene complete. He missed Beowolf.

Bending to pile the discarded lumber onto a tarp, Nutsbe wished the project had taken longer and required more physical exertion. He needed something more to burn away the excess energy in his system. A lot was going on in his world. The prep work for his team's next mission covered Nutsbe's desk. That needed his full attention; his planning often made the difference in keeping his team safe. Then there was Candace and the trial. And big in his mind was Olivia and her smile. And, of course, just as Kennedy predicted, that low-level hum playing through his mind had a distinctly Russian thrum.

Dragging the tarp to the compost, Nutsbe decided to go in and read—let some author's vivid imagination pull him away from the shit mountain he was trudging up.

Not all shit. There was Olivia. Shit with a flower on top.

Taking off his boots at the door, in sock feet, he walked up the stairs to his bedroom, grabbed his novel, and laid back on a stack of pillows piled behind his head.

A dog would complete this scene.

His parents had always had little dogs, which weren't his style, but a bullmastiff? Now, *that* was a dog Nutsbe could vibe with.

A dog would make noises—gurgling tummy, panting tongue, yipping dream. The house wouldn't sound this silent.

Nutsbe lifted his phone and tapped his app, bringing up brown noise to help him concentrate on his paperback. But what filled his ear was the sound of a motorcycle pulling to a stop behind his house. Nutsbe didn't remember seeing a motorcycle parked in the neighborhood. And this one sounded like it was at Olivia's.

Phone in hand, Nutsbe padded to his bedroom window and, standing to the side of the curtain, lifted it just enough to get eyes on the noise. With a final motor rev and a kick that lowered the stand, a man climbed off the black bike. Clad in jeans and a thick leather jacket, he dragged his helmet off his head, tucked it under his arm, looking around with a practiced eye.

This wasn't a casual turn of the head. This was someone scanning the environment for anyone who might be paying attention. He hadn't looked at the house yet. And Nutsbe remembered the sidewalk conversation where Bob thought Olivia looked tired. She had mentioned motorcycles. And yes, motorcycles were new. That one, pulling into her drive, was new.

Nutsbe tapped the phone to bring up the Iniquus switchboard.

"Iniquus communications. Identification."

"Nutsbe, Panther Force." It was against Iniquus' policy for employees to contact first responders. It had a bit to do with legal ramifications and reputation. It was mostly about clear communication and a web of professionals that could deploy to handle the event smoothly and efficiently. Iniquus had capabilities that local governments could only dream of having.

"I'm at my personal residence," he said as he watched the motorcycle guy put his helmet on the back of his bike, walk knowingly to the backyard, and begin to search under the rocks, pots, and mat, assumably for a key.

"What is the nature of this call?"

"Possible breaking and entering at the neighbor's house directly behind mine."

"I have your GPS location on the board. I have the house behind yours as 8398 Millrace."

"I believe that's correct. Gray house, raspberry-colored door. I'm witnessing a man looking under pots and rocks and feeling along window ledges." He put the call on speaker and opened the video to record. With the camera facing Olivia's house, Nutsbe continued to narrate. "He's lifted a rock. He just broke the kitchen door window. He's reaching in." Iniquus Communications recorded all calls. This data could become evidence in court. "The door is now open. The owner's car is not in the driveway, over." He switched from an informational call to an operational one.

"Nutsbe, be advised that Alexandria P.D. is en route to that location, over."

"Received. Over." Nutsbe let the curtain fall back in place. He sat on the edge of his bed, bending to pull out the tennis shoes he kept there for quick access. He tugged them on and laced the second shoe when he heard high-pitched barking.

Nutsbe wasn't subtle when he dragged the curtain back. There was the man with Henrietta in his arms. She was squirming and fighting him, her teeth bared and lunging.

Nutsbe was moving. Out the bedroom door, grabbing at the handrails, he vaulted down the stairs, tore down the hall, through the kitchen, and out his door.

As he ran, he stuck the phone into the hidden chest pocket designed at the exact height and width to insert his smartphone and record his actions. The elasticity in the fabric anchored the phone in place despite physical action. "Are you getting this? Over," he asked as he pulled the new fence door open.

Thank god for the new fence door.

"Video and audio, receiving clearly. Recording. Over."

Nutsbe stepped into Olivia's yard. "Hey, what's going on?" he yelled, hoping that the guy would freak, drop Henrietta, and take off for his bike.

Henrietta squirmed around to see Nutsbe. Then, using the guy's surprise, she got her back legs against his ribs and shoved. Slithering from his grasp, she bounded toward Nutsbe.

Crouching with wide arms like a goalie at a soccer match, the man cut off her line of escape. "Come here, Henny. Come to Daddy. Come on, sweet girl." He tried to croon, but his voice was a sawblade of menace.

Henrietta was doing her best to escape. Zig-zagging this way and that, her eyes held wide, showing the whites, she stayed just out of the man's reach while trying to work her way toward Nutsbe.

When Olivia talked about her pup, it was so obvious that Henrietta was well-loved and the kind of support for Olivia that Nutsbe had begun to want for himself. It enraged him that anyone would try to take Henrietta from Olivia.

"This is B.S." Nutsbe took another step forward. "Stop chasing that dog."

As the motorcycle guy turned to assess him, he stepped under the bright glow of Nutsbe's automatic security lights. Nutsbe saw that the guy had been badly beaten. The bruising on his face was fresh enough that the contusions were just beginning to turn colors. His eyes were bloodshot from impact. Dried blood had coagulated into a black scab beneath what looked like a broken nose.

Henrietta darted past Nutsbe into his backyard.

Nutsbe shoved the door. It slammed, locking automatically.

Now, it was Nutsbe and the biker alone in the backyard. Nutsbe had no quick exit route. His shoes sunk into the moist ground, so he knew he'd be slow off the X.

Shifting his weight only made the muddy mess worse.

"What the hell are you doing?" The guy stormed. "That's my dog." He jutted a pugnacious chin, breathing heavily from the exertion of the chase.

"I don't think so," Nutsbe kept his tone even. He was being recorded, and that was incentive to cool his rhetoric. "If she is, she doesn't seem to like you much."

"I'm taking her to the vet. She hates the vet." He took a step forward. "How about you open that door and give me my dog back."

"You're taking her to the vet on a motorcycle at eight-thirty at night?"

Lifting his arms like he would throttle Nutsbe, the man ran for him.

Nutsbe put one hand on his fence for stability as he lifted his knee to his chest and shoved, catching the guy in his stomach and forcing him backward.

As the biker landed on his butt, legs in the air, head in the mud, Nutsbe paid attention. From the fall, it was hard to tell. This guy might be an amateur, but it might also be that he was caught off guard, and his head was already clanging from an earlier beatdown.

"Dude, cut it out." Nutsbe tried to de-escalate. "You don't want to fight me. It looks like someone beat the shit out of you already today."

The look in the biker's eyes said he had an agenda. And Nutsbe was getting in his way.

Nutsbe watched the guy's hands for the sudden appearance of a weapon. If he pulled a gun, Nutsbe was doomed.

Sirens sounded up the road as Nutsbe took a sidestep and sank again. This was going to suck for sure if that cop car didn't show up fast.

The guy got to one knee and posted his forearm on his thigh. He looked away and waved a hand as if in surrender.

A moment later, the guy was launching himself at Nutsbe, trying to get in a sucker punch that Nutsbe averted by leaning out of the way. The crack of angry knuckles splintered the wood on his fence.

"Ouch, that had to have hurt." Nutsbe kept his tone even. "How about you take a step back?"

The guy gave a single shake of his hand and yipped to relieve the pain. Something the hell sure was motivating the guy. He rounded with a hook that Nutsbe pressed away.

The siren drew closer, and a second one joined the cacophony at a distance.

The man lifted his fisted hands and pummeled Nutsbe as Nutsbe did his best to block and parry. "I need that dog. Give me my dog." Yeah, despite the bad start, this guy was trained. Nutsbe would say ex-military. When the biker kicked toward Nutsbe's shins, he jumped out of the way, throwing himself off balance.

Nutsbe did his best to step and dodge. Since Iniquus had all this on tape, Nutsbe didn't want to do anything that would signal that he was the aggressor and he refrained from landing his own punch. With as much anger as Nutsbe had firing in his system right then, he wasn't sure the man would survive the contact. A manslaughter charge would only make this day that much more complicated.

As the attacker got a foot up on Nutsbe's thigh and shoved, Nutsbe grabbed at the cuff of his jeans, curling his fingers into the fabric, letting himself go with the strike's momentum. This did two things, limited the damage to Nutsbe's body and dragged the guy off his feet. Nutsbe twisted the man's heel, glad he'd primed his muscle memory using this move when he was fighting Chuck just that morning.

The twist of his foot forced the attacker onto his stomach. Nutsbe clambered on top, wrapping his hand around the man's head and shoving his mouth and nose momentarily into a puddle.

Nutsbe kept the guy in this stress position just long enough that the guy realized he could drown. When he stopped squirming and submitted, Nutsbe let him turn his head and gulp in some air.

"Police!" Nutsbe heard a take-charge alpha voice. "Don't move."

Nutsbe slowly ducked his head to look under his arm. Not seeing the officer, he gasped out, "Operations. Is that Alexandria P.D.? Over."

"Affirmative. We've accessed your house security cameras. By our count, there are two police vehicles. Three officers, weapons are at retention ready, and high guard. Over."

"Copy. Over." It was good to have eyes on.

Following the officers' directives, Nutsbe found himself up against his fence, spread eagle. "Name?"

The nut job was getting cuffed beside him, and Nutsbe didn't want to give his name. "My company called this in. They can provide you with my information. Anything you need beyond that can be addressed with my lawyer."

"Lawyer, huh?" The police officer laughed. "The guy is lawyering up before he's even in cuffs. Whelp," he said, "put your left hand behind your back. Leave your right hand in place."

"My name is Mickey Pauley," The attacker said. "This is *my* house. He has *my* dog in his yard, and he won't give her back to me."

Sure enough, Henrietta was on the other side of the fence, barking her head off.

"Is that right?" the police officer asked Nutsbe as he clapped a cuff around his wrist, none too gently.

"Lawyer," Nutsbe said on an exhale. Mickey Pauley was either lying his head off, or he was probably the soon-to-be ex-husband and didn't belong anywhere near here. "Operations," Nutsbe said, "Check with Bob, Cerberus Team Alpha, for the lawyer's name and phone number we were assisting earlier this evening." Nutsbe didn't want to use Olivia's name lest this guy was lying, and he could use the information to squirm out of charges. "Please apprise her of the situation. Over."

"Hey," the Pauley guy yelled. "Who are you talking to? What's going on here? Officer, look at how he's hurt me. Look at my face. I need an ambulance."

Nutsbe shook his head as the officer patted him down, got below the knee, and startled. He pulled Nutsbe's pant leg past his sock and took in the prosthetic leg. He scratched his nose and stood.

Today was one for the books.

"I'm checking your pockets for weapons." The officer who had cuffed Mickey Pauley started going through the guy's pockets, pulling out his phone, his wallet, and a pouch of tobacco.

"Officer, are you listening to me? Look here." Pauley raised his shoulder and leaned to the side, lifting his jacket high enough to expose the police badge clipped to his belt. "I want to press charges against that man. Every charge available to me."

Nutsbe wondered why the guy had kept his badge secret until that moment. All he could think of was that he didn't want his commander to know this went down.

Pauley turned his head and spat at Nutsbe's feet. "I want him to go down hard."

Yeah, buddy? You're just another name on the list.

11

OLIVIA

IT WAS remarkable to Olivia that the night sky was just now getting dark. Today felt like it had gone on for an eternity.

She went from court to Candace's, home to tend to Henrietta, and then on to the office. Walking down the hallway to Steph's office, Olivia hoped their witness had been located. If they had not, a Plan B needed to be laid out.

Candace's house was the surprising chocolate spread that made today's shit sandwich palatable. *Mmm, no, those aren't words that should go together in a sentence.* But the sentiment there was correct. Bob, Beowolf, and Nutsbe each had a steady wholesomeness.

Olivia had done meet and greets with other dogs and other witnesses, but never with a horse like Beowolf.

It seemed to Olivia that Beowolf was the perfect dog for Candace. And that was important.

Tomorrow would be interesting.

She'd specifically told Judge Madison that Beowolf was a

bullmastiff, and he seemed a-okay with all of it. She wasn't sure that the judge had a clear picture. Time would tell, Olivia thought as she knocked on her boss's door.

"Good you're here." Steph looked up from the pile of papers on her desk. "Let's get right to it." She pointed her pen toward the armchair.

When Olivia sat, she immediately slid her heels out of her shoes. There was too much walking today, and she would have blisters. Tomorrow, she'd like to wear pants and flats, but this particular judge was very old school and had his own view of how people should dress for court. Granted, he was eighty. Olivia went along to get along. She saved her brownie points and points of contention for when they served her best. And that was never over the dress code.

"It looks like Congress might be trying to get involved in our foreign extremist's case."

"How do you see that playing out?" Olivia asked.

"I have a meeting set up on Tuesday next week to talk to them about it. What have you got on your calendar?"

"Divorce," Olivia said. "That day, I'll be in court for me. I've penciled that in for the whole day. You just never know what can happen."

"I forgot that was coming up." Steph laced her hands and rested them on her stomach as she leaned back in her chair with a grin. "Big congratulations."

"Yes, thanks," Olivia smiled back. "It's going to feel really good. Just have to get the signatures on the paperwork."

Steph lifted her chin. "You look like crap, by the way."

"Fair," Olivia said, brushing a hand through her hair. "I haven't been sleeping at all." And looking like crap was how she met Nutsbe? *Wonderful.*

"Serious," Steph had been a friend for many years, and

the concern on her face was genuine, "is the upcoming divorce trial keeping you up?"

"No, it's motorcycles," Olivia said, fatigue weighted her voice.

"More?"

"Every night for what—more than a week now? These motorcycles have started up around midnight. Super loud. Super obnoxious."

"At your house?"

"Not my house." Olivia sank deeper into the chair. "They're going around the various roads in my subdivision."

"Isn't that a noise ordinance issue?"

"Could be. I don't know. With the carjackings going on in the city, do I want to pull cops off their patrols to stake out motorcycle noises?"

Steph had that glassy-eyed stare she got when she reached back into a fold of her gray matter to pull out some factoid. "Hmm. Probably, I just have the grand jury on the brain."

"I'm getting some water. Do you want some?" Olivia stood. "What were you just thinking about?"

"Yes, to the water, thanks." As Olivia bent over the minifridge to grab two bottles, Steph said, "I was thinking about things with the Middle East and motorcycles—but it's a CIA story."

Olivia twisted the cap off and handed Steph the water. "Let's hear it." She sat down and took a sip from her own bottle.

"Mmmm, hang on." Steph pulled out her phone and tapped the keyboard. "Yup, here we go. On August 7th, a terrorist—number two in his organization—was gunned down in his car. He and three friends died instantly. Let's see here. The assassination took place on the anniversary of the

African twin attacks on the US embassies in Kenya and Tanzania."

"Where are you reading this?" Olivia asked. "I haven't seen anything in the papers. What has this got to do with motorcycles?"

"I follow intelligence folks on social media," Steph put her phone on the desk. "I want to know right away if they are picking up anything to do with our case."

Olivia leaned forward. "Are they?"

"They know our case is moving forward. Nothing interesting or new. But about the attack on the seventh, the I.C.—Intelligence Community—has been low-key talking about how the CIA was the one who committed the assassinations. They said the CIA had hoped to keep it super-secret, but somebody's ego got the best of them, and they spilled to a reporter."

"They said they were CIA?" Olivia swiveled in her chair, trying to find a more comfortable position.

"No, they said they," she used finger quotes, "'happened' to be there and had witnessed the event." Steph reached into her bag of chips and popped one into her mouth. Then pushed the bag toward Olivia. "Help yourself."

Olivia lifted a no-thank-you hand.

"According to the I.C., the witness described what happened with details that the average citizen walking down the street would not have in their vocabulary, like that they 'clocked the shooter.'"

"What does that mean. That's not in my vocabulary either."

"Apparently, standing looking forward is twelve o'clock. He *clocked* this person at his two." She held out her arm like she was the hand on a clock and then turned her head to line up her view. "That's my take, anyway. The shots were fired from a gun fitted with a silencer."

"How would they hear shots if the gun had a silencer?"

"It doesn't silence," Steph explained. "That's a misnomer. It just makes the shot quieter. Suppressor's a better term."

"Huh." Olivia changed her mind and reached for some chips. "I've never had that come up at trial, but if I do, I know to do more research. Seems like that was someone who knew what they were doing. I don't think I'd be counting shots as much as ducking and running."

"And they knew to follow their trajectory. The witness told the reporter that six went into the car, killing the four people, and two more hit a nearby vehicle that was empty."

"But what's this got to do with motorcycles?" Olivia plucked a tissue from the box on the side table and wiped the fat and salt from her fingers. She was hungry and looking forward to a bag of hot carbs she could pick up at some drive-through. Had she eaten today? Olivia didn't remember eating.

"According to the I.C. folks, it was done by two motorcycle assets on the behest of Uncle Sam."

"For the U.S.? So it wasn't like a tier-one team dropped in. They're saying it was the CIA roaring around on motorcycles?" She tossed the tissue into the can. "What is that government saying?"

"Yeah, interesting. Apparently, they're trying to cover it all up because they don't want their citizens to know that a hit took place on their soil and that it happened in some upscale part of the city. The motorcycles driving up, taking the shots, and moving on says the assassinated terrorist was living there amongst their elite, and the government did nothing about it."

"Okay, but how does a government cover something like that up if it's on social media?"

"They're saying that it was a robbery gone bad and that

this story about the CIA is all made-up bunk. The people absorbed that. Their government conditioned the citizens to accept events like that as propaganda."

"I see. I guess better a robbery than an assassination. And you were thinking, what? What's good for the goose is good for the gander? Maybe the extremists are sending motorcycles to my neighborhood to look for me to do a tit-for-tat since I'm trying to imprison one of their spies?"

"Bit of a stretch, admittedly. I wasn't saying that at all. I said I was *thinking* about a thing with motorcycles—but it's a CIA story."

"Okay, back to the reason I'm here. Did anyone find our witness?" Olivia asked.

"That would be a no. And I did bring it to the FBI's attention. So I guess there's no point in meeting tonight. We can take this up again after the Offsed trial is finalized. But I would appreciate your reading over that file and giving me your thoughts on next steps."

"Good enough." Olivia stood.

"Hey, Olivia," Steph said quietly. "If the extremist organization did get hold of our witness, and if they applied advanced interrogation techniques to get him to share information, our names would come up as people who know the story. Do you have good security on your house?"

"I—"

Both women turned toward the tap on Steph's door. Steph's paralegal stood there, wide-eyed. She shrank back out of the door jamb to reveal the police.

Olivia instantly knew the officer was there to speak to her. Her body braced for terrible news. Had the Offseds found Candace's hideout?

Steph stood up from behind her desk. "Officer, can I help you?"

12

Olivia

Olivia glanced at the plate over the door to assure herself this was the right conference room. She paused long enough to square her shoulders, set her game face in place, and then pressed through the door. "Olivia Gladstone," she announced in her prosecutor's timbre as she strode forward with the overbright clickety-clack of her heel echoing off the terrazzo floor.

Two suited men rose from the cheap laminate table. One was an ill-fitting off-the-rack, and the other suit was bespoke.

Ill-fitting stretched out a hand. "Detective Wannamaker."

Bespoke stepped closer with a manicured hand extended, not prissy, more like an attention to detail. "Sy Covington, Iniquus Senior Counsel."

Olivia was only mildly surprised that an Iniquus lawyer was here. As soon as Olivia had taken her phone off airplane mode as she got into her car to drive to the station, Iniquus's switchboard rang through and briefly explained that there was an attempted break-in at her house—the same information she'd received from the officer who had shown up at Steph's door. Without any other details, Olivia thought that Nutsbe had seen the crime and called it in to someone.

But why hadn't Nutsbe called Olivia himself?

Olivia dropped her glance to the metal folding chair between her and Covington.

Covington pulled it out in a very old-school manner but didn't press her for an acknowledgment of the gesture, nor did he make a show of helping her to push the seat in. He merely settled back down in front of a closed leather briefcase. A tablet was positioned on top.

Olivia turned to the detective. "I was told there was a break-in at my house, and two subjects were detained."

"That's correct." Wannamaker flipped pictures upside down and slid them her way. "Can you identify either of these men?"

Olivia picked one of them up and held it with her fingers pressing along the edges. It was a mugshot of Nutsbe dressed in the Iniquus uniform he had been wearing at Candace's. This had to be some kind of mistake. Nutsbe?

Well, at least she better understood Covington's presence.

Seeing Nutsbe staring stoically into the camera, holding a blackboard with its white plastic numbers, was a gut punch.

What in the actual heck?

A streak of mud slashed across his face; the five o'clock shadow made him look tired, but otherwise, he seemed okay.

She just couldn't fathom—Nutsbe was breaking into her house? There was a reasonable story; she was sure of it.

The next picture she scooped up was Mickey. Of course, it was. He said he was on the way over to her house. And she'd felt the premonition—danger, violence—she didn't have a lock on what that sensation was other than that she should keep a clear and copious distance. In his mugshot, Mickey looked like he'd been stomped into the ground, picked up, pummeled, and stomped into the ground again. Had Nutsbe done that?

She frowned at the image.

Mickey was a fighter. One of the things he liked best about working on the force at D.C.P.D. was finding a criminal who wanted to fight back. Since Mickey had a gun, a baton, pepper spray, and backup, he usually walked away with scuffed knuckles.

And he learned to never gloat to Olivia because she had threatened to go public with his behavior and find a prosecutor in D.C.—even though it would be tough to do—that was willing to bring brutality charges against a cop.

Olivia hadn't married Mickey as a police officer. He joined the Army while they were dating. After they married, he went to war; she went to law school. In the back of her mind, Olivia had blamed some of Mickey's violence on his time overseas. But since he was a mechanic, it was more likely that it was just a part of his personality that he'd learned to hide from her, which was condoned and even cheered on in his work culture.

Olivia sent a glance toward Covington. He wasn't offering her anything in his expression that provided her with information. "This," she said, pointing to the first photo on the table, "is my neighbor, Nutsbe. And this," she put the second photo down and stabbed a finger at her soon-to-be-ex, "is Mickey Pauley."

She raised her brows and drew them tight, staring straight at Wannamaker. "What's the story?"

Covington cleared his throat, drawing her attention around. "I have a phone recording and a videotape of the incident," he said. "It will probably answer a lot of your questions."

"I think—" Wannamaker began.

"Perfect," Olivia interrupted him. "Let's see it."

Covington tapped the tablet on; it was already queued to the beginning. "Possible breaking and entering at the neighbor's house directly behind mine." Olivia heard Nutsbe's voice. She'd recognize his rich bass anywhere. The image must be from his upstairs window. Olivia tapped pause. "How did you get this so quickly?" she asked Covington. "Who is Nutsbe talking to?"

"Iniquus communications, ma'am. When an operator calls in, they record everything to provide evidence and context should it be needed."

Nutsbe called Iniquus, not 9-1-1. That was interesting.

Olivia tapped play. After a minute of discussion, the video continued with Nutsbe jogging out of his house, across his lawn, and pushing open a door in his fence—a door in his fence? There was no door in his fence. She rewound and watched that part again. There was a door in his fence. *Huh.* With the door open, Olivia watched as Henrietta scrambled out of Mickey's arms.

Henrietta had always hated Mickey.

Mickey was chasing her around like an idiot, trying to catch her. Then she was racing for safety past Nutsbe into his backyard, and the door slammed shut behind her.

The camera lens turned. Mickey, bent as if to make a football tackle, roared toward Nutsbe. Nutsbe merely lifted his foot, and Mickey went flying. Olivia tapped the screen and slowed the motion down to a crawl. She wanted to see every detail.

From the angle and movement, Nutsbe had to have his phone on his chest, maybe in a pocket.

She slid the cursor back to the point where Nutsbe came through the fence door. She paused when there was a clear enough picture of Mickey to see that his face was already damaged, and he hadn't yet approached Nutsbe. She moved forward in the fight. Nutsbe knew what the hell he was doing. He was a good fighter, but except for that first distancing kick, he was not throwing down. He was merely defending. It was evident that Nutsbe had done nothing against the law.

Why was he arrested?

At the end, she licked her lips and handed the tablet back to Covington. "Thank you. That was very helpful." She turned to Wannamaker. "Why was my neighbor arrested?"

"We didn't have the tape yet," Wannamaker said. "And Officer Pauley was pressing charges. He told me that he had come home to find Mr. Crushed breaking into his house, that his dog had escaped, and that Mr. Crushed attacked Officer Pauley. That the dog ran into Mr. Crushed's backyard, and Mr. Crushed shut the door, trapping her there."

"So breaking—" Olivia started.

"Attempted breaking and entering with the intent to do harm, assault and battery, trespassing, and larceny of a dog." Wannamaker stroked a hand along his chin. "We just need some information from you before we decide what to do."

"Here's what you'll do," Olivia said. "You'll let Mr. Crushed go home and get some sleep."

"It's a little more complicated than that," Wannamaker said.

"Oh?" Olivia sat back and crossed her arms under her breasts.

"Officer Pauley is pressing those charges."

"Assault and battery are off the table. Clearly, Mickey was already damaged goods, and clearly, Mr. Crushed was defensive, not offensive."

"That was an initial charge," Wannamaker said.

"You agree the evidence shows that Mickey arrived already battered. And that it was Mickey who broke the glass on my door. Mr. Crushed did not approach my home."

"Correct. There's trespassing and dognapping still on the table," Wannamaker clarified. "Officer Pauley said it's his house and his dog. He presented pictures of his title that he accessed on his phone, and there were pictures of him and the dog."

"Interesting." She dug her phone from her purse. "Sorry, let's go back," Olivia said, scrolling through her files. "What is Mickey charged with?"

"Nothing. We let him go."

"Of course." Olivia sighed. She'd found the correct file; she just needed the right paragraph to share. Skimming over the words, she said, "So you let him go. Before I got here. Before I could weigh in?"

"We did."

She looked up. "You sent the officer to my office. It was an extra step. Was this a courtesy because of my job?" Olivia asked the detective.

"It was."

"And yet, knowing I was on my way here. You didn't wait. I'm assuming that it was Mickey's badge that let him head out that door. You are aware, aren't you, of the percentage of domestic abusers that are employed by the police?"

Wannamaker cleared his throat.

"And you didn't want to ask me what my thoughts were. Detective, that's a choice you might want to reconsider in the future." She drew in a long breath.

Olivia needed to keep her demeanor professional no

matter how much she wanted to yell at Wannamaker for his stupidity. "What did Mr. Crushed say through all of this?"

"Nothing, ma'am. He lawyered up and was silent."

Brilliant. And disciplined. That was exactly what everyone should do around the police—keep their mouths shut.

Olivia stretched out to pass her phone to the detective. He accepted it, looking down to see what she had for him. "While it is true that Mickey Pauley is on the title, we have a separation agreement. When I moved out two years ago, we stipulated that I wouldn't go to what had been our marital house where he lives. And he would have no access to our jointly held rental house that I made my home. It's in the agreement and signed by the judge. I can also point out where he kept his cats, and I took my dog. There is no joint custody of the pets. That's a class five felony to try to take my dog, and I am pressing charges against Mickey Pauley." She planted her hands on the table, fingers splayed wide as she pushed her anger onto the surface. "He knowingly made false statements to the police. I'm sure you will want to bring charges. He was trespassing on *my* property." Olivia fought to keep her tone even and calm. She thought she was pulling off the charade of Ice Queen. "I want to press charges. He was breaking into *my* home. I want to press charges." She lifted her hand to stab a stiff finger onto the table for emphasis, punctuating each word as she said, "He was there with malice after a threatening phone call to me." She sat back and crossed her arms under her breasts, hard eyes on Wannamaker so he knew this wasn't a soft ask and he could just shuffle the paperwork off to the side. "I want a restraining order."

"You can get me a copy of this file?" Wannamaker slid Olivia's phone along the table until it was back within her reach.

"Sure, but it's filed with the court, and you have easy access to that," Olivia said, lifting her phone and wiggling it at Covington. "If you need this, I can make it available to you. Just let me know."

"Thank you," Covington said.

They just let Mickey go, unfathomable.

Olivia turned back to Wannamaker with a glare just this side of pugnacious indignation. "Mr. Crushed has permission to be on my property and to invite my dog to his house. I want him released from custody, and all charges dropped. I am the only one under present legal circumstances with any right to determine who has access to that property and my dog."

Wannamaker hefted himself tiredly to his feet and shuffled out of the room. "Hang on."

13

OLIVIA

OLIVIA TURNED TO COVINGTON. "I'm sorry about all of this. How did Nutsbe even know that Mickey was breaking in?"

"He heard a motorcycle and said that you'd been bothered by the noise circling the neighborhood late at night for over a week now."

"That's true," Olivia said slowly. Were Mickey and his riding pals out trying to wear her down? Mickey knew she was a light sleeper. And that going without sleep wore on her.

Olivia sat quietly mulling. She was caught on Henrietta fighting to get out of Mickey's arms.

Why was Mickey trying to dognap Henrietta?

Thinking back to his begging phone call that she shouldn't have answered, Olivia had to conclude that Mickey wanted to use Henrietta as a ploy—a lure—to get them in the same place for some reason.

He'd sounded desperate when he'd called earlier, begging to see her. Olivia had assumed he was panicking about the divorce being finalized. He had a whole future mapped out for himself—a financial future—and Olivia, the sole heir to her great aunt's fortune, played a starring role in his aspired-to multi-million-dollar lifestyle. So yeah, he had an incentive to stop the divorce.

And he had *tried* to stop the divorce.

But after two years of stalling, they were days from their marriage *finally* being over.

That earlier sense of terror washed over Olivia again. She had been a criminal prosecutor for over a decade and knew the calculation. The only way that Mickey could keep the future millions was for Aunt Jo to die. Then, because of how the will was written, Mickey had to wait at least twenty-four hours after Aunt Jo's death to kill Olivia, or the fortune would go to a woman's shelter. If a double homicide was his plan, he had until Tuesday and court to make it happen. As a cop, Mickey knew how to get the job done. And he knew he might even be able to rely on the support of his fellow brothers in blue to make any evidence or investigation disappear.

But what explained Mickey's face?

He looked like he might have finally run up against a criminal who could outfight him. But that couldn't be right. When he changed his uniform, he would have at least washed his face, right?

Olivia grabbed her phone. Shooting a quick "excuse me" toward Covington, she dialed her Aunt Jo. She could hardly breathe as the phone sounded once, twice, three times, panic rose, four—

"Hello?"

"Oh! Thank goodness." Olivia put a hand over her heart. "Are you okay?"

"I was just about to head to bed to read for a bit. This rain has made me feel creaky."

"Aunt Jo, I need you to do me the biggest favor I've ever asked of you." She moved her shaking hand to her forehead as she stood and pulled her shoulders back, trying to give her lungs more room to function.

"What is it that you need, Livy? You sound agitated. Is something going on?"

"Aunt Jo, I need you to listen to me. This is urgent. I'm afraid you're in danger."

"How—"

"I'm going to make a hotel reservation for you, Aunt Jo. And I'm going to send a taxi to your house. It will be there in about ten minutes. I need you to pack a bag fast. Just throw in your medications, computer and chargers, comfy clothes, and toiletries. Don't overthink it. If you need anything, I'll get it for you later."

"Olivia—"

"I need you to stay at the hotel until my divorce is finalized next Wednesday. Okay?"

"Mickey?" Aunt Jo whispered.

"Is out of control. And I don't know if he's heading your way. *Please* only go out the door when the taxi shows up. You're too far away for him to be to you yet. Just pack fast. And this is extremely important, Aunt Jo, you can tell your friends that you're away, but for your safety and mine, that is *all* you can tell them."

"Oh, dear."

"The cab is coming." Olivia could hardly push the words from her mouth. What if something happened to her beloved aunt? What if that something was caused by her marriage to Mickey?

"Yes. I need to dress then." Her aunt's voice warbled.

"Aunt Jo, I'll take time to explain and apologize later. I'm hanging up now. I love you."

As soon as Olivia tapped the button to end the call, she was scrolling for the name of the Philly hotel Jaylen had told her about, which was safe and comfortable with a good restaurant. She used a new credit card from a new bank to which Mickey had no connection. Then she pulled up the taxi app and sent a car heading to her aunt's house—fifteen minutes. Thank goodness her aunt lived in Philly, which was a good two hours away from Alexandria.

With all that in motion, Olivia plopped back in her seat, sending a tight-lipped smile toward Covington.

"It sounded like you handled that well." His southern drawl was warm and slow. It was a balm. Olivia bet he could lead the jury by the nose in a courtroom. "Is there anything I can do to help?"

"No." She shook her head. "But thank you."

The door opened, and Wannamaker leaned in. "If you'll follow me, Ms. Gladstone, the magistrate can talk to you about a restraining order now." He shifted his focus. "And Mr. Covington, they're bringing Mr. Crushed here to join you. The charges have all been dropped."

"And Mickey Pauley?" Olivia asked.

"I have to talk to the judge to get an arrest warrant. That's next."

Olivia stood. "Mr. Covington, I'd like to say something to Nutsbe before you leave, if I may." She didn't wait for an answer but gathered her purse and phone to follow Wannamaker to the magistrate's office.

It was a fairly quick process. Olivia knew the drill from helping many witnesses along the way. As she headed back toward the conference room, Olivia found Covington and Nutsbe standing at the entrance, waiting.

Covington was on his phone, looking out toward the parking lot. When Nutsbe turned her way, she saw relief light his eyes. The fatigue fell off and was replaced with a smile.

Olivia wanted to run into his arms and hold him tight, to thank him for protecting Henrietta and for putting up with Mickey's bullshit.

But Nutsbe was a K9 handler, a neighbor, and a brand-new acquaintance. So she walked over with her hand on her heart, contrition on her face, and said, "Nutsbe, I am so, so sorry."

Covington looked up from his phone and focused first on her, then Nutsbe. "This is urgent. I need to go."

Nutsbe stretched his arm long, pressing the door wide for Covington. "Good luck."

Covington raised his hand as a goodbye and strode into the night, seemingly unfazed by the cold drizzle.

When Nutsbe turned toward her, she lifted her keys toward the parking lot. "Can I give you a lift?" He didn't answer; he just followed along beside her.

What do you say to a man who just fought your husband for your dog? She landed on the mundane. "I haven't eaten yet. Have you?" She liked that he walked close to her. It sort of felt couple-ish. Once again, her fingers itched to reach out and slip into his hand.

"I know a good pizza place on the way back to our neighborhood. Will that do?" he asked with a smile. It was a nice smile. It conveyed that he didn't blame her for this. And that he was grateful for the ride.

"Fat and carbs? Perfect."

She drove through the rain while Nutsbe ordered the pizza to go. Both of them liked the same topping, bacon and pineapple. That was interesting since so many found pineapple on a pizza controversial.

The small talk was very small. There was probably as

much on his mind as she had on hers. Nutsbe seemed to be engaged in watching out the side mirror, turning every once in a while to look out the back window. Did he think that someone was tailing them?

What if it was Mickey?

"There's a new door in your fence," Olivia said as Nutsbe pointed toward the entrance to the strip mall.

"It felt selfish to have Henrietta suffering from fence envy," he said lightly. "It was a quick fix. No big deal."

"I'm sure Henrietta disagrees, especially tonight." Olivia pulled into a parking space across from the Italian place.

"I'll give you the punch code when we get back. That way, Henrietta can hang out whenever she wants. She's in my yard now." He glanced out the window and then back to Olivia. "There's a good-sized roof over my patio. She's not getting wet." Nutsbe unclasped his buckle and reached for the door handle. "I'll run in. Anything besides the pizza? Canoli? Salad?"

"But—" She wasn't sure what the but was. Just maybe he shouldn't be running out in the rain after everything else he'd been through that night.

"Your feet'll get wet," he said, "and your toes will get cold. I don't have that problem." Before Olivia could say anything more, he was out the door with a light jog toward the sidewalk.

Olivia snatched up her phone, dialed Jaylen, and, with alarming speed, spilled the events that had taken place that evening. It was a relief to get the story out of her system, like unscrewing the top on a soda and enjoying the satisfying sound of the gas hissing out.

"Wait! Take a breath." Jaylen sang into the phone in a lullaby tone.

"Oh. Sorry. Are you putting Tilly down?"

"She's putting up a last fight against her drooping eyelids." There was the sound of a kiss. "Aren't you sweetheart? It's so exciting to be awake and exploring the world. It's so hard to shut your eyes. But Mommy really needs you to go night nights."

"Should I call you back? Is my voice waking her?"

"I have my earbuds in," she sang. "And her eyelids are heavy. She'll be out any moment now. This is what I got. You left the police station, and you're getting pizza."

"Yes."

"And you're with your next-door neighbor, Nutsbe—the one who is all kinds of uncomfortable around a crying woman—that Nutsbe?"

"Yes."

"Why was he in your backyard? You have that huge fence back there. He'd have to have walked—yeah, I don't get that."

"He was making a door in the back for Henrietta so she could go run around his backyard when she wanted to hang out outside. It was really very kind of him."

"Dog poo and all? He was down with that?"

"I guess." Olivia laced her fingers and pressed the heels of her hands against her temples, feeling the throb in a steady, insistent beat. "He didn't talk to me beforehand."

"Do you feel comfortable with that?" Jaylen asked. "I'm a little ambivalent. It could be nice, but it could be creepy, right?"

"Creepy? No. Having met Nutsbe, that didn't cross my mind. First, the door saved Henrietta and possibly me—I don't know what Mickey was up to trying to dognap Hen like that. Second, people have doors in their fences. I don't have to use it. There was no presumption, just an invitation. And third, he's just too solid of a guy, you know? There is nothing about him that puts up even the tiniest of red flags. Especially because Henrietta doesn't like men, and she loves Nutsbe. She looks forward to his jogs and mopes when he doesn't run by. But I will tell you I'm processing this for the first time. When I found out about the door, I thought it was his coping reflex."

"Yeah, sure, people reflexively cut doors in their fences all the time." There was the squeak of hinges from Jaylen's rocker as she lifted up. "Tilly's out like a light. I'm going to lay her down in the crib."

Olivia stretched the seat belt out and adjusted it across her chest. "It was the crying thing when we met this afternoon. He was struggling with the tide of cathartic emotions. I think it really bothered him that he couldn't do anything about all the pain."

"It was the witness crying, right?" Jaylen asked. "Not you?"

"Me? Why would I cry? When have I ever cried?"

"I'm just trying to follow why you think that your witness crying made him reflexively cut a hole into the back of his fence so Henrietta could go poop on his lawn."

"Yeah. That might be a leap." Olivia looked through the rain toward the restaurant door. She should have just pulled up and parked along the curb. "In my mind, he felt bad and needed to do a good deed to balance his world. And when I say that out loud, that feels right to me."

"Whew! Done for the day. Heading for a glass of wine and a piece of chocolate." There was the snick of a door. Okay. "I'm in the kitchen. I have my computer fired up. Send me a picture of this guy."

"I don't have a picture to send you. It would have been weird for me to take out my phone and take a picture of him. And no, Jaylen, I didn't get a copy of his mug shot. I think

Iniquus will get a judge involved and make that go away. That group is very secretive."

"Social links?"

"Nope." Olivia turned her head and scanned the parking lot.

"Nope as in he doesn't have one?" Jaylen asked incredulously. "That's suspicious."

"Nope, as in I didn't ask, and I didn't look." With all the carjackings in the paper, Olivia didn't love sitting out here with her engine running, even if the heat from the vent felt good. She put the car in gear and backed out. "Can you imagine how inappropriate that would have been?"

"Not that inappropriate, you're neighbors. You have a community group to share neighborhood news, right? I'll look. What's his full name?"

Olivia focused over her shoulder as she wheeled herself around. "Thaddeus Crushed. That's on his court paperwork. He told me I can call him Nutsbe."

"No Nutsbe anythings. Thaddeus's diminutive is Tad. Okay, there are five Tad Crusheds. That's hard to say—Crusheds. Here's one. He's in his seventies, it seems. Columbus, Ohio."

Olivia was silent while she edged up to the curb and then backed to be right in front of the restaurant door so that when Nutsbe came out, he could jump in and not get even more wet. Throwing her car into park, she said, "Not him. I'd guess late thirties or a young-looking early forties."

"African American?"

"No. From his build, he's of German descent, maybe? Northern something." Olivia wasn't sure if turning her engine off or leaving it on was safer so she could peel out and get gone if someone approached her car. "What kind of last name is Crushed? English?" Olivia asked as she decided to leave the engine on, the car in gear, her foot on the brake.

"Don't know. Probably something that got changed on Ellis Island. Okay, the rest are Avatars. But did you say he worked for Iniquus? Well, shit. That's why I can't find him. I read somewhere that they act like, I don't know, super spies or Delta Force operators. They don't have a public face. They're all very secretive, cloak and dagger."

"It's security protocols. Like me on social media. I lock everything down. I use an avatar and a fake name; very few people know where I live. You and Mickey Shithead."

"That makes me uncomfortable that he knows where you are," Jaylen said.

"They're putting together a warrant for his arrest, and I have a temporary restraining order. So he should get picked up here in the next few hours."

"I don't want to talk about him. I want to know more about Nutsbe. Much, much more interesting. *Infinitely* more interesting. Did you see his hands?" Jaylen asked.

"Yes, why? Are you asking about a wedding ring? No ring. No white place where he didn't tan."

"Ha! You looked," Jaylen laughed. "Caught ya. So good. But it wasn't what I was wondering about. Do you think he still has fingerprints? Don't spies acid them off?"

"Bob said he was a counterpart, so I'm guessing Nutsbe coordinates operations and sends his tactical force into the field. He probably works in the office," Olivia said, turning the heater up another notch. "Okay, here's a question for you. Have you ever heard the term bissextile before? There are so many changes with LGBTQI terms, it would probably be good to know this one."

"Are you sure you heard that word said correctly? Bissextile? Who said it?"

"Nutsbe. Something in passing. He was making small talk about Beowolf with my witness and mentioned that Beowolf had just had a birthday. His dog turned four last week. She said her birthday was two weeks ago but hadn't celebrated. Then Nutsbe looked at me and said, 'I don't celebrate my birthday often since I'm bissextile.' And when he said it, he winked at me. Does that make sense to you?"

"You didn't look it up?" Jaylen asked.

"I haven't had time yet."

"Hang on." A moment later, Jaylen's laughter was bright with amusement. "That's fabulous. Bissextile has to do with leap year. His birthday must be February twenty-ninth. That's what he meant by not celebrating often."

"What now?" Olivia's lips stretched into a bemused smile; she also registered relief. *Interesting.* "That little shit."

"It's pretty funny, actually."

"It's a *little* bit funny," Olivia admitted.

"Anyway, it's good that he's a Pisces. Well, in bed, at least."

"Yeah?" Olivia looked over at the door, hoping Nutsbe would come out soon. "Why's that?"

"Reading: Non-judgmental, creative, romantic—but not in the run around kind of way. They're intuitive in bed. They can figure out what their lover wants. Water sign. So," Jaylen said, "I'd say you have shower sex in your future if you decide to enjoy this guy."

"Okay, what about out of bed?" Olivia asked.

"You're really into this guy," Jaylen accused her.

"I'm not. I'm curious. I've never met anyone like Nutsbe. He's ... something. I'm too tired to find the right adjectives."

"And it's not like he'd be a rebound," Jaylen said. "You've dated since your legal separation. That one guy, Chad."

"His name was not Chad. But your point is well taken. We'll see. Now is not a good time to even consider a date. Hey, Jaylen, he's back with the pizza. I'll talk to you tomorrow. Bye."

"Olivia."

"What?" Olivia moaned as she flipped the locks to let Nutsbe in.

"It's been a rough day for you in court," Jaylen said gently. "Take a breath. Eat the pizza with the guy. Have fun. Relax. It's been a soul-sucking case. But it's almost over, right? What more could go wrong?"

14

Nutsbe

Last night had been interesting in the best sense of the word.

It had gone from shit show to something that made the whole Mickey Pauley circus well worth it.

When Nutsbe brought the pizza to the car, both Olivia and he were famished, and they ended up eating in the parking lot under a light. He'd thought of it as cozy, intimate, yeah, even a little romantic, with the rain forming a curtain of sound around their car; the streetlights, refracted by the torrent, glittered outside the window.

That could have gone on a lot longer, and he would have been glad. But Olivia's eyes were tired. So he suggested they head home.

Knowing that a piece of cardboard would protect Olivia's door and Mickey Pauley was in the wind, Nutsbe wished he could extend an invitation to use his guest room. Having just met her that morning, Nutsbe didn't think Olivia would accept an invitation to sleep at a stranger's house. He didn't want to push her away by being too forward. And she certainly had the wherewithal and the savvy to pack a bag and go to a hotel until she fixed the window and could have an alarm system installed.

After dropping Nutsbe off at his house, and picking up Henrietta from his backyard, she'd rounded the block, pulled into her garage, and gone in. And he hadn't heard her leave again.

When the rain stopped around twenty-three hundred hours, Nutsbe heard the now familiar rumble of motorcycle engines—two of them. They carried on for over an hour before the rain sent them home again.

Then, it was just the flash of floodlights that blinked him continuously awake.

Nutsbe had used the robotic system to adjust his security lights and cameras to take in Olivia's backyard. He set the sensitivity to high and quickly learned that on the other side of his fence, an ecosystem of nocturnal animals trounced across her yard.

It reminded him of the case where he had monitored a client's home, and the team thought dogs were setting the system off. Adjusting the lights to form an animal corridor so the flashing lights didn't wake that client or the neighborhood had proven to be a near-fatal mistake, allowing the bad guy to belly-crawl into place. Boots on the ground and a sick sense in Nutsbe's stomach saved her life.

What Iniquus needed was an AI system that could read the heat signatures and only flip the lights on when the intruder was the size of a human. He'd talk to the tech department and see if they had something like that in the works.

After the first time the floodlights flashed, Nutsbe swiveled around to quickly manipulate the clasp that anchored his prostheses, then leaped to the window to scan. After that, Nutsbe flung his sheets and blankets to the side and went to bed wearing his prosthetic legs, ready to jump into action.

The thought "if someone is coming for her …" clenched his stomach and made something low and vicious hum under his skin. He thought back to the postures of the Cerberus tactical dogs, waiting for the appropriate set of circumstances to fly through the air and sink their teeth. They longed for it. The only thing holding them in place was painstaking training. Yeah, that intensity in the eyes, that bunching of the muscles—that was him.

Nutsbe had always been arm's length from violence. He dropped the bombs from fifteen hundred feet. He managed the missions from the TOC. He fought on the mats where he could tap out.

Last night was the first time he'd faced a real-world fight. Like the tactical K9s, he had kept his cool, thought strategically, and done the right thing regarding force application. He was proud of the way that had all gone down.

But maybe he was like a dog, too. That first taste of blood might have awakened his animal instincts. He'd wanted the fight. More precisely, he'd wanted the fight that would protect Olivia. And in this instance, Nutsbe knew the best weapon wasn't his fighting skills or something he could snatch up and wield. Nutsbe's weapon of choice? A strategic mind and access to one of the best information systems in the world.

Now that it was morning, Nutsbe dressed in sweats and went for his morning jog, waving to Henrietta, who sat in her usual place in the window.

No sign of Olivia.

Home again, showered and dressed in gym gear, he

headed into his home office, where he fired up his computer. He had an hour before he needed to get on the road.

After a quick look into the court records, Nutsbe found the outstanding warrant for Pauley's arrest for last night's incident. Check that box.

Mickey Pauley was indeed a cop—surprise, surprise, he worked for the D.C.P.D., so just over the Virginia border, where he held a security clearance and was a sharpshooter when they needed extra eyes on the roofs when foreign dignitaries were visiting.

It looked like Pauley had turned down promotions, stating he liked being out with the public. Nutsbe guessed that, with Olivia's salary, if Pauley liked doing patrol, there was no reason for him to push himself up the ladder. Nutsbe knew cops who liked being right down in it with the community. He also knew cops who liked the physicality of knocking the suspects off their feet.

Yeah, there were a lot of streetfighter moves to Pauley's attack last night.

And here was a long list of complaints for brutality—all dismissed. No mention of Olivia's being involved with his career or working to clear his name from the accusations.

Olivia said she was almost free.

He liked her. More than liked her, Nutsbe couldn't stop thinking about her—a first for him.

Nutsbe just wished they'd known each other a little longer and a little better so he could be a bigger presence in her life between now and that divorce court date without feeling like he was muscling his way into her situation.

Nutsbe's phone pinged with a text.

. . .

Covington: They tried to serve Pauley last night at his house. He wasn't there. The server waited at the police station. Pauley didn't show up for his graveyard shift. Keep your head up.

Ping.

Covington: Spoke with Special Agent Kennedy early this a.m. about your arrest. Also made him aware of your name in court records. My office is working on getting you wiped from the police system. Given the circumstances and your clearance level, we should be able to get this done today.

Ping.

Covington: Our AI systems are scanning social media and mainstream media. Since Pauley's paperwork includes the address of the incident along with your name, this could put a bullseye on your house. You'll be kept apprised so you can act accordingly.

Nutsbe: Appreciated.

Before he could lay the phone down, it rang. Kennedy was on the line.

"Nutsbe here."

"Hey, early, sorry, I'm about to jump into a meeting. I talked with Sy Covington this morning. We're grateful to be looped in."

"Yeah," Nutsbe said. "Anything new on your end?"

"There is, actually. We might have found out how Russia got your name."

"Oh?" Nutsbe drew himself up to sit rigidly in his captain's chair.

"A little more digging. And if we're right, that's not information we can share over an open line. Even if Iniquus encrypts all communications, there are still people out there with the technology to sniff the air. And someone could have followed you from the police station last night to get close enough to do just that. Are you still at home?"

"I'm leaving here for a meeting in a few minutes. I'm not sure I'll be at Iniquus today. Listen, my neighbor drove me home from the police station last night. A couple times, I thought someone might have been following us."

"To your neighborhood?" Kennedy asked.

"Hard to tell on a rainy night. If someone followed us, they had skills, maybe a team."

"Russia wouldn't know you were at the police station, not yet."

"That's what I keep telling myself." Cold tingled over Nutsbe's scalp when he said that. It was the feeling he got when he tried to blow sunshine at a situation that didn't warrant positive thoughts. "I hope it's just a dose of paranoia sauce," he added lamely.

"It's to be expected," Kennedy said. "You know how to get me if you need anything."

SITTING on the faux leather bench, Nutsbe ate a breakfast sandwich and waited on Marvin.

Gadgets and parts filled the office. Paused projects littered the tables. It looked like a mad scientist's playroom. Marvin was a robotics engineer who teamed up with a reconstructive surgeon and an orthopedic surgeon to develop the protocol for osseointegration surgery, implanting hardware directly into the bone so an amputee could easily attach their prosthetic legs. The cool thing about their team was that it included a neurologist, kinesiologist, and a software engineer who specialized in AI.

Years ago, hoping their research could benefit soldiers injured on the battlefield, the working group went to Afghanistan to see the injuries as they presented when the PJs climbed out of the heli with the soldiers. They were touring the combat surgical hospital where Nutsbe's rescue helicopter landed. And that team performed Nutsbe's operation. They were testing new surgical techniques that preserved as much muscle and nerve tissue as possible, gathering it up at the end of his residual leg so that now, those systems could inform the software in his robotic prostheses through a series of sensors.

That AI system, to Nutsbe's way of thinking, made a world of difference in his recovery and day-to-day life. He liked being involved in the research and feeling like he was contributing.

The research was making a difference now as the teams' work was put to use in Ukraine and other turbulent areas.

After Nutsbe had worked through his recovery and had the great good luck of signing on with Iniquus, Nutsbe found himself a few miles from Marvin's research facility. Making it easier for Nutsbe to continue to give his volunteer feedback on the team's continuing efforts.

This morning was Nutsbe's monthly check-in and stint as a lab rat.

Seeing through the open door that Marvin was coming up the hall, Nutsbe shoved the last bite of breakfast in his mouth, wiped his fingers, rolled the papers into a ball, and shot it across the room into the trash.

Marvin stood in the door following the trajectory. "Two points." He held out his hand. "Good?"

"Good enough."

Marvin plopped into his chair and set a pair of lower-limb prostheses on the ground.

Nutsbe lifted his chin toward them. "Fancy."

"Yeah. They got a little imaginative with the airbrushing on the robotics' cover." Marvin moved the limbs over to Nutsbe. "These are loaners. So let's start here." Marvin rubbed his palms back and forth, then set his hands on the chair's arms. "In the past month, was there anything you decided not to do because of your prostheses?"

"My team was in Estonia and went out on the bogs to walk around."

"Bog walking?" Marvin shook his head incredulously. "Does that come up much?"

"First time." Nutsbe grinned. "I declined."

"I've seen videos of people on the bogs. And falling into the bog ponds. That was probably a good call on your part." He moved the prosthetic legs in front of him. "I don't think they'll help with any bog walking scenarios, but they have updated smart accelerometers we'd like you to try. Also, there are software updates that are supposed to help you with unexpected disturbances you might encounter on your path, making the encounters a smoother, more natural process and, at the same time, increasing your stability."

Nutsbe pulled up his pants legs and exchanged the sets.

"With these," Marvin said, "if something were to hit your leg, it'll lock out parts of the system to help you maintain balance. This could be helpful if, for example, you're lifting weights at the gym or if you're on the mats sparring. It can tell the direction and level of impact. Then the AI system will determine if it's best to stabilize you in an upright position, which is more robotic, or if it's best to allow your body to accept the impact more naturally, perhaps letting you fall."

"Sounds dangerous."

"You have a thought behind that assessment?" Marvin asked.

"Not to say that these things will kill me." Nutsbe kicked them out. "But that's hard to predict."

"With the limbs of my birth, who's to say that my legs will always do the right thing at the right time?" Marvin asked, watching Nutsbe attach the final sensor pads to his thighs. "I could trip in front of traffic tomorrow, get killed by a bus."

"Always sunny, Marvin."

"Here's the thing, you may never know that it was put into play. It might keep you upright when you would otherwise have fallen. We hope you'll find that it will help you navigate sudden impact."

"It's a trust issue. I'll try them out and give you my opinion—see if my confidence in the system grows with use. If I had them last night, I'd already have feedback for you."

"Last night?" Marvin leaned back in his chair. "Is it work or is this something you can share?"

"Someone was up to no good in my neighbor's yard. We had a few words. It ended in a fight."

Marvin did a quick scan of Nutsbe. "You don't look worse for wear."

"There was a lot of ducking and weaving on wet grass. He was kicking at my legs, and I was trying to stay out of range. That kind of agility, that's the kind of thing this helps with, right? Stabilization in sub-optimal conditions?"

"In theory." Marvin frowned. "And your stability?"

"About as good as the assailant's. We were in a backyard where things were spongy—not bog spongy, mind you. And once this got ramped up, there was a lot of mud."

"You were wearing boots?" Marvin asked.

"Tennis shoes. So I had traction on the sole."

Marvin lifted one of Nutsbe's lower leg bionics to look it over when Nutsbe's phone sounded with the Cerberus tone.

"Let me get this. It's work." He swiped the call open. "Nutsbe here."

"Bob here. Olivia's office called. She's in court, and Candace is pulling the flu symptoms again and wants the office to let the judge know."

"Where does that leave us?" Nutsbe asked.

"You're on the way between Iniquus and Candace's. I could get Beowolf to you in about ten minutes. And you could go over there and help Candace to feel safe."

Nutsbe's throat constricted. "Is she crying?"

"Olivia mentioned panic, not sobbing. Even if Candace is wearing a kryptonite necklace, you need to suck it up, butter cup." Bob chuckled. "Candace needs you."

Nutsbe's whole muscular system clenched, and he arched back. "Okay, let me get changed into my suit." He turned to the door where he'd hung his bag. "I can dress and meet you downstairs. You can switch Beowolf to my vehicle. I can grab my go bag and paperwork and head over to her house."

"That's the plan. See you in about twenty."

Nutsbe put his phone beside him on the bench. "Sorry. We have a client that needs assistance. I'm going to have to come back and try your new system for you another time. How about I call tomorrow and check your schedule?"

"Why don't you keep those and leave me these?" Marvin pointed at the prostheses Nutsbe had worn in. "I'd like to check them out and see how well they stood up to that fight. Check the data on the chip. That's real data that we can only try to simulate here. And it's important stuff. We want soldiers who want to return to the battle to have the opportunity."

Nutsbe stood to retrieve the garment bag. "Yeah, did you see in the paper that the Army appointed their first double amputee to serve as a garrison commander?"

"Really?" Marvin sent him a grin. "Good stuff. Now that's what I'm talkin' about." Marvin pointed toward Nutsbe. "You shouldn't feel any difference in your normal day-to-day. The system would kick in under some of the more extreme events you might get caught up in."

Nutsbe tucked the bag over his arm and reached for his phone on the bench. "Extreme, like what?"

"Beyond bog walking?" Marvin asked. "I don't know what the hell you guys are up to at Iniquus."

15

Nutsbe

Olivia had explained where she liked to park on court days and how she left home early in order to get her coveted spot by the trees. Other than this small public lot, there wasn't much in the way of quick-access parking once the courts and local businesses got going for the day.

Iniquus Automotive Department had sent two vehicles over early that morning to hold spots for Candace and Nutsbe. Whenever a tactical team was on protective duty, automotive performed this function to ensure their principals had the least possible exposure.

Now that Beowolf had weaved his magic and calmed Candace enough that she was willing to go to court, Nutsbe waited for Candace to back out of her driveway. He had Automotive on the line, letting them know they were en route. Drivers would stay in the placeholder vehicles and pull out just as Candace and Nutsbe drove in.

Nutsbe had been right about needing the two spaces. He

would have gladly driven Candace to and from, especially if sitting in the vehicle and petting Beowolf would have helped calm her nerves. But Candace wanted the control. If the need for flight arose, she wanted her keys and her wheels with no attachments to someone else's agenda.

Nutsbe got it. He even agreed with it. That's why he'd made the arrangements as they were this morning. And why he didn't put up the fight that he could tell she was expecting.

Candace followed her GPS to the lot, pulling in slowly as instructed. And with Nutsbe on the phone, giving her the go-ahead, she pulled into the newly-opened space, then waited in the car for him to park next to her and unload Beowolf from the back.

Nutsbe rounded to Candace's door. She was clinging to the steering wheel, staring straight ahead. After a moment, he knocked lightly. She visibly swallowed and pushed the door open.

As Candace climbed from her car, Nutsbe took a moment to scan the parking lot. Everything looked quiet. The people who had left the courts for lunch and those on the afternoon dockets were making their way up the sidewalk to the front entrance for the afternoon sessions.

Nutsbe pulled a couple of clean rags from the side pouch on the go bag he had hooked over one shoulder. He used a rag to clean inside and out of Beowolf's slobbery lips, then tucked the cloth in his belt and handed a second one to Candace. "Precaution." He smiled and tried to project confidence to help Candace feel safe. "I didn't tell you before, but you look very pretty. I think the jury will better understand what happened to you without the spikes." He touched his ear. "That's one man's opinion. I'm sure that when you get home, putting on your steel shoes is going to feel good."

"I can't remember the person who bought this dress. She

is so remote from me now." Her frown tugged long, and she held her eyes wide.

"Whale eyes" was the term when a dog held their lids that way, a sign of mounting anxiety.

Beowolf lowered his head, pressing Nutsbe out of the way to get over to Candace.

Crouching, Candace wrapped her arms around his head. "Hey, buddy. Thanks."

Nutsbe had a tickle on the back of his neck. He lifted his head and did another scan as he said, "You have your driver's license?" Woods to the left, parking garage to the right, roadway to the rear, and straight in front was the side door to the courthouse. They'd have to go round to the front to gain entry.

"Yes."

"Do you have anything with you that might be considered a weapon?"

She came to her feet. "You and Beowolf."

"Okay, yes." That didn't sit quite right with Nutsbe. Yeah, sure, if this Offsed guy or anyone else was coming after Candace, he'd interfere. Beowolf—beyond his breeding of tackle and squash? It wouldn't be great if the court dog suddenly bit a chunk out of someone's leg. "No knives, even like a box opener or a multitool?"

"No."

He pointed to her bag. "You'll need to leave your phone in the car."

"I will not. My phone is always in my pocket. I'll just put it on airplane mode."

"They'll stop you from going in and tell you to take it back to your car. I'd just leave it in the car, to begin with. As a matter of fact, you might want to consider leaving your purse in the trunk and taking only your keys in with you. It would simplify things at security. If you don't have a pocket, I could hold on to them for you." He patted the strap of his pack.

She sighed.

"I know. It feels bad. I get that. I had to leave my phone, too. It's such a part of our existence. Not having it readily handy is strange. But we play by the rules. We go through the motions. You answer the questions, and then your part is over. This part, anyway."

"Over will feel good."

NUTSBE FOLLOWED Olivia's instructions and arrived at the courtroom door without mishaps or extra stress taking Candace and Beowolf—in his work vest emblazoned with a blue "COURT SUPPORT ANIMAL" patch—through the security check. The "WORKING DO NOT TOUCH" Candace knew, was a directive for others. They didn't want Beowolf to be distracted from his job, focusing on Candace. She could touch Beowolf as much as she wanted.

After giving their names, the bailiff opened a door to the left. "You can wait here until the witness's name is called."

It was a closet of a room. Almost all of the floor space was covered with a table and chairs. The dark green walls made the space claustrophobic, making it feel like they were trying to hang out in a storage closet. Nutsbe had to put one of the chairs on top of the table and signal Beowolf under to make room for the three.

After a moment, there was a tap at the door, and Olivia poked her head in to identify herself before she fully opened the door to join them.

"Everyone doing okay? Nutsbe? Candace?" Olivia leaned over to look under the table. "Hi, Beowolf."

Olivia looked cool, polished, and professional in her navy blue suit with a matching blouse. "Before the lunch break," Olivia said, "the jury received instructions about a dog in the courts. Candace, while you testify, I'm just reminding you that Beowolf will be with you on the stand, and Nutsbe will be right in front of you. He'll be there to handle Beowolf should any handling be necessary. Candace," Olivia wrapped Candace's cold, white fingers in her hands, "this is hard. I want to acknowledge that. You are brave. You are strong. You are supported. You can do this."

"I feel safe with Beowolf in with me. If he's not in with me, I feel like I might have a severe case of amnesia and not remember."

"Okay." Olivia squeezed Candace's fingers again, then pulled her hand away. "We talked about the consequences of that."

"I'm aware of the consequences. I'm not an idiot, Ms. Gladstone. I'm trying to do the right thing and to stay alive." She hid her hands under the table. "If Kyle Offsed is put in prison for life, what would it matter if he killed me right here on the stand today? He'd still go to prison for life. No difference."

"Well, luckily, that's not a problem. Beowolf and I are going to be right there with you." Nutsbe turned to Olivia. "The judge knows Beowolf is a bullmastiff?" Nutsbe asked, hoping that his size wasn't the thing that would make everything go haywire for Candace's testimony.

"I did tell the judge that it was a mastiff. I'm just not sure that he understood. He strikes me as a cat person." She smiled, then turned back to Candace. "Since you'll be called first thing, I'd like for us to go ahead into the courtroom. That way, when the judge comes in, you're just moving from that seat to the witness chair."

"Is *he* in there?" Candace's shoulders came up to her ears.

"Offsed?" Olivia asked. "Not yet. So this would be a good time for you to move in and get settled. Remember, besides Beowolf and Nutsbe—and me—there is an armed bailiff in the room, and there will be physical space between you."

Candace's face drained of color.

"You've got this." Olivia squeezed Candace's arm. "Once this is done, it's done. You don't have to anticipate it anymore." She stood and opened the door.

When Candace got reluctantly to her feet, Beowolf scrambled out from under the table and pressed through the door at the same time she did. He seemed to be signaling that he'd stick with her no matter what. And from the look of resignation on Candace's face, she accepted that and was ready to face the Devil.

Together, they moved up the carpeted walkway.

At the front of the courtroom, Olivia's paralegal stood up and vacated the protected seat.

"Thanks, Gail," Olivia said. "I'll see you at the office later."

And there they were. Beowolf taking up the side aisle, Candace holding onto Beowolf's ear, and Nutsbe bracing for the kryptonite assault that was surely coming.

For the moment, there was calm.

Nutsbe focused his attention on Olivia, organizing herself at the prosecutor's table in front of him. Her demeanor was different here—how she held her body and her facial expression. She had to be wicked smart and badass to have risen to her position. Even so, even here, there was something approachable to her attitude.

Nutsbe—from his experience in the courts as a witness to the many cases that involved Iniquus security's interventions—found these qualities played out better with a jury of one's peers. No one wanted to feel like someone looked down on them. Friendly but professional, respectful, and capable—these attributes made a difference in a case.

Nutsbe turned his attention to the door opening behind the judge's bench.

A woman moved into the courtroom and walked over to the bailiff. There was a whispered conference. The woman waddled back through the door to the judge's chambers, shutting it firmly behind her.

The bailiff moved to the front of the judge's bench, looking first at Olivia and then at the defense attorney.

"Ladies and gentlemen, Judge Madison was called away to a family emergency. Court is in recess. Please check in with the courts by seven o'clock in the morning to see if the trial will continue tomorrow."

Candace whipped her head toward Olivia. "That's it? No court today?"

"No. I'm sorry. I know this is hard, but we—"

Without letting Olivia finish, Candace turned on her heel and hustled from the courtroom with Beowolf trotting beside her.

Nutsbe flipped a wave toward Olivia and started after them. He was this side of jogging to keep up.

Breathlessly, Candace reached her car and turned to Nutsbe, her palm up, waiting for her keys.

He dug into his go bag. "I'll call the courts and talk to Olivia. How about I call you with the plan for tomorrow?" he asked. Holding the keys over her outstretched hand, Nutsbe paused to catch her eye. He wanted some kind of commitment from her.

"Yeah, sure. Tomorrow." That didn't have the sticking power he'd hoped for. As soon as Nutsbe dropped the keys into her hand, Candace jumped into her car, slammed the door, and peeled out of the parking space.

Nutsbe stood in the middle of the parking lot, watching Candace drive like a bat out of hell to the road, taking the turn so fast that the rubber screeched as the tires tried to grip the roadway. He wondered if she'd just keep going or if she'd be there when the trial started up again.

Beowolf stood beside Nutsbe and thrust into his hip, turning Nutsbe to the side. "Okay, normally that would have dumped me on the ground, but this new equilibrium software system seems to have worked."

Beowolf shuffled to the side, then thrust his head, pushing Nutsbe again.

"Cut it out," he said. When he looked up, he saw Olivia coming into the lot. A gust of wind roared up. Her hair blew into her face, and she tried to capture the strands in her hands so she could see.

A last shove from Beowolf and Nutsbe headed over to her. "Dude, that wasn't necessary. And you're in vest. That's not very professional. When I saw her, I'd have gone over." Nutsbe raised his hand as a hello.

As Olivia came to a stop by her car, Nutsbe reached her, and luckily, Beowolf was walking like a gentleman on a loose lead. "You didn't get your favorite spot under the trees today," he said.

"Yeah, I started out later than I'd hoped, and this was the last spot. I was lucky to get it, though." With her keys clasped in her hand, she lifted her wrist to her forehead, shielding her eyes from the sun. "Hey, do you happen to be heading home?"

"I can be, why?"

She looked down at Beowolf, then gave him a scritch. "You are so handsome. Do you know that?" She looked up to find Nutsbe's gaze. "I have a big ask and feel weirdly damsel in distress saying it out loud."

Nutsbe grinned.

"On my way over here this morning, something sounded wrong with my car. It felt a little scary. Whew!" She laughed as another gust rose up and whipped at her suit. "That's strong!" With her purse on her shoulder and her hair held in a fist, she leaned against her car. "My mechanic said I can bring it in the morning."

"Did any of your dash lights come on?" Nutsbe looked at Beowolf who had become rigid with concentration. His eyes were on the parking deck that Nutsbe was facing. A quick flick of his attention told him nothing unusual was happening. Maybe a cat or bird was up on the wall.

"No. The noise started up as soon as I hit the highway." She explained. "It was the strangest whacking noise coming from the back of my car."

"A tire?"

"My thought. But it didn't affect my steering. My tire pressure readouts didn't go down. Once I got here and parked, I walked around and looked. Nothing stood out to me as odd. The noise, though, was unnerving. After last night and everything." She flicked her hand through the air. "In the back of my mind, Mickey did something to my car to put me in danger. Hey, did you change your spotlights to keep an eye on my yard?"

"I did. Lots of raccoons." Nutsbe smiled.

They stopped talking while the next gust blew through. It lifted the drool from Beowolf's mouth and sent it flying like a loogy onto Nutsbe's suit. Good thing that Iniquus fabrics were all treated and most anything that got on them could be easily wiped off.

"You want me to take a look at your car?"

"Thanks, but I have that appointment with my mechanic. It's right around the corner from my—well, our houses. If you're headed home anyway, maybe you wouldn't mind following me? If I end up having to pull over on the shoulder to call a tow truck, I'd rather not be on the side of the road alone."

"Why don't you drive mine? And I'll get yours home to you."

"Oh." She looked startled by the idea. "I can't drive your car. I don't know how."

"You don't know how to drive a car?"

"Like with my hands." Olivia held out open palms as if that gave him more information.

"Ah, okay Well, this one is from the Iniquus pool," he pointed over to his vehicle, "and it operates like any other." If Olivia had seen him jogging in the neighborhood, then she knew all about his prosthetic legs since he usually wore shorts.

Beowolf gave an exaggerated yawn and was panting as he focused forward. His scruff lifting. Nutsbe scanned again—nothing.

"It's a normal car, then?" She pressed.

"It's not a normal vehicle, no. It's an Iniquus vehicle equipped for me with hand controls per the law, but that doesn't affect the pedal control. There are a number of vehicles in the Iniquus pool that can be driven with hand controls. Our operators can get banged up on the job, and it just makes sense to have vehicles available while they recover. Or for me. Besides those controls, Iniquus does special modifications on all of its fleet, so none of the vehicles are what you might call normal."

"Like what?" Olivia asked, curiosity painting her voice.

"Run-flat tires, for example."

Beowolf was on his feet, a low warning rumble in his chest. Nutsbe followed his line of sight. "What have you got, buddy?"

Beowolf stomped his foot.

"I don't see it, boy." Nutsbe slowed his breath as he methodically scanned, and sure as shit, a flash of reflecting light winked at him.

See that once, and it locked into the brain as a death signal.

Sniper.

Nutsbe spread his arms protectively as Beowolf bit into Olivia's sleeve, dragging her down to the ground.

Nutsbe threw himself on top of them, shielding the two with his body.

As they hit the ground, a man behind them screamed with horror-filled surprise.

16

Nutsbe

Twisting to peer over his shoulder, Nutsbe found an elderly man seated on the ground just within view. His legs stretched out in front of him. He bent, his hands gripping around his thigh. Blood gushed through his fingers.

"Stay here. Stay down," he ordered. "Beowolf, stay!"

An arterial spurt. If Nutsbe took the time to drag the guy, he'd bleed out before they reached cover.

Nutsbe whipped his go-bag forward, yanking a tourniquet from the front pocket. Holding it between his teeth, Nutsbe rested his weight on his hip and did a side crawl that kept his head as close to the ground as possible, pulling his thighs toward his chest, then lifting and thrusting.

The man turned gray as his blood pressure dropped. Nutsbe pressed him to lie down lest he pass out, adding a concussion to the emergency. With practiced hands, Nutsbe secured the tourniquet above the wound, then tightened it hard until he could see that the blood had stopped flowing.

Looking down to tell the man they needed to move fast, Nutsbe found him out cold. It had to be from the sudden blood loss.

There was nothing that Nutsbe was willing to do about that now.

He scrambled around behind the man, assessing. Five foot ten, maybe two hundred and fifty pounds? He wasn't small, that was for sure. Nutsbe hadn't trained to drag this much weight and didn't want to try it from standing when his head would present a clear target. Nutsbe decided he'd continue his side crawl, a move he had developed from the SEAL combat swimming sidestroke. He could do it with some efficiency, but would it work here?

Nutsbe caught the guy by his shirt collar and made the first pull. They gained mere inches. Putting the back of his hand under the man's nostrils to see if he was breathing, no whisper of air tickled his skin.

Nutsbe saw three choices.

He could risk it and try CPR here.

He could keep dragging and hope for the best.

He could consider the rescue a lost cause, give up, and seek safety.

Nutsbe pressed and dragged again, getting the same limited results.

"Argh!" Olivia yelled. And Nutsbe shot a look her way. She was in a bear crawl with her ass in the air, Beowolf had his mouth around her arm, and he was dragging her toward Nutsbe.

There was a splintering crack that jerked Nutsbe's head up. The rear window of the car beside Olivia's shattered, and then a bullet hit the passenger's side window where she'd been crouched.

Nutsbe's heart gripped.

Crap, that was close.

Nutsbe pressed again, and with gritted teeth and the growl of a powerlifter, he shoved hard into his leg.

With Beowolf's jaw wrapping her arm, Olivia stumbled, unable to stand. With her hands on the ground in front of her, Beowolf forced her along.

As she passed them, another bullet pinged and ricocheted, hitting the man in the leg below the tourniquet.

Shitshow it is, then.

Beowolf pulled Olivia between the cars where Nutsbe had aimed.

"Olivia, stay there. Do *not* come over here." He pressed again, gaining another few precious inches. "Olivia, did you hear me? Stay put!" Nutsbe yelled, lest she try to come and help.

Beowolf's hot breath was on his neck. Leaning forward, he sniffed the man's hair.

Nutsbe had been silently counting the seconds since he found the guy unconscious. This was it. The time that an average person could hold their breath underwater. After this, the chances of reviving the man—saving his life—drained away.

Beowolf's massive mouth bit at the man's shoulder, grabbing up the fabric of his suit jacket. He pressed into his haunches, and the man slid.

"Good job, Beowolf. Good job."

Nutsbe watched Beowolf's body shift and tried to time his own pull, so they were in sync. There was a rhythm of pull and scramble.

Moments later, surprisingly, Nutsbe found they were between the cars. One last drag got the guy's feet behind a tire.

"Olivia," Nutsbe shout-whispered over the blare of car

alarms. "I need you to keep as much of you as possible under an engine block." When Nutsbe pointed to the car straight behind him in the asymmetric lot, he saw she had her phone in her hand.

How did she have a phone coming out of court? His mind flicked past that thought as he reached out. "Can I have that?" It was more command than question.

"I was going to call 9-1-1," she said, holding the cell phone up to her face to unlock the screen and then stretching it out to him.

Nutsbe quickly tapped out the number for Iniquus communications, put it on speaker, and laid the phone on the man's crotch.

A woman's efficient voice brightened the air. "Iniquus Communications. Identification."

"Nutsbe, Panther Force, Code red. Code red. Code red." Nutsbe maneuvered around until his legs were under the car to his side so that he could be in position to assess the situation. "Track GPS coordinates to Cerberus K9 Beowolf. Over." He scrubbed a knuckle up and down the man's sternum to see if he would revive.

Out cold.

Nutsbe looked over at the puddle and smear of blood and tried to guess how much fluid the man had lost.

"Copy. We have your GPS coordinates placing you beside the federal courthouse. Over."

Nutsbe pressed two fingers to the man's carotid and got nada. "Affirmative. Active shooter. The sniper is on the roof of the parking garage. At my location, we are two males, one female, and one K9 between the cars. Over."

Nutsbe loosened the guy's tie and tore at his shirt, making the tiny white buttons fly like shrapnel, exposing a pot belly and a torso covered in thick gray hair.

"Sending emergency vehicles to your location. Number of injured? Over."

Nutsbe yanked off his suit coat and tie, quickly folding his shirt sleeves up his arms to the elbow. He measured off the location of the man's xyphoid process, laced his fingers, and positioned the heel of his hand over the man's chest. With the first thrust, he sent an assessing look toward Olivia, who was getting onto her knees, encumbered by the narrow cut of her skirt. "Olivia, were you hit?"

"Me?"

"Check yourself over. Use both your hands. Touch every part of your body. You're looking for a hole or blood."

As Olivia followed Nutsbe's directive, he saw her bloody knees.

"I have a male, mid-sixties, gut shot wound to his left leg. Femoral tourniquet applied. Mark the time." He thrust downward. "Unconscious. Not breathing. I'm applying CPR. Over."

From his phone came rock music timed to the tempo of an effective thrust.

Nutsbe looked over his shoulder. "Olivia." He waited for her to look him in the eye. "Okay?"

"I'm fine." She leaned over the man's head. "This is Judge Greenway," she said with alarm. Shuffling to the side, Olivia positioned a leg on either side of the wheel, her skirt stretched wide. "Should I do mouth-to-mouth?"

"Yeah, good." Nutsbe was breathing hard as he thrust down the required two inches. The sharp stones ground into his knees.

"Actively monitoring. Over," the Iniquus communications officer said.

Beowolf stepped carefully along the far side of the judge, then came to sit to Nutsbe's left. As Nutsbe leaned forward into the compressions, the dog's body would effectively shield Olivia. "Good boy." They caught each other's gaze, and there was no mistake; they were partners in keeping Olivia safe.

Nutsbe had a flicker of hope as the first rescue siren screamed in the distance.

Help was coming.

But with the shooter still aiming at the cars around them, could they all survive the wait?

17

Olivia

Sensory overload fried Olivia's nerves.

The bullets that burst the cars' windows set off their alarms, shrilling to the owner to come and check.

No one was coming.

As soon as Judge Greenway collapsed, distant yelling told Olivia that everyone had scrambled for safety. As far as she could tell, their little knot hunkering between the cars were the only people still outside.

The only human targets.

Oh, those car alarms, with their bright wails that pulsated and glared! They whipped about on the buffeting gusts and echoed off the hard sides of the surrounding buildings. Each joined in at a different point, none aligning with their neighbor. It was a constant nerve-jangling discordance.

From her phone, the upbeat rock music kept Nutsbe steadily at work. Red-faced from exertion, sweat-slicked his skin. He had to be exhausted. She wished she could relieve him, but the shuffling and maneuvering in this cramped space would take too much time away from their work.

Nutsbe had the muscles for this job. Not pretty muscles—not show muscles, power muscles. Muscles trained to do things like this—save people.

Day two of Nutsbe's heroism.

Rescue sirens blared and squawked, surrounding them on three sides. The fourth side was a railroad with no access. They seemed to have formed their semi-circle and stopped at too far a distance to be particularly helpful.

What they needed was a gurney, a chest compressor, and an airbag.

She was the airbag.

Olivia, once again, turned her head cheek to nose, drew a breath in through her mouth, then turned to seal her lips over the judge's mouth and exhaled. That breath forced his lungs to visibly expand. The sharp prickle of emerging beard was like sandpaper, making her lips feel raw. She turned her head and breathed in fresh air, then turned back to force life past cold blue lips.

But this time, as she blew, vomit bubbled up the judge's throat, filling her mouth.

Thrusting back, gagging and gasping, gobs of his half-digested food fell from her lips. Olivia made the mistake of looking down at the puddle of coffee and sweet rolls. And something red and chunky.

As her own stomach churned and bucked. Olivia was vaguely aware that Nutsbe had rolled the judge to his left side and was sweeping his airway clear.

As another wave of vomit spewed across the parking lot, Nutsbe scooped the puddle away from the judge. And when that wave receded, Nutsbe cleared his mouth again.

"Vomit," Nutsbe called for the Iniquus person's benefit.

The phone had dumped from the judge's crotch to the black-top. "I have a pulse and a breath." His voice was filled with victory and exhaustion.

Olivia, trying to still her wobbling stomach, watched as Nutsbe bent and folded the judge into the rescue position she had practiced in her yearly first-aid class but wasn't sure she'd remember how to do now that it was necessary.

Nutsbe kicked his bag and a water bottle rolled out. He moved toward the judge's feet and washed his hands, then dried them on the drool towel strapped to the bungee cord on Beowolf's work vest. "Good boy. That's my good boy." Nutsbe patted his side, then scratched his ears.

Nutsbe's steadiness through all of this helped Olivia immeasurably.

He handed the half-empty bottle and towel to Olivia and said. "For cleaning up. I have another one for you to swish your mouth out." He turned to Beowolf, waiting patiently like the best of the good doggos. "Beowolf, follow."

With his supply bag looped over his arm, Nutsbe crawled past the judge's head to an area with enough space to put his back to a bumper. There he sat with his knees bent, catching his breath.

Beowolf padded over to Olivia, sniffed her over, and then gave her a swipe of his tongue before lying down at Nutsbe's feet. She noticed he was no longer watching the condominium's parking garage, and Olivia assumed the shooter was gone.

Reaching into his bag, Nutsbe drew a water bottle out and handed it over.

Olivia duck-walked farther away between the cars, filled her mouth, and spat. A few more swishes and the water tasted less sweet in comparison to the bitter bilious puke that had filled her mouth. Her nervous system began to reset.

When she waddled back toward Nutsbe—her suit skirt stretched tight against her thighs—he had a roll of mints in his open hand.

She glanced toward the judge. Reflective emergency blankets made him look like a baked potato. "Wow." It was the only thing Olivia could think to say.

"You did awesome. I am so proud of you."

She shook her head as she popped a mint in her mouth. "Do you think the first responders are on the way over to us?"

"Not yet. They're looking for the shooter."

"But he's gone, right?" she asked.

"My guess."

Olivia cast her gaze around. Not that she could see anything but cars.

"You can either hunker in or run for it," Nutsbe said. "Your call."

Olivia focused on Judge Greenway. "You could get the judge out of here?" That didn't seem probable. He was a big guy, and it had taken both Nutsbe and Beowolf to drag him. Olivia felt terrible for not helping. But Nutsbe had asked her not to, and there was probably a good reason.

"I'll stay with the judge. You need to do the thing that is best for you."

"I'm not running for it." She plopped onto her butt, sending him a quivering smile. "I like having these engine blocks near me."

Nutsbe grinned. "You did learn a thing or two as a prosecutor."

"This is a strange experience."

"Yeah, I have to say, I've never been shot at in a public parking lot by a sniper before."

"Snarky." Olivia laughed. "I like that."

"You doing okay?"

"I could use a bathroom." She pulled her legs out from underneath her and stretched them long. Her knees were scraped like an elementary school kid taking a tumble off their scooter. Her shoes were over by her car. She'd come out of them when Beowolf dragged her to this side of the parking lot. Olivia leaned over and kissed Beowolf. "You're my hero, too. Thank you for protecting me."

Beowolf moved his head onto her lap, lifting first one brow, then the other endearingly. Olivia stroked her hand over the smoosh of his wrinkled forehead.

Nutsbe checked his watch, doing a pulse count on the judge. He lifted the phone and said all the right things—respiration, color, lack of responsiveness.

"We're safe now, don't you think?" Olivia asked.

"I think that depends on the goal," Nutsbe said.

It was *not* what she wanted to hear.

"If that was an assassination attempt, and it was a miss, the shooter might have ditched the weapon—or not—and have come down to patrol the parking lot to finish the job."

Olivia froze.

"I don't think that's what's happening. If the guy thought a close, predictable shot was possible, he would have taken it. The shooter wanted the protection of distance and had an exit route planned. We don't know if the target was acquired or not."

"If he was successful or not—" Olivia wiped a hand over her head. "Mickey is a sniper for the police department."

"Don't get ahead of facts," Nutsbe admonished her. "You're a prosecutor, so lean into that. No jumping to worst-case conclusions."

"Fact, the judge needs medical help ASAP. I mean, how long can you leave a tourniquet on?"

"We have no control over that," Nutsbe said.

"Are you scared?" she asked.

"Concerned? Sure. Scared? No, I'm okay. But it is a frightening situation." He looked at the judge. "I think we're in the hunkering down part of this event. The shooter's probably running and hiding. The police will have to clear the area before they can greenlight the ambulance to come in. I think we're going to be okay."

He caught her gaze and held it for a long time. He held out his hand to her. "Are *you* scared?"

Nutsbe was right; this was a frightening situation. She had been terrified up to the point where she started the artificial breath. Doing something proactive had helped until the puke. How was she now? "Weirdly, no, not scared."

He scanned down to her legs. "I'm going to take care of your knees, okay?"

Olivia didn't want to let go of his hand. And it looked like the bleeding had stopped. But Nutsbe reached for his magic bag of helpful things.

He moved toward her feet.

When he pulled out a medical pouch, Olivia focused on the keychain attached to the zipper pull.

Nutsbe drew out gloves from the front, then pulled them on. He opened the bag. A plastic sheet went on the ground for him to use as a sterile spot. Nutsbe laid out the things he would be using, including a pair of plastic shears that would have made it through the metal detector.

"I'm going to edge your skirt up." He moved her skirt to her mid-thigh. "I'm going to cut your hose and then remove them. You'll start bleeding again. The fibers have dried into the scabs." Now that he was this close, they could hear each other without yelling.

Though the wind would sometimes gust and whip away

their words, it also whipped away the smell of puke, and Olivia was grateful.

Olivia distracted herself as he first slit a hole that allowed him to begin cutting around her thigh by pointing at the photo on the keychain. "You all were having fun."

"It was a great time," Nutsbe lifted her leg and placed it across his thigh to cut around the back.

"No cake or balloons. It didn't look like a birthday party. What are you celebrating?"

"That's my Live Day last year. Some pals I hadn't seen in a while showed up to surprise me."

"I don't know what that means, 'Live Day.'"

"That's the day I lost part of my legs. But I didn't lose my life. Every day since that day is like a bonus."

"How did that happen?"

"My convoy hit an IED in Afghanistan."

"But I thought you were Air Force, right? How is it that an Air Force pilot got caught up in a convoy IED attack?" Olivia thought this was shaky ground. She didn't know the etiquette here. And she was afraid that Nutsbe might feel that she was gratuitously digging for details that were none of her business. "Is it okay to ask?" She frowned. "I mean, I'd like to know. Not in a curious way, but more in an 'I think we're becoming friends' kind of way, and this is a big deal—an inflection point in your life."

"Yeah, that's the way I took this conversation."

Friends? Olivia thought. Not really, no. She felt that there was something more there. Something that could be special and important, emerging like green shoots from the winter soil.

For her, anyway.

"Is it classified?" she asked.

"Nope." He worked his fingers into the top of the hose and gently pulled the fabric to her knee. With care, Nutsbe worked to dislodge the fibers from the cut that had already crusted with a wide, coagulated scab. "The fresh blood will help clean out your wound from any tiny rocks and dirt." He slid the rest of that pantyhose leg off, and it was bizarrely seductive. Olivia chalked those sensations up to survival hormones, a bit of a crush, and that she'd only read of such things in her bathtub smut novels.

"How did I get hit?" Nutsbe asked. "String of bad luck and miracles. This is going to burn." He swiped over her knee with an alcohol pad. "Not the best first aid practices, but it'll have to do in a pinch." He turned the pad over and swiped it on the other side while Olivia tried not to wince. "I was flying a mission in Afghanistan. There was a massive sandstorm and high winds. Those storms could come up unpredictably. At the time, I had been skimming over a mountain range, trying to keep my bird in the shadows so I could poke out and drop my load without the guy manning the surface-to-air missiles seeing me in time. They could hear me for sure. I'm assuming it was the debris in the air that made both my engines cut out. I made an emergency landing in the middle of Taliban territory." He tore the packet of petroleum jelly and swiped it over her cut. "They sent the SEALs to save my butt and blow up the plane."

"Wow."

"A little bit wow, yeah." He placed a cotton square over the cut and reached for the cling bandaging. "I never needed rescuing before. It's an odd sensation. In the Air Force, we're on a team but also alone." He lifted her leg and tucked it under his arm, trapping it there.

For Olivia, this was one of the most confusing moments of her life—being turned on by his gentle touch and attention while focusing on understanding the desperate straits he'd survived and not knowing if the sniper was still actively stalking the area now, looking for someone to put in his crosshairs. She wished she had control, that she could focus on a single thought or emotion—but obviously, her nervous circuitry was misfiring.

"There are skills I have that the SEALs depend on. I have done more than my share of bomb runs to protect them or cover their tracks. But that day, I was completely dependent on their unique skills. The relief is something incredible—there's a profound sense of debt and brotherhood."

Nutsbe wrapped the bright blue cling bandaging around her leg, setting her leg back on the ground to start again on her other side.

Olivia sucked in a stuttering breath, then released it in a rush.

"You okay? Hanging in?"

"I'm not going to cry, I promise." She wasn't a crier, but this might just be the time to start. It seemed like it would be a good way to let go of this pressure in her head and chest.

Their eyes met, and a slow grin spread across his face. She wanted to kiss him. That was inappropriate given the circumstances, not the least because of her need to brush her teeth and gargle with something very strong.

That look from him was what she needed, not tears.

Nutsbe gently slid the cool sheers between her flesh and the Nylon.

"Were you hurt putting the plane down?" Olivia asked.

"It was a bumpy ride in, but I was fine. After the SEALs blew up the plane, they had another mission to jump on, so they got me as far as the first convoy they could find outside the wire. That convoy would give me a ride back to the fort. From there, a helicopter was supposed to take me back to my base."

He gently worked her stocking down her leg.

"But the convoy didn't make it," she whispered.

"It did not. The truck in front of us flew up in the air, and whatever it hit seemed to trigger along the chain behind us. That was bad. Four vehicles."

"Wait. So the terrorists were able to rig it so that when the lead car got to the explosives, the entire convoy blew?"

"Wicked crazy stuff. That's exactly what happened. So, yeah." He paused for a long time, scrutinizing her face; his mind seemed hard at work. Finally, he reached over and tapped the mute button on the phone. He licked his lips and said, "I've only ever told one other person this part of my story." He paused as if he were reconsidering, then said, "Here it is. When I was lying there with my limbs fucked up —excuse my language."

"Seems appropriate here."

"This is kind of out there." He looked around, focused up at the sky, then back at her. "I'll just tell it like I did that time before. As a kid, my grandmother always knew when I was up to no good. Even if I was just thinking about it, the phone would ring. It was always Nan asking me what the hell I thought I was doing. It's important to know that she died when I was a Doolie at the Air Force Academy—that's freshman year. Okay, fast forward to after the convoy blew. I opened my eyes, and Nan was kneeling beside me. She was yelling at me. Cussing me out." Nutsbe paused with a lopsided smile, but Olivia could see he was trying to wrangle his emotions.

"You should also probably know," his voice had turned husky, "that my Nan was a rule breaker. She liked to drink and liked to smoke. So she didn't look like an angel with wings and a halo. She was herself with white hair and long red nails, cigarette in her fingers, highball in hand." He shook a finger in the air and made his voice wobble. 'What's wrong with you? You know what to do. Get your tourniquets on your legs.'" Nutsbe quickly turned to look at the judge, then back. "She said, 'It's not your time, young man. Don't you even think about it. Get yourself out of this junk pile and get yourself moving to the north. Move it.' I did as I was told. In my household, growing up, the kids didn't ever ignore Nan. I wasn't about to start ignoring her then. Olivia," he put his hand over his heart, "she saved my life. Everyone who was with me was already dead. I was lying there in shock. I wouldn't have crawled off my X if it hadn't been for her. Wouldn't have gotten far enough away when the second RPG hit the wreckage, nor when the Taliban moved in to make sure the job was complete. That's that part of the story."

"That's crazy wonderful." Olivia wasn't blinking.

"Wanna hear something even more freaky?" He popped his brow at her.

"Absolutely." She wanted to know *everything* about this man.

Right now, Olivia was filled with profound gratitude for Nutsbe's grandmother.

"One of the marines later told me that an old lady in a pink pantsuit had told him where to find me in the trees. The marine scanned over to where she was pointing, and when he turned back to ask how she got out there in the middle of nowhere, she was gone. Why was a woman in pink pants in the middle of Afghanistan? He said he was afraid she'd set him up for an ambush, so they went in slow. He was able to describe her to me. It was Nan. It was *definitely* Nan."

Olivia believed his story with every fiber of her being. But the implications of that belief ... She'd have to think long and hard about all of this. His story was overwhelming, all of it. "I am retrospectively terrified for you. What? How?"

"I was glad as hell when the Marines got there. MIA is tough on families." His whole body visibly tightened as he scanned her face. "Am I hurting you?" Nutsbe looked down at her leg in his hands.

Her heart squeezed so tight it hurt. "That's gratitude you see on my face. I'm thankful to your Nan, that you made it through, and selfishly, but honestly, I'm so glad you're here with me right now. But no tears. I keep my promises."

That seemed to reassure him. But Olivia knew the rest of his story wasn't a secret because he unmuted the phone. "Those Marines called in the PJs. That was the start of the next set of miracles." He turned and slid closer to the judge. "Checking vitals on Judge Greenway, over."

"Standing by, over."

With her knees cleaned and bandaged, Nutsbe pulled off his gloves, did the checks on Judge Greenway, and called out the numbers.

When Nutsbe settled back beside her, he reached for her hand again, and they laced their fingers. "Next miracle," he said. "A group of researchers had come to Afghanistan to see the state of the wounded soldiers as they were brought from the battlefront to surgery. Right doctors with the right skills at the right time for me. I was a very lucky guy. I got to be a guinea pig for some new amputation protocols that made all the difference in my recovery and ability to ambulate."

"Thank you for telling me. A Live Day is a wonderful thing to celebrate." She squeezed his hand, then looked over at the Judge. "How do you think Judge Greenway's doing?"

"Air going in and out, heart pumping. From there? Hard to tell," Nutsbe said.

Beowolf's head popped up at attention, and they both jerked around when an officer yelled, "Hands! Hands!"

18

Olivia

Beowolf lay at Olivia's feet as she stood by her car.

She had given her name, but Nutsbe had cleared his throat before she said anything else. She was the witness to a crime. From her prosecutorial work, Olivia knew well that it was best to be quiet. She needed two solid nights of sleep and time to process before she should open her mouth. And she said as much to the officers, then she turned away.

Nutsbe said, "Beowolf follow." It was his turn to give his name, and it was sweet that he was sending Beowolf along as her guardian angel. "You are, aren't you? An angel?" she asked, and Beowolf raised both eyebrows. "You knew what was happening. I wonder how. Nutsbe knew you'd locked onto something. You were pulling, and he was tackling. And I'm alive." She put her forearms on her hood. "I might not be alive," she whispered.

Because her car was part of the crime scene, the police

wouldn't allow Olivia to drive away until after the CSI had collected their forensic evidence.

That would take at least a few hours.

A television crew pressed against the yellow crime tape that the police had strung. They had their cameras rolling, and Olivia noticed that Nutsbe had produced a baseball cap from his magic bag and pulled the bill low over his eyes. He also kept his face averted.

Olivia thought back to Jaylen trying to look Nutsbe up on social media under the name Tad Crushed and talking about how Iniquus kept a zero profile.

Jaylen! Olivia lifted her phone, swiped, tapped, and was instantly greeted with an "Olivia?"

"I'm alive and, for the most part, unhurt," she said in a rush. "Are you listening to the news?"

The phone was silent longer than expected, and Olivia had to look at the ticking timer to ensure the line was connected.

When Jaylen spoke, fear painted her words. "You were there for that? I told myself that you were in some safe room inside the courthouse. What the heck was happening?"

"Shit, Jaylen, can I just start off with what a freak I was?"

"How's that?" Tilly screamed into the phone, and Jaylen raised her voice to talk past it.

"What's wrong with Tilly?"

"She's mad that she asked me for an egg, and I made her an egg, but she didn't like how I took the shell off. Ignore her. She just needs to let go of some stress. I've got her in my lap now, and we're rocking. I'm wearing my earbuds, so I can hear you if you can hear me."

"Did you see that Judge Greenway was hit?"

"They're speculating on the news that it might be about this big case he has running with Chinese Mafia ties."

"That was fast. I mean." Olivia looked over at the press, then looked up at the faces pushed into the windows watching from above. Law offices. Anyone with a smartphone could have focused in and seen his face anywhere along the timeline.

"Go back. How are you a freak? Did you pee on yourself? I would have."

Olivia glanced around her and lowered her voice to a whisper. "Okay, imagine this: The judge is unconscious, leg in a tourniquet sprawled out between the cars. Nutsbe and I are hiding with him, waiting for the police and the ambulance. And Nutsbe was doing first aid on me."

"Wait," the fear was back in Jaylen's voice, "you're hurt? Were you shot?"

"Me? No, I scraped my knees like when we were kids and tripped on the playground." Olivia planted her elbow on her car and leaned her head onto her palm; the other hand held her phone to her ear, and Beowolf sat with his back to her like a protective sentinel. "It was no biggy, except that it was *such* a biggy."

"All right, not even *I* can follow that."

"It was—and I would only admit this to you—*erotic*." Olivia scraped her teeth over her upper lip. "Jaylen, I was so damned turned on while he hovered over me, *sliding* my hose off." She looked around again to make sure that no one else could hear.

"He slid your pantyhose off in the middle of a parking lot? *He* did it?"

"He did it, but it was a whole thing. He kept me modest, but that didn't help. He had these shears, and he cut the—*Whew.* He was lifting my leg, bandaging my damned knees. He was so focused and tender. I can't remember a time in my life when I wanted to grab a guy and just act like a spring rabbit in the wild."

"That's quite the picture—Tilly, please don't pinch me. That hurts Mommy. And I don't like it—Yeah, Olivia, you remember we learned about that in psychology."

"Did we?"

Beowolf budged back a bit, and his body supported Olivia's legs. She was grateful; it made her feel less wobbly.

"I don't remember particulars," Jaylen said, "the take away is something about fear of dying makes a human want to quickly procreate. I could look it up."

"Please don't. It felt so wrong. I'm so embarrassed that I was putting out weird vibes."

"Was Nutsbe responding to them?" Jaylen asked.

"Hard to tell." She could now feel the tiny stones under her bare feet. Olivia needed to find her shoes. "He was smiling at me. And he kept me distracted from the event and focused on him by telling me ... some things. I just hope he thinks I was terrified, and that was the weird sizzle coming off my skin."

"But that was factual, wasn't it?" Jaylen asked. "I mean, I'd be terrified."

"He's walking over here." Olivia changed her tone from whispering secrets to passing basic information. "I knew this would be on the news, and you'd be freaked out. I wanted to let you know I was okay. Nutsbe's heading over here. He asked me to go to Iniquus to talk to his commander about this. I'm not allowed to drive out of here yet. But when we can, he's going to drive my car home so he can listen to that noise from this morning. Can you call my mom and tell her all that and that I'm fine?"

"Will do," Jaylen said. "Call me later. Love you. I'm so glad you're alive."

Olivia swiped off and then stared at the phone. Yeah, she was glad she was alive, too.

"Olivia?" Nutsbe was beside her, and she looked up into rich hazel eyes warmed with concern.

"Yes?" She slid her phone back into her purse. "All done with the police?"

"You're shaking." He observed. "That's adrenaline coming out of your system."

She looked down to see her hands trembling violently. Olivia blushed. Was she not living up to expectations? He wasn't trembling.

"Human nature." He rubbed his hands up and down her arms, and more than anything, in that moment, Olivia wanted to step closer to him, have him wrap his arms around her, and hold her tight. But she was still very aware that she was vomit-spattered, and who in their right mind would want to snuggle with that?

When the wind kicked up, he brushed the hair from her eyes. "Do you have everything you need from your car? I'll drive to Iniquus, then if you're up to it, you can drive my pool car home. Iniquus will pick up this one," he pointed over, "when the tape comes down."

"But—" She looked around. Yeah, when they made the plan earlier, a leg of the journey was unaccounted for.

"I'll get someone from my team to drive me back to pick up your car, and we'll just move along with the plan we were making when all this started."

She turned back to him. "Like nothing happened."

"Not like nothing happened. Something awful happened. This is just a route to get us from Point A to Point B because we can't stand here in the parking lot forever."

Olivia blinked at him, trying to get her brain in gear.

"Honestly, I'd appreciate you letting me handle the cars.

When things are spinning out of control, it's good to have a smaller issue, something easily fixed with a little effort and attention."

"Yeah," Olivia said. "I get that. Like the new door in your fence?"

Nutsbe put his hands on his hips and looked down at Beowolf. There was an endearing bashfulness about the move.

"You're not great around crying, I've observed," Olivia said.

"Women crying?" He brought his head up to catch her gaze. "Can't stand it."

"Is there a story there?"

"Not that I know of."

Beowolf turned around to face the judge. Stabilized and packaged for transport, he lay under the reflective blanket on the gurney.

"I've been that way from as far back as I can remember," Nutsbe said as the paramedics wheeled Judge Greenway toward the ambulance staged on the road. "You ready? Iniquus left a car for me up the block away from this mess."

"So efficient. It reminds me of house elves. And a hotwash, huh? I've had people on the stand mention them. I've never been through one before."

Nutsbe was wiping the drool from Beowolf's chin. "This isn't exactly a hotwash. A hotwash is when you come in from a mission. And then you review what went right, what went wrong."

"Which we're doing." Olivia bent to get her shoes where they lay on the ground when she'd stumbled out of them. "Mission Beowolf. Right?" Nutsbe held her elbow as she slid her foot into one shoe, then the other.

"Then we decide what needs further training, decide if new protocols need to be developed for next time."

Without hose, Olivia's skin pinched, and she had to run a finger along the inside of her shoe to settle her foot in properly. "Please, god, let there never be a next time. I get it. Not really hotwash. Okay. I'm a little disappointed." She stood on both feet. The walk to the new car was going to give her blisters, such a petty grievance. "What do we need to talk about at Iniquus?" She stepped forward and stared at the wide pool of blood that the police were photographing.

"The trajectory of the bullet, for one."

"Coming right at the judge." She frowned.

"Coming right at us," Nutsbe corrected.

She twisted to look up at him. "How's that? The judge was yards away."

Nutsbe turned Olivia and wordlessly used his finger to draw an arc from where the sniper had been down to the blood where the judge had stood.

"Right." Olivia gave an emphatic nod. "The judge. It hit him in the leg." That last part trailed off. Olivia recognized that something was wrong with her thought process.

Nutsbe moved around behind her, stretching his arm forward so she was lined up with his finger. "Would you agree that's where we were standing when Beowolf pulled you down?"

"Yes." Her lungs lost their elasticity. Air couldn't go in, and air couldn't go out. A shiver traced her spine, jolting her body.

Nutsbe put his free hand on her arm to steady her. "Watch the arc again." He traced his finger through the air.

Olivia turned and grabbed Nutsbe's arm with both hands, staring up into his eyes. "If we had been standing there, the bullet *wouldn't* have hit the judge in the leg. It would have hit one of us instead."

That was a kill shot.

19

Nutsbe

Nutsbe offered his arm to Olivia, and she took it, walking alongside him, her hip brushing his as they moved easily together.

He'd prefer to hold her hand, but he had to be ready if he needed to jump into action.

Beowolf trotted along on a loose lead. As they made their way to the SUV location Iniquus had sent to his phone, Nutsbe was using Beowolf as his barometer, watching to see if he was predicting an impending shitstorm. Right now, Beowolf's posture seemed relaxed.

"Hey, Nutsbe, how would Beowolf have known to drag me to the ground the way he did?" Olivia asked as they moved down the sidewalk.

"Beowolf lives at the Cerberus Kennel with the tactical dogs, so I'm not sure what he's seen other dogs do and picked up from dog-to-dog mentorship. And beyond hospital visits and court support, I'm honestly not sure what Beowolf's trained to do. Certainly not tactical stuff." Nutsbe pointed to the left, so Olivia would know they were rounding the corner.

"Like?"

"He doesn't fast rope out of helicopters strapped to an operator's ruck."

"At two hundred plus pounds?" Olivia looked bemused. "That would be tough."

"It's possible Beowolf was in a training group to spot the reflection on a scope. That makes sense to me. Back at the parking lot, he was acting agitated for a while before he grabbed you. I focused up where he had been looking and saw the glint just as he started to pull you to the ground." Nutsbe thought it was good to keep Olivia talking. In all the years that his team had been pulling victims out of life-or-death situations, he noticed that they always did the worst when they shut down and went silent. Nutsbe was going to encourage conversation.

"And then you jumped on the pile," she murmured.

"Again, I just met Beowolf, I don't know his training, but I can tell you that the K9s that go out with my team are all trained to watch the weapon's finger. As long as the finger is in a safe position, a weapon won't get a bite. Move the finger into the trigger guard, and the fur missile launches without command and gets that wrist locked down between, say, two hundred pounds of bite pressure, and the attacker cannot flex the finger."

"From that distance, he could discern that tiny movement of the finger? That seems improbable."

"I have no idea."

"And he bit me. No, he didn't bite," Olivia corrected. "Dragged me to the ground. It was a strong enough grip—what should I call it?— I had no choice but to move where he wanted me to go. But he didn't pierce my skin."

"His breed tackles and traps."

"That's one way to describe it. It was unexpected, for sure. I didn't know what was happening."

Nutsbe pointed at the SUV painted the Iniquus branded charcoal gray.

Before they reached the vehicle, Nutsbe decided to go ahead and ask the uncomfortable question. "Do you think that could have been Pauley up there?"

Another thing Nutsbe had learned over his years with Iniquus, if you're asking a survivor about something with a lot of emotion attached, it was best to do it while moving. That way, some of the sparking energy could dissipate.

"It occurred to me, yes," Olivia said without hesitation. "He has the skills and the motivation. But going back to the arc you drew. I'm not a thousand percent that either you or I were the specific target. I know these irregular wind gusts are confounding. And it makes sense to me that the bullets were landing erratically in the area and not in a sniper's 'one-inch box at a hundred yards,' which is their standard requirement. But that one-inch mastery can only happen when the air current is predictable, and the calculations can be done."

"True," Nutsbe acknowledged.

"The Offsed brothers have been threatening my team. They'd have some skills—mmm, I don't know their skill level. They like to practice shooting with a militia group."

They arrived at the vehicle, and Nutsbe reached under the running board to extract the magnetic box with the car's fob. He swiped open his phone app and tapped in the code that would turn the radio waves on, activating the fob's connectivity. Pressing the button, the vehicle chirruped as the back gate lifted.

Rounding to the back with Beowolf, Nutsbe discovered a dog bed and a blankie ready. "Beowolf, load." Nutsbe put his hands under Beowolf's rump to help heft him up. Once Beowolf smelled the beef jerky treats that Automotive had left for him, he scrambled the rest of the way up just fine on his own.

As Nutsbe closed the hatch, Olivia climbed into the passenger side and pulled on her belt.

Nutsbe slid under the steering wheel and adjusted the mirrors before sending Olivia a check-in glance. He pressed the engine button and flicked on his directional light, then waited for a break in traffic to merge and head down the road. Over here, away from the crime scene, everything seemed to be humming along like normal.

"It could have nothing to do with any of us," Olivia continued where they'd left off. "It could be a random shooter who thought that he'd sit on the roof and take potshots at the federal judges. Something could be moving through the courts that didn't align with his politics, and he might have just lumped everyone into the same pot. Could have been stochastic terror."

"He?" Nutsbe looked at her, then flicked on his turn signal.

"Statistically, we're looking at a white male under forty."

"And you have something going to the grand jury?"

"Yeah." She brushed at her skirt. "I can't talk about that."

"Would those players land on this list? Are they motivated and capable?"

"They are, yes. Motivated without doubt. Capable? Definitely." She pulled down the visor to look in the mirror, then fussed with her wind-knotted hair.

Nutsbe didn't share—couldn't share—that it might have been he who put Olivia in the crosshairs. Could Russia or Albania have done that? Improbable. It wasn't their style.

Could it have been the FBI? Absolutely. Yeah. Definitely their style.

As if reading his mind, Olivia spoke the words he'd been thinking, "The FBI will be knocking on our doors. It will be tricky because there is so much that I can't share with them." She slapped the visor back in place. "I'd like to change the subject, please."

"You choose." Nutsbe was paying close attention to the flow of traffic around him. He didn't know if he was still primed from the sniper or what was happening, but a prickle across his scalp told him to stay vigilant.

Olivia watched him work the gas and brake pedals. "So how is it you can drive the car? I'm trying to work it out in my brain. I have a friend who has M.S., and once she lost sensation in her feet, she had to give up driving a standard car. She had the assistive technology installed for her hands."

"Let me start by telling you that I can, at any point, use my hands. I've trained extensively and been tested for proficiency in using my bionic limbs. There's just no leeway in state law, so I am required to have the hand capability. That's this here." He pointed. "Now, to answer your question, the surgeons I was telling you about in Afghanistan?"

"Yes."

"They kept as much of my nerve and muscle tissue as possible in my residual limbs. Later, they mapped out what touch point triggered what sensation in my brain. When they touched here, it felt like my pinky toe. If they touched there, it felt like my heel. So that's one set of sensors. Then, other sensors read the muscles in my thighs, knees, and glutes. The AI system determines the movement associated with which sets of muscles are firing. The software puts it all together, and while not perfect, it's darned good. That group keeps making strides forward." He sent her a smile so she'd pay attention to his play on words. "Today, I'm field-testing new prostheses. They have a system they're experimenting with to help with stability. So far, high marks."

"Science being accumulative." She let that thought trail off, then said, "Another friend, acquaintance really, she has an ALS diagnosis. She's watching this research group who just did their first brain implant. It's supposed to be going really well. The implant is attached to a computer, and the patient can communicate and access the computer by thinking things. Can you imagine the impact on someone with, say, quadriplegia or Parkinson's? I can think of a host of other issues that might really benefit."

"An incredible achievement if it's safe." Nutsbe focused on his rearview as Beowolf got to the back of the cargo space and stared out the window, panting.

"In the future, I wonder if something like that could somehow get integrated with prosthetic limbs. Maybe someday cyborgs might actually be a thing."

Yeah, the magical *what-if*. One of Nutsbe's least favorite topics. "I don't need that," he said evenly. "I work with the research scientists because I'm one of the few who can help them. They were there for me at a time when they could make a huge difference in my life, and I'm extremely grateful for the opportunity to pay that back. But I'd be fine either way. Alive is good."

"Alive is good. Yes." She was quiet for a moment. "So what risks?"

He glanced her way.

"Besides infection and other obvious things, you seemed to have more than that in your voice when you said, 'If it's safe.'"

"Extrapolate out from this story: I have a friend whose pregnant wife and baby were kidnapped. The criminal hacked into her car's computer system and was able to follow her GPS. When she was on a remote stretch of road, they used the car's computer brake system to stop her vehicle. The criminal walked over with a gun, and there was nothing his wife could do but comply."

"What?" Olivia screeched. "They had outside control of her car?"

Maybe the wrong thing to bring up at the wrong time. He'd switch it back to medical. "Can you imagine if a bad guy could hack a medical pump? A pacemaker? A brain with a new sensor?"

"When the enemy is inside the house," Olivia whispered.

"Exactly."

"Yeah, that's a lot to weigh into the equation." She looked down at her hands knotted in her lap and seemed to force herself to ask. "Is your friend's family okay?"

"Smart woman. Very pragmatic. She figured a way out. Iniquus has a program for our significant others on how to handle situations. She put that training to good use. And she saved her family."

Olivia scooted around in the seat, looked out the back window for a long moment, and then faced Nutsbe. "Would you train me?"

"To be a significant other?"

"I-I-I," she stammered.

Nutsbe reached over and squeezed her arm. "I'm giving you a hard time. You're asking about what to do when? If you were getting carjacked like she was?"

"Yes, carjacking. It's a major problem in D.C. right now. The other day, the thieves shot that dad. I know they will often bump your car, and when you get out to exchange information, someone runs up, jumps in, and takes off. I know that you're supposed to let them go."

"Right," Nutsbe agreed.

"The guy happened to be standing at the door." She skated a hand out. "I'm not blaming the victim in any way. I'm just saying that sometimes things go okay, and sometimes they just don't. We don't have any control except, in my mind, in trying to be kind. So I guess my question is, what should I do beyond trying to be a good person and not give karma a reason to create havoc?"

Nutsbe nodded. "Okay, some carjacking basics."

"Just a minute. Nutsbe, could we go back to the first part of this conversation?"

He looked over to her and pulled his brows together. He didn't know what she meant by 'the first part of this conversation,' but her tone told him she had some big emotions brewing, and he gripped the wheel.

"I like you. And so I need to say this." She licked her lips. "I don't have your lived experience, and I'm going to make mistakes and say the wrong things. I'll learn with time. I hope I haven't offended you so much that you'll avoid me. It's not my intention—"

"You know what, Olivia?" Nutsbe grinned. *She liked him.* "As long as you're not crying, we can talk most anything out. Classified is off the table, of course."

"Okay, how about we talk about why you keep looking in your rearview mirror like that?"

20

Nutsbe

Should he tell her?

Olivia had handled everything else that day like a rockstar.

But he knew so little about her. People had their breaking points, and Nutsbe didn't want to push Olivia past her capacity. Especially if this was a nothing burger.

What he had was that prickle across his scalp and Beowolf's vigilance. With all the doggo yawns going on back there and the panting, Beowolf was stressed; Nutsbe got that.

What he hadn't heard yet was a warning rumble.

"Right now, I'm driving with situational awareness." That was true. "When we operate an Iniquus vehicle, we're trained to do it tactically." That was also true.

"What does that mean?"

"Have you heard of OODA loops?" Nutsbe asked, trying to check his mirrors without being obvious.

"OODA? No. Sounds like Udon noodles."

"It's a thought process they train into combat pilots. OODA: observe, orient, decide, act. It allows the pilot to make the split-second decision, overcome hesitation, and do what's necessary: drop the bomb, evade the rocket, or pull the ejection lever."

"You didn't do that in Afghanistan when your plane failed, right? You said you landed it?"

"Landing is the preferred way to get down from the clouds. For about a third of pilots who attempt it, ejecting breaks their spine. It's a doomsday scenario."

Right now, Nutsbe was in the observational part of that OODA equation. Yup, he was pretty sure this pair of motorcycles had been following them from the courthouse.

"Hey, Olivia." Nutsbe purposely modulated his voice to sound casually conversational.

"Yes?" She glanced his way.

"Candace said she was hiding at that friend's house because the perp has brothers."

"He does. Two. And they're every bit as menacing as Kyle Offsed. But Kyle is the only one Candace can identify as being at the crime scene. And he's the only one I have enough evidence to bring to trial." She looked out the side window while playing with the ring on her finger. "When they're around, it's almost like I can taste the latent violence." She looked over at Nutsbe. "Even Judge Madison is concerned. That's why I'm allowed to keep my phone on me at all times." She paused. "I wonder what happened to cause him to leave with the family emergency. Of course, Judge Madison is an intensely private guy so unless the issue continues to interrupt court, I'll never know." She reached down and did something with her shoe. "It occurred to me that if we had been in court, we would have missed the whole sniper scene. Not knowing why the judge had to leave, one could start developing conspiracy theories. But I do know that his mom has been in and out of the hospital this last month. I'd lay money on something happening with his mother's health."

Nutsbe glanced at the red toggle emergency switch and considered flipping it on as a precaution.

"What does your gut tell you?" Olivia focused on Nutsbe. "Do you think we'll be back in court tomorrow? Oh, wait. Can you even go? I didn't ask about your schedule. Beowolf is a last-minute dog, after all."

Nutsbe tipped his head left and right, loosened his shoulders, and prepped his body. "Hang on to that thought. I want to focus on these Offsed brothers. Do you think that they might actually cause you harm?"

"They're both on parole. They'd be back in jail for a very long time if they did."

"Right. But in the meantime, you could be hurt or killed. And they'd have to be caught and tried. Do they happen to have motorcycles, do you know?"

"Yes. They do. Candace thinks she's spotted them near her house, that's why she's staying at her friend's house. Are you thinking about the last few nights of noise? It occurred to me that they were trying to intimidate me. But that's pretty far-fetched." Her hand shot out and gripped Nutsbe's arm. "Do you think that's what Mickey needed to talk to me about? Do you think that's who beat the crap out of him the night you were arrested?"

"No idea," Nutsbe said. Well, this wasn't good news. It would be nice to ask Mickey, though. "Do you know if they've taken Mickey into custody yet?"

"My office is supposed to text me if word comes in. And there's been nothing about it."

For a while now, the motorcycles hung back far enough

that they couldn't be heard over the rest of the traffic. He'd catch flashes of them far back in his mirror. Now that he'd turned onto the empty road heading toward Headquarters, Nutsbe could hear them again.

Rounding the curve where a speed adjustment wouldn't be as visible, Nutsbe took his foot off the gas pedal. He kept his focus on the rearview. And there they were.

Olivia heard it now. She twisted in her seat. "Oh shit. Do you think it's them?"

"If it is, it's hard to imagine that they'd do anything out here. We're almost to Iniquus." Nutsbe reassured her. "It's a protected campus. If they're still following us when we get near the security gate, our cameras will pick up the license plates, and we can identify the owners." He resumed his speed. He didn't want to spook them. Nutsbe wanted those pictures of the plates. "If these two follow us all the way to Iniquus, we'll take steps." Nutsbe's focus slid to the red toggle on the instrument panel, and Olivia followed his gaze.

"What's that red toggle thing for?"

Nutsbe grinned. "It opens up a can of worms."

"Helpful worms?" Her voice was equal parts curious and worried.

"This is an Iniquus vehicle. Iniquus tracks their fleet. That toggle would light me up on the board. They'd be moving assets into place. Remember how I used your phone to keep Iniquus looped in? That toggle opens up that comms line. It allows me to explain the situation and effectuate the right response. For example, if satellite is available, they'd watch from the sky and advise."

"Movie scenarios." Olivia exhaled.

"Real-world scenarios."

She turned around. "They're still following."

"At a specific distance. If I speed up, so do they. If I slow down, so do they. It's poor tracking craft."

"Do you do that?" Olivia yanked her seat belt so tight Nutsbe was afraid she'd cut off her circulation. "Follow people? Track them?"

"I track them on my computer. I'm not an operator. I train like an operator, so I understand what's possible and what's not possible in the field. Movies are make-believe, and I can't ever just imagine something can be done. We're not actors. There's no fake blood to wash off at the end of the day, as you've experienced earlier."

"That's," Olivia pushed her hair from her face, "frightening."

"More frightening than what you do day in and day out with criminals like Kyle Offsed?"

"This case was actually my gentle case. I have another one that makes me feel really scared for the first time. There's a big damned dragon my office is trying to slay."

"What can you tell me about that?"

"Nothing other than they just seated a grand jury."

As they approached the underpass, the car that had been a good distance ahead of them swerved to the center of the road and came to a sudden stop just inside the mouth of the tunnel, effectively blocking the road.

Nutsbe braked as his hand toggled the emergency switch.

The motorcycles roared up from behind. And there was the Beowolf rumble that Nutsbe had anticipated; motorcycles equaled bad guys.

"Iniquus communications. Identify yourself."

Four men swarmed for the car and were running toward them. "Nutsbe Crushed. Panther Force. Code red. Code red. Code red. Ambush. Possible carjacking."

As they raised their hands and Nutsbe registered their

firearms, he yelled, "Guns. Guns. Guns." His foot moved from brake to the gas, and he managed, thanks to his ongoing vehicular evasion training, to floor it with enough finesse that he didn't spin the wheels.

The SUV rocketed forward.

The men in his path were too busy jumping out of the way to point and pull the trigger.

The open doors were a mirage. Nutsbe only needed to calculate the side of the car body, the side of the underpass, and the width of this behemoth of an SUV. He thought maybe it was possible.

His only other out was backing up.

He could do a lot in his car with evasive driving, but he wasn't there with his lower limb or hand control agility to whip the car around in a one-eighty to get out of Dodge.

Nutsbe didn't bother to register what the motorcycles were doing—if they, too, had whipped out firearms.

Forward it was.

His brain flipped to its survival mode, slowing time.

The vehicle scraped along the cement, scrubbing the mirrors from the sides, sanding away the paint. The screech of metal stabbed at his eardrums in the momentary darkness of the underpass.

Olivia screamed, throwing her hand over her face as they crashed through the back door of the white car. With the first impact, their SUV bucked and juddered. Nutsbe was afraid that he wouldn't make it through the front door without momentum.

But he should not have doubted the power of an Iniquus vehicle.

The front door of the ambush car peeled back and popped, dropping to the ground. Nutsbe's back tires lifted and rolled over it, dropping them back down with a bounce.

"Impact," Nutsbe said in the rock steady voice he used when Panther Force was in a hot situation—calm was survival.

He kept the pedal down so the abrasion was damaging, but they didn't get stuck.

They popped out the other side of the underpass.

It felt like it had been going on for long minutes, but mere seconds had passed from observation to action to outcome, and he didn't see anyone standing in the road, trying to get a bead.

Nutsbe's next observation was that the motorcycles didn't follow them past the damaged vehicle.

He'd been narrating this for the communications officer. "We're through the underpass heading to the campus. Over."

Yeah, that had been almost impossibly tight. Nutsbe wouldn't have made it through if the guy had been inches closer to the center. He would have had to crash into the back, hoping to pop the criminals' car out of there like a cork. Had it twisted, Nutsbe would have trapped their SUV, and what came next wouldn't have been pretty.

He reached out and rubbed Olivia's knee. "Hey, you're okay. You're okay."

She had her hands knotted into her hair, her eyes wide.

He was going to give her system a second to reset.

The criminals had that strategy down. It looked planned and rehearsed for grace and flow. Ex-military? Ex-FBI? Those men had made tactical shapes in the way they advanced, sitting into their hips, whipping guns to their chests, acquiring a target, and punching their weapons out as they extended their arms. Yeah. Tactical.

He went through it again in his mind's eye.

Men swarmed from three car doors in a cadence. The front door popped open, and the front passenger ran back.

Once he cleared, the back doors opened, and three more men piled out. Foot on the ground, pivot, run.

That left the doors open for a quick exit and the driver ready to peel out. What was the operational goal?

"You're okay." He sing-songed, as much for him as for Olivia.

Stealing this vehicle would be a coup. It was worth about eighty-five thousand dollars. If they were coming for the car, would they need to leave the driver in the getaway car? He'd have to think about that strategy and talk it out with his team.

If that crew was coming for either him or Olivia, they'd be pissed that they didn't catch their mouse in the trap. And possibly more importantly, they'd have to report back. And someone was gonna be enraged that there was a failure because failure gave everyone a heads up, and surprise was now going to be that much harder.

Anger begat pain and violence.

Nutsbe's foot was still heavy on the gas.

Yes, Iniquus vehicles had bullet-resistant glass. But did he want to test it?

Hell to the no.

"Nutsbe. I am two clicks from the gate. Coming in hot. Over."

"Received. We will continue to monitor. Over."

Nutsbe drove aggressively for the Iniquus campus. And they were ready for him as he squealed around the corner.

Roaring through the open gate, Nutsbe finally lifted his foot from the gas and let the vehicle coast to the guest parking lot.

"Hey, Olivia. We're here. Are you okay?"

"OODA loops," Olivia whispered.

Nutsbe pulled calmly into a parking space right in front of the atrium door. "I've concluded, Olivia, that you're a dangerous woman to be around. I can honestly say that being your neighbor is more dangerous than anything I've done as a member of an Iniquus tactical force."

"I'm sorry," she whispered. She was white as a sheet and shaking with good reason. He was a little shaky, too. Today had been a lot for a nervous system to process.

"Look, I don't know what's going on here. Are things coming at you? Are they directed at me? We both have jobs that can put a crazy's target on our backs. Heck, it could be happenstance, just a run of wrong place, wrong times." He repeated his earlier thought, but it tasted wrong on his tongue.

"It doesn't feel like that." She didn't raise her voice above that whisper.

"You okay?" Nutsbe asked, turning off the engine. "Anything I can do?"

"Honestly, I could *really* use that bathroom now."

21

Nutsbe

Beowolf was back at his kennel playing with his pals, and Panther Force was back in the war room with their thinking caps pulled on, going over the knowns with Olivia.

Now, there was nothing else to be said.

They'd spent the last hour examining the events that had occurred since Olivia's soon-to-be ex had put a rock through her kitchen door window.

It was a lot.

Olivia showed her prosecutorial chops as the team listed the complications on their whiteboard.

There were imbalances in today's disclosure.

Olivia mentioned that she was on a team that had just seated a grand jury in a significant case and wasn't at liberty to discuss it. She'd mentioned that she was in the final days until a contentious divorce. And lastly, there was the Offsed trial, which both Olivia and Nutsbe were involved with now.

On his side, Nutsbe disclosed nothing.

That Russia, Albania, and a retired senior FBI honcho might want him eradicated was left unsaid.

The sniper? Olivia was right; everyone agreed the wind made it difficult to tell if it was a professional or a disaffected Joe Schmo shooting from the parking garage roof. They needed to wait for the crime scene reports to better evaluate.

The motorcycles that were following their SUV into the ambush?

They weren't amateurs; they knew to hang back.

They weren't professionals; they made beginner mistakes.

The motorcycles were an in-between.

But that was assuming that the riders were doing something nefarious. With the rearview film on the big screen, they decided it was a valid option for the bikers to stay a certain distance from the SUV in front of them when it was erratically changing lanes and speed, the way Nutsbe had done to test his theory that his vehicle was being followed.

Neither Olivia nor Nutsbe could identify the sound of those bikes as the ones that had been harassing their neighborhood.

At least with the back-camera footage, they could get the make and model. Nutsbe put that on his to-do list.

The ambush?

Definitely a dedicated crew. Again, the criminals had tactical training, which was evident to everyone. And the police had already brought Panther Force up to date on that car. It was a fast turnaround because it was an M.O. that the D.C.P.D. had been chasing all over the capital city and was now spreading to Northern Virginia.

Were all the ambush criminals ex-military? Ex-law enforcement?

Impossible to say with their video alone.

It could very well be a street gang that someone trained up.

"We go away to help out Strike Force for one night—one night—and this is what you get yourself up to?" Thorn chided.

"I got bored without you and went looking for a little excitement," Nutsbe said, checking his phone. "Hard to blame a guy." It was security calling in.

Nutsbe had interacted with the police on three occasions in less than twenty-four hours, and it didn't surprise him in the least when the front gate was on the line asking permission to allow Special Agents Kennedy and Finley to head up for a meeting.

They hadn't even bothered to send a text to see if he was in the building.

Commander Titus Kane tipped his gaze to Thorn. "Automotive brought a new vehicle around to visitor parking, now that Nutsbe made a mess of the last one." He sent Nutsbe a grin before focusing back on Thorn. "Olivia was going to drive the new vehicle home. Do you want to walk her down?"

"Will do." Thorn stood and faced Olivia. "Ma'am, it's been a trying day. I can either get you the keys, or I'd be happy to drive you."

Sending Thorn a tired smile, Olivia said, "I think my nerves have settled. I won't inconvenience you. But thank you." As she followed along behind Thorn, she caught Nutsbe's gaze. "You're still able to help me with my car? How about I order takeout for two?"

Olivia had handled everything since he'd met her with an interesting combination of compassion and ice in her veins. Nerves of steel, the kind of woman who would talk about issues without opening teary floodgates, rational and even. It was crazy that she'd been on the other side of his fence for *years*, and he'd not known it. All that time ...

Nutsbe had just watched something similar happen in Estonia, where not just the right people lined up, but also the right place, right time. It made Nutsbe wonder. Maybe he was just meeting Olivia now because her marriage was about to end. It was a thought that brushed through his mind and vanished.

Right now, both his heart and his head appreciated Olivia Gladstone's sudden appearance in his life, even with the volatility. "I can't guarantee what time I can get there." He waggled his phone. "I'm not sure what my friends are on the way up to talk to me about."

"Okay then, I'll see you when I see you." Olivia looked like there was more she wanted to say, but she rolled her lips in, gave a nod, acknowledged Kennedy and Finley, and followed Thorn into the hall.

Nutsbe stood back as the special agents made their way into the war room.

"That was Olivia Gladstone. She's a U.S. prosecutor," Finley said. His focus moved toward the board, scanning down the storyline. "Hell of a day you two had."

"One for the books." Nutsbe moved back to his chair. The special agents were familiar enough with the room that they didn't need special manners.

"Really interesting that she's been involved in all this." Deep in thought, Kennedy pulled his brow together as he took his chair.

"You know her, Kennedy?" Titus asked. "You're Eastern Europe. Why are you finding her presence interesting?"

"Nothing classified." He sat and considered those words. "Nothing that I've been read into anyway. But I'm just back from Germany, and her name came up in passing. I looked her up just last week."

"In Germany?" Nutsbe asked.

"And interestingly," Kennedy pulled his ankle over his knee as he settled in, "there was a motorcycle component to why I was invited to that meeting."

Titus leaned back in his seat, crossing his arms over his chest. "For clarity, her name was spoken in conjunction with motorcycles?"

"Her name was mentioned—and knowing your clearance levels and professionalism, I'm going to share this with you. I think I might have heard something I wasn't supposed to know."

"It stays in this room," Titus said.

"All right." Kennedy swiped his fingers down either side of his nose. "Eastern Virginia sat a secret grand jury looking at a possible assassin functioning within the U.S. The DOJ has already been scraping up associates, several of whom have been working as unregistered foreign agents. The extremist organization will be pissed if the prosecutors get the true bill to press formal federal charges. The concern is that once charged, the man will turn State's evidence and share the terrorist organization's internal secrets. We know that group is actively trying to thwart that outcome."

"Olivia said she has a grand jury seated, and she's unable to talk about it," Nutsbe said, his arms folded over his chest, his gaze intent. "That information may be accurate and current. How would anyone in Europe have figured it out?"

"Hard to say." Kennedy drummed his fingers on his knee. "I heard rumors, and I'm repeating the rumors back to you."

"What has that got to do with motorcycles?" Titus asked.

"At that same meeting, there was a briefing about an American terrorist active in Germany. German authorities believe that an extremist organization has been using an American on a motorcycle to attack Jewish targets in Northern Germany. A leader of a major Jewish community group has been specifically targeted."

"An *American* terrorist in Germany," Titus asked. "Is he acting on ideology?"

"Ideology." Kennedy let that word drag out. "From what Interpol is turning up, he's getting a hefty payday. Interpol knows the biker is responding to commands from out of the Middle East, and they're actively seeking the biker's arrest. It muddies relationships when an extremist organization can get people from countries with friendly governments to commit crimes. It's a positive for an adversarial country when they can get criminals from one Western ally to hurt another Western ally, right? If and when arrests are made, and that hits the papers, it creates bad feelings and diplomacy issues amongst friends."

"What has this American biker done exactly?" Nutsbe asked.

"So far, he's thrown Molotov cocktails that have only created minor damage but major terror," Kennedy said.

"And they're sure it's this American?" Titus asked.

"They have him on video. They just can't find him. But various intelligence agencies are picking up his name in a lot of chatter about a missing dissident with dual German citizenship. We know there was a fatwa against that dissident. They believe the American was able to entice the guy out of hiding to attend a dinner. No one knows what happened to him after he left the restaurant with the American biker."

"Let me just go through this," Nutsbe said. "As you were listening to this conversation about Olivia and the American biker—"

"Different parts of the conversation," Kennedy said.

"Okay, but were these two concerns spoken back-to-back?" Nutsbe pressed. "Is it possible that this was a stream-of-consciousness conversation that aligned two disparate things because somewhere in their mind, they drew a connection?"

"I get what you're saying, Nutsbe." Kennedy's gaze rested on the ground as if he were going back in his memory to revisit the meeting. "The intelligence community thinks the dissident was assassinated, not kidnapped. They're looking for a body. That's one thing. Another is that we already knew the extremist group was involved in terrorist acts. For example, that same group hired a local thug to go after our US national security advisor when he was visiting Germany. The attacker showed up outside of the security advisor's hotel suite with an assault rifle. The Secret Service acted, and the man was arrested. From his interviews—and this is where my counterparts were looping me in—it was discovered that this particular extremist organization is increasing its policy of going after low-level dissidents worldwide. The goal is to send a message that *any* level of opposition is intolerable. And as an example, they mentioned Eastern Virginia had recently seated a grand jury that has something to do with dissident assassinations."

"And they mentioned Olivia's name," Titus said.

"I understand that Stephany Abner and Olivia Gladstone are running a team," Kennedy affirmed.

"Olivia said her grand jury was classified," Titus said. "I'd keep this information as need to know."

"Got you." Kennedy nodded his agreement.

"I hope Olivia and her team are all taking precautions," Finley said.

Titus leaned forward to catch Kennedy's gaze. "Might be nice if the FBI went by and had a little chat with their office, don't you think?"

22

Nutsbe

Kennedy held Titus's gaze for a long moment, steepled his fingers, and said, "I'm reminding you that we agreed that the Olivia Gladstone information was part of a privileged conversation. If anything is to be shared, it will be at the discretion of the U.S. government, not Iniquus taking the reins." Kennedy relaxed his hands onto his knees and turned to Nutsbe. "As for you, Nutsbe, we picked up your name on two different police reports today. Not really playing this with a low profile."

"Any thoughts about whether today's events could be tied to the Russo-Albanian-FBI case?" Nutsbe asked.

"It occurred to us." Finley pointed toward the board. "Could I take a picture of your notes?"

"They're speculatory in blue and known in red," Titus said. "You can have them as part of your deal with Covington. Share and share alike."

"Agreed." Finley stood and walked toward the whiteboard.

"While you look at that," Nutsbe said, "let me ask you this: Any chance the FBI wants to keep me quiet? Do you know of anyone who might be taking potshots at me as I leave the courthouse where my name is listed and of public record?"

"I'm not saying it's impossible." Finley held his phone up, methodically taking pictures of sections of the whiteboard.

"It's not a Russian M.O.," Kennedy pointed out.

"But just like the extremist organization story, with the American on his motorcycle, any of the possible players could have hired out." Finley turned and walked back to the table to sit next to Kennedy. "You remember the case Panther Force worked on with the militia group in West Virginia, where some of the members got caught up in the Russian scheme to get computer gamers to take patriotic actions, that is, step in and do their dirty work for them?"

"We remember," Titus said.

"Russia, Albania, or McMahan, any of them could have made the hire," Kennedy said. "All of them would have the right connections to make that happen."

"Then we have no idea in what direction Nutsbe needs his defense up," Titus said.

"Witness protection program," Finley kidded. "We can get the marshals involved."

"Hell to the no, we're not getting the marshals involved." Nutsbe stabbed a finger onto the table punctuating each word. "These last two days are starting to make my mind spin. It's like the flying monkeys in The Wizard of Oz. It's coming in from all sides. You guys didn't just come down here to do a welfare check. What's up?" Nutsbe asked.

"We know how Russia got hold of your name. And going forward, you, and more broadly, Iniquus, will want this information. It's classified. My superior, Frost, permitted me to read you into this part. And since the FBI often works hand in hand with Iniquus," he looked at his watch, "I've got an appointment here in a minute to explain this to your command and head of IT."

Nutsbe reached up to rub the corner of his eye. "All right, let's hear it. They didn't hack our computers. Did the FBI get hacked?"

"Not to our knowledge," Kennedy said. "While Iniquus has leaned into AI from the beginning, you know that's a double-edged sword. Like anything, the good is quickly overshadowed by people with less-than-golden intentions. In this case, AI sound technology is the problem. We believe they got your name through your fingerprint."

Thorn walked through the door, moved to the table, and sat facing the special agents.

"We're about to learn how Russia got hold of my identification through sound," Nutsbe filled him in.

"Shit," Thorn said.

"Sound and fingerprints?" Nutsbe turned to Finley. "My fingerprints are on file with the FBI for security clearances. I don't use my fingerprint as biometric identification. I think it leads to a dangerous trail. You never know what the engineers are going to figure out next."

"There is now an AI system," Finley said, "that automatically identifies a person's fingerprints through the swipe of a finger on a touchscreen apparatus—computer, smartphone, tablet. When swiping, the gesture creates a friction sound that is captured and analyzed using a localized algorithm. The AI system can infer from the sound irregularities and interpret the noise to create a reproduction of individual's fingerprints."

"The sound," Nutsbe was flabbergasted, "of me swiping my finger on a screen."

Titus turned to Thorn. "Would Arya know anything about that?"

"Negative. Arya studies large animals with low resonance sound waves. And even if she knew anything about it, would I allow you to talk to her about a terrorist? Hell no, brother, I would not."

"Is this swipe-sound technology accurate enough to be used in a court of law?" Nutsbe asked.

"At this stage," Finley said, "it's helping both the good and the bad guys comb through the haystack to pick out the possible needle. Once you're on their radar, the next steps can be taken to refine and confirm."

"The FBI has gamed this out," Kennedy said. "Since biometric fingerprint security is widespread, if the AI capability continues to advance, illegal market fingerprint authentication information could criminally generate about a hundred billion US dollars in the next decade. Businesses and people who work in sensitive fields have been cautious about revealing their fingerprints. Some people in intelligence have become very aware of their hands in photographs. CIA, DIA, and FBI are all coached on this now. The right camera shot, an excellent computer system, and the finger pad could be enlarged and focused to expose the fingerprint for exploitation. But why put assets out in public, working to capture that picture? A viral app—one that requires you to swipe—so think, game, screen, anything with a downward swipe—and the AI can capture the sound and create the print for hundreds of millions of people and hold them on file. Make that app free, let it go viral, and you could build a computer bank of players' biomarkers very quickly."

Nutsbe laced his fingers, resting his hands on his head. "I swiped something."

"You did," Kennedy said quietly. "We think at least twice."

"Do you know what it was?" Nutsbe asked.

Finley leaned forward. "We believe that Russia captured your print most recently when you talked to Iniquus client Amanda Bradshaw."

Nutsbe moved his hands to the arms of his chair and leaned forward. "I know the name. I met her once in person, and she contacted me once with a security question. She was a student who was doing research at the August Helsinki meeting when Panther Force was doing close protection for State."

Titus said, "Panther Force was contracted by her university to provide kidnap and ransom support if needed—which it was not—we played no role."

"Nutsbe introduced himself," Kennedy said. "It's in his reports."

"That's right," Nutsbe agreed. "I introduced myself, but not by name. I said I was with Iniquus Panther Force and that we had a connection to her university. I didn't go into any details beyond that."

"One of the last photos from the meeting had you in it," Kennedy said. "You were in your Iniquus uniform, shaking Bradshaw's hand. She went to Moscow to visit her grandmother and was arrested. Her grandmother called the U.S. consulate, and we began to monitor her phone. Since that arrest, she called and talked to you, sending you a link." Kennedy paused, turning to Titus. "Any word on her well-being?"

"Nothing we can share," Titus said. He turned to Nutsbe. "Amanda was arrested in Moscow on espionage charges."

Nutsbe scowled by way of response. "You said Russia had my Thaddeus Crushed name. Amanda doesn't know my name. But you're right, recently, she called the Iniquus help number given to her university. Communications would have directed the call to my phone. She wanted me to check on a website for her."

"We monitored and recorded that interaction from her phone. We believe they took your swipe from the Bradshaw call as the collection point," Kennedy said.

"Why do you think that? That swipe on my phone would have given them nothing to make Russia curious about me," Nutsbe insisted.

"Alone, no," Kennedy agreed. "However, we think that McMahan was monitoring Hoxha's computer. This is how we see it playing out: In Helsinki, when you met Amanda, you were in an Iniquus uniform, and a picture of the two of you was taken and forwarded to her phone."

"Okay." Nutsbe nodded.

"After her arrest, Russians went through the phone, and in that picture are you, Amanda, and the Russian president."

"That's right, he moved through that room. We didn't approach him."

"The Russian investigators latched on to that picture and asked Amanda for your name and affiliation."

"She would say she doesn't know my name, but I work with her university," Nutsbe filled in.

"She had to have remembered your affiliation with Iniquus. Iniquus has done a lot of damage to various Russian schemes. The SVR would recognize the Iniquus name. If we were in the Russian investigator's shoes, we'd want to know your name *explicitly*. So they got Amanda to call you. That we know as fact. Like I said," Kennedy pushed forward in his chair, "Intelligence was monitoring her phone after her grandmother informed the consulate of her arrest."

"Okay," Nutsbe's mind was mile-a-minute trying to piece this together.

"The goal, we believe, was to get you to swipe the screen and, in that way, obtain your fingerprint to compare to their data bank."

"But Amanda wouldn't know who to ask for," Nutsbe insisted.

"She could have described you to communications," Finley offered. "And she could narrow it to Panther Force."

"True. Okay, so they got the swipe. Still, how did they put it together with my name? Wait a minute. The FBI knows about this because you all use this AI advancement. Of course, you do." Nutsbe leaned back in his chair, looking up toward the ceiling and thinking. "And McMahan would have wanted to keep a close eye on Hoxha from the beginning to see if that connection was trustworthy before McMahan got himself tied up in anything." His voice faded as he tested that theory in his mind. *Could it be?*

"Bingo," Finley said. "You were on Hoxha's computer, weren't you?"

Nutsbe sat up to look at Finley. "I was. And I swiped. And McMahan would have had those prints. This was years ago, before he did anything illegal with Hoxha. I was only on his computer once. At that time, McMahan could have had someone look at the IAFS to give him my name. Back then, he might have backburnered it because Iniquus was working on the company's Montenegro retreat security, so my involvement wouldn't have raised any suspicions. And again, McMahan wasn't doing anything wrong. If he was watching for me to swipe again, I never did. Just the one time."

"And at some point," Thorn added, "he could have handed the information over to Albania or Russia. I'm getting the picture."

"Bingo again," Finley said. "In this working scenario, Russia had your fingerprint and the data from the FBI. They would know your fingerprint was associated with Hoxha and McMahan."

"Hoxha anyway, and years ago," Nutsbe insisted.

"Year's ago. And uninteresting at the time. But things have become complicated for all the players in that scheme since then."

"Right," Nutsbe said.

"And when your Amanda-swipe matched the sound pattern of the print on Hoxha's computer, suddenly your name rises to the top like cream. After the Amanda call, intelligence started hearing your name in dangerous circles."

Nutsbe wasn't a fan of the sensations around his jaw and neck. It took effort to remain stoic.

"That's what we believe happened. And when we know more, we'll share more." Kennedy stood and pointed to the board. "Thank you for your notes. We're going to keep working on this situation." He turned to his partner. "Finley, anything you need to add?"

"Not now, no." He lifted his phone. "After speaking with Command, I want to go back to the office and think about all this."

The two men lifted their hands as a parting salute and left.

"Amanda Bradshaw," Titus said. "Son of a bitch."

23

Nustbe

"Now that the room is cleared," Nutsbe said. "Amanda Bradshaw was arrested? Why the heck was Amanda Bradshaw in Moscow, to begin with?"

"You haven't read the paper today?" Thorn asked.

"Been a might busy. How about you catch me up?" Nutsbe asked.

"You had left for Estonia," Thorn said, "so you missed this part. Amanda decided that since Helsinki was so close, she'd pop over to Russia to visit her grandmother."

"But Moscow?" Nutsbe shook his head. "In this atmosphere?"

"We strenuously discouraged her from going. Free will," Titus said.

Nutsbe turned to Thorn. "The university didn't weigh in?"

"They didn't offer guidance. Bradshaw seemed to think that only Americans with high name recognition were getting picked up. She was a student. I pointed out that other students came to some very bad ends at the hands of governments where America had little to no diplomatic presence."

"Let me guess," Nutsbe frowned, "she said they were foreigners, and she had family."

"Grandmother, to be exact. And that's where they arrested her, at her grandmother's apartment."

"That's what's in the paper?" Nutsbe asked. "When was the arrest?"

"Two weeks ago," Titus said. "It looks like she spent one night with Grandma and the second night at the prison. Word is just now getting out to the public."

Nutsbe leaned back and focused on the ceiling. "Well, shit. Kennedy is probably right, then."

"What did you land on?" Titus asked.

"When I was in Tallinn, Estonia, Amanda Bradshaw contacted me via the switchboard. She asked me if I could check a website to see if it was safe for her to open on her computer. Bradshaw mentioned something about research for the university. She said she didn't want to mess up her new security clearance. And since we do that for her university's contract, I followed through, no big deal."

"You opened it and decided it was fine?" Thorn said.

"I did because it was."

"But you swiped through while she was on the phone with you?" Titus said.

"I did."

Titus's nod was grave. "You have that information in a report?"

"I logged it and reported on it. We can hand the info to our cyber team and get them to take a look."

"I'll bring it up with Command first," Titus said. "See how they want to handle this. Off the top of your head, this was in the last two weeks, so after her arrest?"

"It fits Kennedy's timeline. I flew back to D.C. from Estonia for a few days to attend meetings and pick up K9 Max for Halo. And that's why I can pinpoint this exactly. It was the day I came back to join the team in Estonia. It was the night of the Tallinn fire. You all were downstairs having dinner, and I was doing reports in my room."

"What was on the site?" Thorn asked.

"A nothing burger site. I remember thinking that it wasn't worth her while." Nutsbe shook his head. "Russian prison. That's no damned joke. This situation with Amanda is out of our hands, right?" Nutsbe turned back to Titus. "The State Department is negotiating her release?"

"She's on their radar. We warned her about this very situation." Titus didn't look up from his phone, where he was searching through a file. "State Department wants us to butt out. They have the Special Presidential Envoy for Hostage Affairs involved."

"Honey?" Nutsbe knew that Honey Honig had been rerouted and hadn't returned with the rest of Panther Force. He often worked alone when he was negotiating a hostage release. And Nutsbe hadn't had time since the Panther Force wheels landed to move through the roster and account for everyone's workload.

"At this point, there's nothing we can do. There's no way to get in and grab her out. If she was sent to her grandmother's to await trial, that would be one thing. This ... Nothing to be done except stick our nose in and complicate the situation." Titus seemed to have found what he needed and sent it on to the person who needed it. His focus returned to Nutsbe. "But based on other Americans being held on trumped-up espionage charges, she's never coming home."

"I think I have the photo that Kennedy told us about." Nutsbe opened his phone. "Our protectee took it and sent a copy to both of us because it isn't every day that a Russian president walks through the room." Nutsbe held his phone out. "Do you think that guy with the black case carries the Russian equivalent of the nuclear football?"

Titus looked at the picture, and his face brightened with a rare grin. "That, my friend, is paranoia in action. When the Russian president takes a shit, this poor guy," Titus tapped the screen, "has to fish the turd out of the pot and carry it in that case."

"It's a shitcase?" Nutsbe pulled his chin back, pulling his lips thin with disgust. "Are you pulling my leg?"

"I shit you not," Titus said. "He's afraid that a foreign government could get his fecal matter and test it to gain his DNA and other information about his health."

"Disgusting." Nutsbe put his phone back in his pocket.

"Exactly," Thorn said.

"Titus, what do you think about the FBI's theory for how my name showed up? I think we're throwing darts blindfolded." Yeah, Nutsbe would admit it; today, his nerves had been mightily taxed. "Why not throw that one more dart out there, too, and see if it hits a bullseye."

"I can't say that I disagree. Fingerprint swipes, I imagine we're about to get protocol saying that if we're doing anything with an external site, we'll need to use a stylus. Another security hoop to jump." Titus stood. "For now, I need to give Margot a call. Thorn, you need to get home and spend some time with Arya. Nutsbe, I'm sure you'd like to get out of that suit. You smell like a goat turd floating in a punch bowl. Go relax. Court tomorrow?"

"I'm not sure yet. But I'm on my way to pick up Beowolf and take him home with me, so things are smooth in the morning if the trial is a go."

"Are you staying at the barracks? It might be good for you to be on campus until things shake out a bit."

"I promised to pick up Olivia's car from the courthouse. And then I'll stay at my house. We don't know who the target is: Random Joe Public, Olivia, or me—"

"Could be all three," Thorn said.

"Until that's cleared up, I want to be around and ensure Olivia is safe."

Nutsbe sat shotgun as Thorn drove him to the Cerberus campus to get the car Automotive had left for him when he picked up Beowolf.

"From the sound of things, you and Olivia are getting pretty tight," Thorn said as he drove past the training fields.

"Tight." Nutsbe tried that word on. That word sounded like "tied." He didn't feel like that was entirely right. "It would be nice to take her on a date once things settle. I enjoy her company."

"Companionship, not relationship?" Thorn rolled his window down and stuck his arm out, letting his hand ride the warm end of summer air. "I mean, you two seemed to have forged some kind of a bond."

"In the trenches, that happens." Nutsbe would much prefer this conversation weren't happening. "I'm just not cut from the relationship cloth."

"I hear you, brother. I spouted the same shit before I saw the picture of Arya, and my whole world shifted."

"Nothing's shifted for me. This is what friendship looks like."

"Right." Thorn sent him a grin. "You're staying in harm's way at your house because of your good neighbor policy."

"Always nice to be on the good side of a federal prosecutor." Nutsbe looked out his window. Bob had Beowolf on a lead and was wiping the ubiquitous drool from his mouth.

Thorn pulled into a parking space. "Especially one that shows up with food."

"Sexist much?" Nutsbe released his belt.

"Food isn't sexist," Thorn pointed out. "Everyone eats."

"Yeah, man, I hear you. Thanks for the ride." He climbed from the car, then turned and leaned in. "Give Arya a hug for me."

"Will do. Stay safe, brother."

24

Nutsbe

"Hey Bob, you have a go-pack ready?" As Thorn drove off, Nutsbe wandered over to the sidewalk where Bob and Beowolf were waiting.

"It's already in the vehicle." He nodded to the SUV manned by an Automotive driver at the wheel and another in the back seat. "Beowolf's ready for bed. He got fed for tonight and had his exercise. He's also had a bath." Bob fobbed open the hatch and then handed the keys to Nutsbe. "He smelled like a sewer when you dropped him off to me."

"Puke. He was lying in a cramped space where I was doing CPR."

Beowolf loped over, sniffed, then turned to sit beside Nutsbe.

"Hey, there, buddy." Nutsbe swiped his hands from neck to chest in a rhythm as he dropped a kiss on Beowolf's wrinkled brow. "You had a bath? All fresh and clean? I'm going to introduce you to Henrietta, and she's a lady. So it's good that you're all spiffed up."

"CPR at the sniper event?" Bob asked. "You've had a rough day. Vomit says the person revived. Are they doing okay?"

"I haven't checked the news yet." Nutsbe left his hand resting on Beowolf's head.

"And you? How are you doing?"

"Better than I might have expected. Olivia and Beowolf were with me. We made a good team. I still have some heightened awareness, fatigue from the adrenaline. All in all, I moved through the double crisis, and it feels like it's in my rearview."

"Glad to hear it." He nodded toward Beowolf. "Beowolf's never really bonded with anyone." Bob slid his hands into his pockets as he observed the K9. "He's buddies with everyone. Loves people." He looked up to catch Nutsbe's gaze. "Didit brought him in and started his career here when they didn't click. He was always a good dog, mind you. Just not *her* dog."

"I get that." Nutsbe wriggled his fingers into Beowolf's fur, and Beowolf leaned heavily into Nutsbe's leg. He could almost feel the stabilizing mechanism engage in his prostheses. "I've seen that in my family. Our pet dogs were either Mom's or Dad's. If it was Mom's dog, that dog would only listen to her and ignore Dad and vice versa."

"Same with Beowolf," Bob said. "We always talked about him as kind of a lone wolf. Unusual for a bullmastiff, really." He pulled his chin back to consider Beowolf as Beowolf lowered himself to lie down. "I've been working with him since he was a puppy, but look where he is. He's not on lead, so he can go wherever he likes. He's lying at your feet, looking out away from you. That means he trusts you and is protecting you. It's un-Beowolf-like. He usually likes to plop down in the middle of the room, so he's the center of attention. Normally, I'd find him here." Bob pointed at the sidewalk between them.

"He's been heroic, Bob. When you hear the whole story, you'll be very proud. But," Nutsbe patted his pocket to check that his phone was in place, "it's going to have to wait. We're going to retrieve Olivia's car from that lot."

"Good enough."

"Listen, Bob, I was wondering if you had the name of a good sensor collar for dogs to move through a locked doggy door."

"Why would you need something like that? Are you planning on getting a pup?"

"I'm not planning, no. I'm considering. But this is for my neighbor's dog, Henrietta. She uses my fenced-in yard. I thought it would be good if Hen could come and go on her own. Say, for example, if it was raining or something."

"It would take some training first for her to use the door, and she'll need to learn a command telling her to go from where she was standing, across an area, and through the door. I'm not saying it can't be done. What breed?"

"Cockapoo."

"Ah. Well. That? Hang on." Bob turned and went into his headquarters building.

While Bob was away, Nutsbe loaded Beowolf into the back of the SUV.

The beeps warning that the hatch was lowering sounded as Bob came out with a box in his hand. "Cockapoos are about fifteen inches. My wife, Anna, got this for her chihuahua, checked the wrong size at the website, and forgot about it until it was too late to return or exchange." He held it out. "Good brand. If this works for you, take it. It's been sitting back in our supply room for over a year, so if it came with a battery, I'd change that to something fresher. You can set it so Henrietta can only go in and is held in that area. Otherwise, what good is the fence if she can dash out and get into the road?"

"Exactly." Nutsbe held up the box. "Thanks. I'll bring Beowolf back tomorrow after court if that's happening or in the morning if it's not. The time depends on how things play out with the judge."

IT WAS HARDER THAN ANTICIPATED, heading back to the sniper scene. Nutsbe thought the pool of blood would probably be there until the fire department came in. It had been a point of dread the whole way.

When they pulled into the lot, Nutsbe was relieved to see that the police tape was down and any biohazard had been cleaned.

Parked, Nutsbe handed off Olivia's keys to the guy in the back. "I'm going with you in her car. We're listening for a thunking noise." He turned his head to the driver. "And you're following us?"

"Affirmative, sir."

Standing next to Olivia's car, Nutsbe was convinced that either he or Olivia was the target. And he was leaning on Olivia being the one in the crosshairs. Nutsbe had been exposed for too long while he wrapped the tourniquet and dragged the judge without getting shot for the sniper to have been targeting him.

Instead, the next set of shots hit the windshield and the mirror of the car next to Olivia's. If Nutsbe had been the sniper and had lost view of his target, those were the shots he would have taken to move his rabbit out into the open or maybe hoping for a fortunate ricochet.

Before the bullets hit, Beowolf had grabbed Olivia and was moving her.

Nutsbe looked at the placement of the various bullet holes. The sniper wasn't a rando; he was well-trained.

Sure, he was considering the soon-to-be-ex. But terrorism was the bell that Kennedy had started clanging in Nutsbe's head. Surely, Olivia knew the dangers of taking on a terrorist organization.

Nutsbe walked forward, tracing Olivia's path.

She had been in the lot's drive space—out in the open—when the next bullet flew. Now, a wind gust very well could have thwarted that shot trajectory. Olivia dove behind the cars, then Nutsbe was dragging Judge Greenway as the second bullet hit the judge's leg.

The tourniquet was in place, and no more blood lost.

The essential information was that the sniper didn't aim for the judge's center mass. And he didn't have Nutsbe's head as the target, though he was right there, upright and the most exposed of the three.

Kennedy called it; sniping was not the Russian way.

And again, while Olivia thought the wind buffet caught the bullets, these holes weren't random. From the sniper's vantage point, the car bodies had to be blocking the three of them. The bullets peppered the windshields of the vehicles around them.

Nutsbe was confident that the sniper was trying to unnerve the group and get them running for cover farther away, or even for the shelter of a nearby business.

And after walking this through, Nutsbe was even more confident that Olivia was the target.

The driver fobbed Olivia's car unlocked, then held the back door open.

Nutsbe pointed his finger to the back. "Beowolf, load."

Beowolf stopped to consider the back bench seat, sniffing and tipping his head before finding a way to get into the space. Poor guy didn't quite fit on her back bench seat and had to put one of his back paws on the floor.

Walking around Olivia's vehicle, he saw there were no bullet holes. He also didn't see anything easily located that would make the noise that Olivia had described. He opened the passenger door and climbed in.

As the driver pulled out slowly, they both listened closely. "You?" Nutsbe asked.

"Nada," the guy said. "Maybe when we get some speed.

The driver was right. As soon as they hit the highway, Nutsbe heard the tire thwack. Not like a flat, just something bizarre and loud. The driver pulled off on the shoulder and put on his hazards.

With his phone flashlight, Nutsbe lay on his back and inched himself under the trunk. There, he discovered half of a bungee cord. The hook was stuck in the wall of the tire and the cord would smack the undercarriage with each rotation.

He called Olivia and told her he was stopping by the tire shop to get it patched.

"I got called into the office, puke suit and all. Can you text me when you think you might be back home so I can be sure to be there? I'll try to time the dinner arrival. Italian? I need a heavy dose of calming carbs."

25

Nustbe

After having the tire repaired, the team was on the last leg of their task. As they drove past his house, Nutsbe saw an Iniquus vehicles pulling into his drive. The Iniquus SUV that Olivia had driven home was in place for Nutsbe, and the other would take the other Automotive guy back to Headquarters.

It was a complicated shuffle of vehicles.

His driver rounded the block and up Olivia's drive.

Since her garage door was open, Nutsbe pointed. "How about you pull in there?" After they parked, the driver handed Nutsbe Olivia's keys and headed over the lawn to catch his ride.

"All right, Beowolf." Nutsbe turned to let Beowolf out. "We're going to see Olivia. And you're going on a blind date with Olivia's pupper, Henrietta." Nutsbe cleaned off the drool and then gathered the lead as Beowolf made his way out of the back, lifting one back leg and then the other to stretch and kick. "I expect you to be a gentleman."

Nutsbe strode up the walk and stood outside the raspberry door, pressing the bell that could be heard outside. The door color was even brighter and more obnoxious close-up, to the point of being comical. A tickle of laughter curled his lips as Olivia opened the door.

"Oh!" she said, stepping back. "You've changed already."

Nutsbe stood on the porch while Beowolf sniffed around and got comfortable. "I have a shower at my office, and I keep changes of clothes handy."

Olivia turned with a come-on-in swoop of her hand. "I'm obviously not as lucky." She walked down the hall past the formal living room on the right and the dining room on the left, decorated with simple lines and muted colors. She headed down the hall toward the back of the house. "How is it you have Beowolf with you? I thought he lived at the kennel?"

"He's having a sleepover, in case the docket updates, and we're on for the morning. It's just easier."

"I have dinner keeping warm in the oven." She stopped by a child's safety gate and squatted. "Hi, Beowolf." She scrubbed his sides. "Come meet Henrietta."

She let them sniff each other through the child gate.

Nutsbe noticed her suit jacket lying over Henrietta's bed.

"Still puke spewed." Olivia had followed his gaze. "I gave it to Henrietta before you came so she could smell you in her house and, luckily Beowolf, too. That way, she could get used to everyone's scents. My friend Jaylen did that when she brought her newborn home, and her pup immediately took to the baby."

"Seems to be working."

Nutsbe looked over at the TV. "Sumo wrestling?"

"Yup. Big fan."

"Really?"

"It's very satisfying, I think, to watch someone respectfully face an adversary, grab hold of them, and pitch them out of a ring." She sent him a smile. "Did you know that some sumo wrestlers eat up to seven thousand calories a day?" She raised her brows. "Yeah, they keep their weight up as part of their job. Interestingly, because of their workouts, they don't have visceral fat to make them unhealthy. I think about that whenever I sit down to a high-carb meal like tonight's. Carbs are stress relieving, sure, but since I'm not in the ring … If you don't mind, I'm going to leave you to monitor the dogs. I need to go upstairs to get cleaned up and changed out of these clothes." She laughed. "Sorry, that sounded very nineteen-forties Hollywood, 'let me slip into something more comfortable.'" She affected a May West accent. Turning to the den, Olivia added, "Either way, that's exactly what I intend to do." Beowolf and Henrietta had curled up together on the rug. "I think they're okay. If you want to wash up before dinner, the bathroom is on the right." She pointed. "Make yourself at home." She held her hands wide, inviting him to go where he wanted. "I'll be right back."

Nutsbe found a place on the couch. Moments later, the shower was running overhead. It took considerable self-discipline to stop himself from imagining a naked Olivia with suds snaking down her water-warmed body. He reached over, grabbed the coffee table book, and focused on those pictures instead.

When she came down, her hair was still a bit damp. Dressed in black leggings, with an overly large rose-colored sweatshirt, she had brightly colored hand-knit socks on her feet.

When she saw him focusing on them, Olivia held up a foot. "My Aunt Jo made these for me."

"Thanks for having me for dinner." He stood. "You sure you want me to stay? It's been a hell of a day," Nutsbe said.

"I'd like you to stay. Mostly for the company," she wandered toward the kitchen, "but there's also my childhood compulsion." She smiled over her shoulder at him. "Even if I'm not doing the cooking myself, it's what we do in my family. Sick? Here's food. Sad? Here's food. Celebrating? Here's food. That way, we don't have to find the right words." She pressed her lips together and looked unhappy with what she'd just said. "Let me try that again. Thank you for your company. Also, if it's not food, I don't know how to thank you for all the ways you've made things better for me and Henrietta over the last couple of days, even though I seem to be the pivot point for putting you in bad situations. I feel both guilty and humbled."

"You're okay, Olivia," Nutsbe said gently. "It's okay."

She blinked at him.

"Just as long as you aren't crying. Everything's okay."

"To that last point, you need to brace yourself," Olivia said, moving to the counter, opening the cupboard, and reaching for the dinner plates. "I got word we're back in court tomorrow morning. I called Candace, and she said she'll go if Beowolf is there." She handed them off to Nutsbe, who put them on the table. "She has a subpoena to show up, but that doesn't mean she won't run away if she feels too vulnerable. And she is key to this case."

"I'm glad she feels Beowolf is a help." He put the plates on the table. "I'll head to her house in the morning." He searched along the line of drawers. "Where do you keep the cutlery?"

"Here in this drawer." Olivia bumped her hip against the counter and stepped out of his way. "Napkins below."

"Hopefully, there will be no tears tomorrow, something else instead—righteous indignation, fury. Those are good emotions to have."

Olivia dumped the salad from the takeout container into a salad bowl. "Can you get the dressing? Fridge. Top shelf, right."

Nutsbe turned as she leaned over the oven to pull out the lasagna pan and enjoyed a momentary glance at her heart-shaped ass before turning back to set the table.

They sat, and for a long, comfortable time, they ate in silence.

"Where are your freckles from?" Nutsbe stood to take their empty plates to the sink.

"You mean DNA-wise? No idea. I'm a mutt." She wiped her mouth. "What about you? Where is Crushed from?"

"It was Havaror," Nutsbe returned for the salad dressing, then headed to the fridge, "an old Norse name."

"I don't get it." She canted her head. "How did Havaror become Crushed?"

Nutsbe scratched his thumb along his jaw. "The family story goes that on Ellis Island when they asked my many greats grandfather for his name, he didn't understand, so he said the last English word he'd heard. We think someone might have yelled, 'I'm getting crushed!' as they left the boat. And so when they asked him something, he just said that."

"Crushed." She looked at him, processing. "Crushed?" Olivia laughed. "That's spectacular. That's an amazing story. Which do you like better, Havaror or Crushed?"

He winked. "I think my many-greats grandfather crushed it when picking a new name."

"Cute." She stood and pushed her chair, turning to stand

in front of Nutsbe. "But you know for sure it was Havaror?" Her head tipped back to hold his gaze.

"We have the family papers," he said.

"Havaror. I wonder what it means. Something like thatcher or blacksmith. It means guardian defender."

"Of course it does." She reached out and put a hand on his arm. Took a step closer as she laughed. "Oh, wait. You're not kidding, are you?"

"Nope." He lifted a lock of her hair and twirled it around his finger. "I like the smell of your shampoo. It smells fresh, like the islands and cocktails on the beach."

"I—" She smiled.

Nutsbe had wanted to taste that smile since he'd met her.

"My last name is Gladstone. I don't think I have a story." She blinked long lashes.

He was close enough now to see the gold and navy flecks in her blue eyes. Her lids closed, and as she pressed up onto her toes, her breasts brushed along his chest. His dick was damned aware of her warm pressure, the softness of her curves. He moved his hands to her hips, wrapping them in his grip and pulling her in tighter. As she lifted higher, bringing her mouth closer to his, Nutsbe lowered his head and slowly swept his lips over hers, feeling the tingle of the barely touching kiss.

Olivia gave the tiniest gasp, a sip of air.

Her hands splayed across his back, holding him in place, pulling him tighter, waiting for more.

Nutsbe glided his palms up her sides, dipping at her tiny waist. Brushing her hair from her face, he cupped her cheeks.

Once again, he skimmed his lips over hers. The soft warmth teased his senses.

Pressing her hips to him, Olivia trapped his cock against

her stomach, humming a needy "mmm" that made his entire body vibrate with expectation.

Her eyes shut; her breath was feathery against his skin.

Tangling his fingers into her hair, tugging gently until she moaned. This time, he held the kiss until her mouth opened to him. Supporting her head in the palm of his hand, he deepened the pressure, his tongue finding hers and letting her decide what felt good.

Need washed over Nutsbe's skin.

It was a disorienting kiss. This kiss was velvet and starlight. It was the kiss of belonging, a kiss that defied any expectation that he might have entertained. It was both lust and redemption. He wanted to explore those sensations and understand why *this* kiss was different than all the others he'd had.

And he also didn't want her to think he was a horny teen without finesse or self-control. He couldn't imagine that she was experiencing the euphoria that sang through his body. So he pulled his emotions inward.

Heart racing, Nutsbe lowered his forehead to hers. It was the best he could do while he regained some semblance of emotional balance.

And Nutsbe was gratified that he wasn't the only one thrown for a loop. Olivia moved her hands to his biceps and clung unsteadily.

"Oh." She exhaled, raising her head and blinking at him.

He wasn't to a place yet where words would come. He tried to read Olivia's eyes, where emotions swirled.

And then, she, too, seemed to retract the surface emotions. "Uhm. Thank you. That was nice. Really nice." She lowered herself to stand flatfooted. She seemed to be listening to her inner dialogue. What she shared with Nutsbe was, "But I have to tell you, my life is complicated right now

—well, usually. But, in particular, right now." Her hands moved from his arms to lay flat against his chest—both connected and distancing.

Surely, she could feel his heart thrumming under her fingers.

"Yeah, I got that impression." Nutsbe struggled to sound casual. He needed to accept the boundaries she was nailing into place.

"So you'd understand if I said that was a really nice kiss. *Really* nice."

"I agree, really nice." This was the brush-off.

"Okay." She took a step back but left her hands where they were. "So we understand each other?"

"Olivia, it's okay." He smiled. He wanted her to experience zero pressure from him. God knew she was right. After what Kennedy had shared about her involvement with terrorists, the case she was trying, the divorce from a fugitive, the sniper—who had the mental space for a new relationship? He was proud of her that she knew her capacity. "We can be friends and neighbors who share a backyard. Oh, hey." He reached into his pocket and pulled out the radio collar for Henrietta. "My next day off, I'll put in a doggy door and teach Henrietta how to go in on her own. On rainy days, you can send her over to my yard to play without you getting wet. She just needs to learn a command, and she can get herself through the gate and stay safely inside until you come to get her."

Olivia dropped her hands. "Nutsbe, please stop being so nice." She took another step back. "Stop with your problem-solving and your consideration." Her hands came up, and she shook them. "I'm not used to it, and it's throwing me off balance."

"Okay." Nutsbe slid the collar back into his pocket.

"No." Olivia put her hands on her head and spun in a circle, then stopped and closed her eyes. Nutsbe waited as she took a breath. It had been a hell of a day for her. And he had no intentions of adding to her mental load.

When she focused on him again, she said. "Thank you for the collar. I'd really like that collar, and I really like you."

"And you really liked the kiss." He smiled. He got it. At least, he thought he did. She was asking for time. His system was doing weird tumbles and flips.

"Yes, I did," she said, lowering her hands to grip them in front of her.

"But it's bad timing." He sent her a slow smile and a shrug. She really was just so damned beautiful.

"That's it?" Olivia asked, her voice bright with shock.

"Was there something more I should say?" Nutsbe slid his hands into his pockets, hoping to make his pants lay flat. His dick hadn't gotten the message that it wasn't playtime.

"Yes, of course. You should tell me that I'm losing out. You're supposed to ask me if I understand how spectacular you are—which, by the way, I do. You should be asking if I know what a catch you are. Then, when I don't change my mind, you're supposed to escalate to 'you're a frigid c-word.'"

Nutsbe's hands curled into fists. "Men say that to you?"

"Men have been pulling that from the beginning of time." She pulled out a chair and fell into it. "I thought you had sisters."

"I think they keep those conversations from me." Yeah, sitting would help. Nutsbe moved to his chair as he said, "I might be overly protective of my family."

"Tad bit?" She winked.

"I remember my sisters talking about a scene in that book they all like—Pride and Prejudice."

"I *love* that novel."

"Funny, I've never mentioned that book without the woman I'm speaking to saying that." Nutsbe smiled and popped his brows. "I know the scene that proves your point."

"Yeah?"

"The weaselly guy was at the breakfast table. The whole family had to leave so he could have privacy to ask the woman—"

"Elizabeth."

"Right. To marry him. But he was doing it like a foregone conclusion that she'd say yes. And he couldn't fathom that she said no."

"That scene, and then later on, the not-so-weaselly hero, Mr. Darcy, did the same thing, only worse."

"How could it be worse?" Nutsbe asked. "I didn't finish watching the movie."

"Darcy basically said, 'You're beneath me. Everyone would be horrified by our betrothal, but I'm willing to put aside your inferiority.'"

"Inferiority?" Nutsbe's brows drew sharply together. "Are you kidding me right now? The hero character said that?"

"He told Elizabeth that despite her inferiority, he was willing to marry her because he loved her most ardently."

Ardently, that was the word. That was what happened; the sensation of that kiss was ardor. That's what that word felt like, all-consuming. Nutsbe pressed his lips together as he studied Olivia's face, the friendliness of her freckles, the intelligence in her eyes. "And women like this book? Wow, what a jackass."

"Right?" She traced her finger over his knuckles, then slid her hand into his, looking down at their laced fingers. "I think women like that book because Darcy realizes how much of a jerk he had been. He was contrite, and he worked hard to redeem himself." She looked up and held Nutsbe's gaze. "Which, in my experience, almost never happens. So there's that."

They sat there looking into each other's eyes, grinning like idiots.

Nutsbe wanted to pull her into his lap, to feel her head on his shoulder, to wrap her in his arms and hold her tightly. Yeah, *protectively*.

Something genuine, and scary, and perfect was going on between them.

And Nutsbe hoped against hope that whatever big and bad was out there, showing up in their lives, it would aim directly at him and *not* at Olivia.

26

Olivia

After another night of tossing and turning, Olivia, dressed in her court suit and tennis shoes, moved quickly down the road behind an exuberant Henrietta.

"I'm up because my kid can't sleep once the neighbor's rooster starts crowing." Jaylen yawned. "Why are you up? Did you have trouble sleeping from everything that went on yesterday? I'd be having nightmares."

"I'm walking Henrietta. Then, I need to get to the courthouse early enough to find a parking spot. I'll tell you, my whole nervous system has been way off since yesterday. I need a reset. Thank god for Nutsbe and Beowolf. Just immense heart-full gratitude. They at least knew what they were doing. I think my best metaphor is that I was a stick just riding the current, swept past any rocks or obstacles."

"Poetic. Picturesque. Go with the flow."

"Exactly. And that flow kept me from any harm. I trusted

it. Was it consistently bad?" Olivia asked. "Absolutely. Did anything bad happen to me?"

"Scraped knees."

"The ache didn't start until bed last night, and, if I'm being honest, that whole bandaging scene was well worth the pain."

"Sort of a reverse sexy-nurse scene. So now you can understand the appeal."

"Absolutely. But I will tell you, my mind raced all night." Olivia sent a glance over her shoulder when a car door slammed. "Not about yesterday, but about Mickey and my cases. I'm worried about my aunt and that she'll stay safe. Just wrung out. Going this long without sleep is breaking my brain."

"I'm sorry. I remember the days when Tilly was new, and she didn't sleep but for two hours at a stretch. I thought my brain was melting inside my skull. A very uncomfortable sensation."

Olivia stopped as Henrietta sniffed the stop sign and crouched for a ladylike pee. "Yeah, just have a lot on my mind. Nothing as precious as a sweet Tilly to care for."

"So, how's Nutsbe?" Jaylen's voice was a teasing lilt.

"Fine, I guess." Olivia whipped her head around as a car passed by. Granny-aged driver, nothing dangerous there. She realized she'd expected it to be the boogeyman.

"What's that in your tone?"

Olivia let Henrietta pull her lead to get them walking again. "Nothing."

"Olivia! You kissed him, didn't you?"

Olivia didn't answer. The emotions from yesterday were humming through her system.

"Boo, he had terrible breath?" Jaylen whispered.

"No."

"He sucked on your tongue like a vacuum cleaner? Remember that guy in the frat, the pre-med guy that made your tongue ache for days after?" Jaylen asked.

"I remember, and no."

"It was like kissing your brother, just a no-go?"

Olivia sighed. She knew Jaylen wasn't going to stop. "I don't have a brother to reference, but in my imagination, *eww*."

"Yeah, pretty much. I kissed a guy once, and it was like kissing a brother. And to be honest, you never know—Tilly, no, ma'am! Tilly, we do not stick our fingers up the goat's nose. Leave Zygoat's boogers alone, please." With a heavy exhale, Jaylen focused back on Olivia. "To the whole date your brother thing, did you know Iceland has an app to keep you from doing the nasty with a first cousin?"

"They need an app for that?"

"The country's so small—three hundred thousand people or so—and almost all of them pool near the capital. There were so many accidental familial hookups that they made an app. In English, it translates to 'incest protector,' or something like that."

"How can the app tell? I mean, photo identity wouldn't work, right?" Olivia asked.

"You bump phones together. 'Tap the app before you tap that.'"

"Gross."

"Yeah, well, worse if you found out that guy you've been screwing around with is cousin Olaf or something. Can you imagine?" Jaylen asked.

"Wouldn't their family names clue them in?" Olivia saw the neighborhood gossip walking her schnauzer, waving a hello hand in the air. Olivia pretended not to notice and turned around, dragging Henrietta away from the delicious smell she was snorting. "Sorry, Hen. I'll let you sniff that tomorrow." Once they'd picked up their pace, Olivia said. "I'm assuming you looked up Icelandic naming conventions. And for anyone else, I'd think they were bored out of their mind to have done that."

"I am bored out of my mind. Thank you for noticing. Your calls throughout the day are my touchstones of sanity." Jaylen laughed. "My *glad*stones. Get it?"

"Cute. Yeah, but Jaylen, this is something you'd do anyway, chase a detail down the rabbit hole."

"Guilty. Okay, in Iceland, there are traditionally no family names. It's usually the dad's first name plus son or daughter added to the end. So I'd be Jaylen Geraldsdottir, and you'd be Olivia Darensdottir."

"Yeah, I like Gladstone better. By the way, you were right. Nutsbe's last name was changed at Ellis Island. It was some Nordic name meaning protector."

"He told you that?"

"Yes, but I looked it up, and he was right."

"See? You do the rabbit thing, too. In the end—Tilly, don't lick that frog, please. Put it down. We look, don't touch —you tried to throw me off the subject of Nutsbe, yet here you are circling around."

"He's too good," Olivia said, starting up her drive. "I don't trust it."

"Teeth pulling it is. Prior to this kiss, did Nutsbe make any advances on you, something besides being neighborly that makes you think he's not too trustworthy? Love bombing you? Gaslighting you? Telling you how great he is?"

"No. Nothing." Olivia fished her keys from her pocket.

"Do you think he likes you?"

She slid the key into the lock and opened the door, letting Henrietta in first before she turned to scan the neighborhood.

She still had bogeyman vibes, which made sense, given how her week went. "Hard to tell."

"Why?"

"Cause he's not love bombing, gaslighting, or trying to convince me he's the best thing that ever walked into my life." Olivia chuckled as she shut the door behind her.

"Okay, get to the juicy stuff. Who kissed whom?"

"I kissed him," Olivia admitted.

"The cad!"

"Stop." She felt guilty about it.

"Did he reciprocate?"

"It was a nice kiss." Olivia unhooked Henrietta and put the lead on its peg. "Right track, wrong timing." *Damn the timing.* "But very nice. *Too* nice."

"How can a kiss be *too* nice? I hear a *tad* bit of regret in your voice. Get it? Tad bit—"

"Yeah, I got it. Well shoot," Olivia moaned. "I've been doing that to him all along."

"What?"

"The tad thing," Olivia said. "A tad bit this, tad bit of that, it's embarrassingly obvious."

"Low-hanging fruit."

"I thought it was kind of intimate, private jokey." Olivia slid into her heels, grabbed her bag, and headed out the door to court. "But no, it's got to be everyone and every day. And he just smiled and acted like I was a clever girl."

"'Cause you are. And you're tired," Jaylen said sympathetically. "You've had motorcycles."

Olivia's phone vibrated.

"Yeah, and I have Steph ringing in. Let me grab that. I'll call you later. Love you."

Fobbing her garage door open, Olivia climbed under the steering wheel as she swiped the call with her boss. "Hey,

Steph. Good morning." She slammed the door shut and quickly locked it.

"Good morning. Heading to court?"

"I am." Olivia pressed the button, and her engine hummed. She'd be driving on four safe wheels, thanks to Nutsbe. It had been considerate of him to step in and handle it. That wasn't something Olivia had experienced with a man before, generosity of time and skill. She kind of liked it.

"So I'm calling with bad news," Steph said.

Olivia stalled, her heart racing. She said on an exhale, "Crap. Is it?"

"They found his body. The police are, of course, treating it like a crime scene. I'll get an autopsy report when it's completed. Reminder, you're on a cellphone."

"I'll be careful And also, crap! Crap! Crap!" Olivia banged her fist on the steering wheel. "To be clear, this is—*was* the person who hasn't attended our appointments these last few days?"

"I'm sorry, yes."

"Okay. Well, that's horrific." Beyond that, Olivia didn't have time to process. She had to put her emotions on a shelf until later. Right now, Candace needed her to focus on keeping Offsed in jail. Putting her car in reverse, Olivia asked, "Are the others okay?"

"I checked on them this morning. They're scared and regretful that they're cooperating."

"But it was cooperate or go to prison until they were decrepit old men. This is the find-out stage of FAFO." Olivia shifted to drive and started down the road before she remembered her to-go cup of coffee on the table next to her breakfast burrito. She could really use the boost of caffeine. Too late now. "Do you think they need to be in protective custody? Do you think we need them in the witness protection program?"

"Very good questions. I'd like to talk to you about that when you're in the office, and we can be specific." Steph paused and then changed her tone from business to personal. "So what's going on? You sound nervous."

"I'm off balance from the string of violent events. I was in the parking lot when the sniper shot Judge Greenway."

"Are you kidding me, Olivia? You were there? I assumed you were in court during all that. Are you okay?"

"Scraped knees from when the court support dog team dragged me to the ground. They probably saved my life, Steph." Olivia stopped and blinked. *Yeah, they almost certainly saved my life. Whew! That's a lot to take in.* Olivia cleared her throat. "And then, on the way to the Iniquus Security campus, our car was ambushed. Nutsbe, that's the dog handler, was like a movie stunt guy, getting us through that. It was a scene straight out of Hollywood."

"Ambushed?" Steph's voice sounded lost.

"The police say it's a new carjacking tactic where they stop in the middle of the underpass and pull guns on the driver."

"Guns, Olivia?" Steph exhaled. "Again? Same day?"

"Same hour. We went from one crime scene straight into the next. The police arrived within a few minutes of our escape. They found the attacker's abandoned car, making a traffic jam. That car was undrivable—Nutsbe ripped their doors off when he got us out of there. The five criminals got away. The police said the car they were using had been carjacked earlier in the day. That victim is in the hospital with a gunshot wound to the hand. They'll recover. It's probably on the news or in the papers."

"I don't know what to say."

"The police towed the other car back to headquarters for their CSI to go over," Olivia added. "Hopefully, that will come up with fingerprints to identify the crew, and they can be found and taken off the streets before they teach others this tactic."

"How do you know all this?" Steph asked. "I'm on the Internet, and the story isn't readily found."

"I was at Iniquus Headquarters to answer some questions about the sniper. It seems their organization has contacts everywhere. Nutsbe was working the phones and then shared what he found out."

"Wait, you were on the grounds of the secretive Iniquus Security Headquarters?" Steph said with a bit of excitement, a bit of jealousy, and a bit of curiosity in her voice. "Who gets to see that? No one. What was it like?"

"Interesting. The exterior is very country club, with southern charm. Inside, it's modern, with clean lines and no clutter. There's a solid hum of good guys doing good things—that's the best I can do right now to describe it. Anyway, the Alexandria detectives said that this attack fits a known M.O."

"You've said that twice. Did you think that someone was coming after you?"

"I have a bunch of targets on my back, and we lost our witness, so that's not paranoia."

"No. You've had one hell of a week," concern colored Steph's voice, "personally and professionally."

"I think I'm full. Though I will say, I'm getting a better perspective of what it is to have life disrupted by criminals—most certainly to a lesser extent than how my witnesses are typically affected," Olivia said. "Right now, I'm focused. I'm going to go hold this trial together with my one witness who, unfortunately, but understandably, has wobbly knees."

Beowolf

"The dog is going to be there?"

"I sure hope so." Olivia pulled to a stop at the light, and her phone pinged. She looked down to a window that said: **Unknown tracking device detected.** She blinked at it.

"Okay. Did they serve Mickey-shit-for-brain's yet?" Steph asked.

"Nope. They can't find him."

"Maybe he went on vacation?"

Olivia lifted her phone and looked at the warning. What did that mean? "I checked when I woke up this morning, and there's nothing in the police system." She squeezed the buttons to take a screenshot, then settled the phone back in her cup holder as she followed traffic through the green light. "Would be weird for him to go on vacation just before our court case and without telling work. He's missed his second day without a call in."

"How worried are you about what he could be up to?"

"Worried enough. On the way home from Iniquus yesterday, I bought a burner phone and called my Aunt Jo from the parking lot, well away from my car. Paranoid or not, I don't want her traced, and I don't know who Mickey is friendly with and what skills they have—putting secret apps on my phone or what have you." Obviously, Olivia was right to have taken that extra step. *Unknown tracking device?*

Mickey knew where she lived and worked. He could easily look up her court schedule. He might have an app on her phone to find her if he found Aunt Jo first. Or maybe to trace her to her aunt. That could be what that warning was about.

Another possibility was that last night, while he was driving her car, Nutsbe had put something on her vehicle to protect her—so he could watch out over her and forgot to mention it at dinner. That would be an out-of-character thing to do. Nutsbe had seemed forthright in every interaction. Still, she'd met him Monday, and here it was Wednesday. Could that be right? She'd known him for about forty-eight hours? That was a mind-blowing realization.

All the same, she'd ask him at some point that day.

"Sorry for your crappy week," Steph said.

"Yup. And you, sorry for your crappy week, too," Olivia said with a sigh. "I'll be by the office after court to discuss that. Thank you for letting me know about our witness."

Parked, Olivia glanced in the mirror and deemed her appearance acceptable. Then, she stuck her phone in her pocket and slid her briefcase along as she exited the car.

There was no line at security, and she breezed through with a flash of her court paperwork, allowing her phone. And right now, Olivia clung to it like a lifeline. Yesterday's sniper hell went so much better than it might have because of that approval. At least Nutsbe was able to communicate with help. Olivia sent a thank you thought to Judge Madison, and hoped that his quick return meant his personal emergency was easily handled.

Arriving at the waiting room door, Olivia tapped before entering; she didn't want to startle Candace.

"No one's in there," the bailiff said.

"Man with a dog?"

"From yesterday?" he asked. "No, ma'am, they're not here yet."

Olivia walked to the security hall, waiting as long as possible.

With five minutes until the case started, Olivia returned to the courtroom, sending a pressed lip acknowledgement to her paralegal, saving the front seat for a missing-in-action Nutsbe.

The jury filed in.

The bailiff stood in front of the bench. "All rise for the Honorable Judge Madison."

Olivia lifted from her chair with a furtive glance at the closed doors.

The judge took his seat and waved his hand to seat the courtroom.

"Ms. Gladstone, you may call your next witness."

Olivia stood. "Sir, my final witness has not yet arrived."

Defense rose to his feet, trying to suppress a smile and look stern. "Your Honor, the prosecutor throughout this trial has been leaning entirely on what we deem to be circumstantial evidence and has wasted everyone's time with the smoke and mirrors of the *so-called* experts who have come in to testify. And now her eyewitness has failed to show up, possibly to prevent herself from committing perjury." He pressed the tips of his fingers onto the defense table. "To preserve judicial economy and federal resources, Defense asks for a dismissal with prejudice and an expunction of these charges from Kyle Offsed's records."

"Counsels will approach the bench," the judge said.

Kyle might go free?

"Your Honor," Olivia began, "the witness bravely came to court yesterday and was ready to testify. As you know, the afternoon session was postponed. I hope everything is well for you and your family, sir. Perhaps something outside of the witness's control is making her late. If the court would—"

Defense jumped in, "The court should consider the pain and stress that my client has endured, exposed to this entire trial of—and I will repeat—nothing but circumstantial evidence and an assault on my client's character and good name. Ms. Gladstone wishes to send my innocent client to prison for life and yet cannot produce a single eyewitness? This is not to be borne."

The judge turned to Olivia. "Ms. Gladstone, I—"

The door at the back of the courtroom opened. Holding onto Beowolf's ears like reins, Candace walked in, making her quivering way down the aisle with Nutsbe supporting her by the elbow.

"I believe the motion is moot, your honor," Olivia said. "My witness has arrived."

"Proceed."

"State calls Candace Hockman to the stand." Olivia sent a glance toward the jury. They edged forward in their seats to watch the procession. Olivia mentally crossed her fingers that this visible entrance wouldn't get Beowolf banned from the procedure. "Judge Madison." Olivia tried to prevent any friction as defense counsel rose with a finger stabbing the air. "A reminder that permission has been granted to allow Ms. Hockman to have a court support K9 with her today."

"K9, not horse," the defense counsel protested.

Candace's face was splotchy red, and her eyes were swollen nearly shut. She must have been crying long and hard. Olivia imagined that Nutsbe had accomplished a miracle in getting Candace here at all, let alone only fifteen minutes late.

In contrast to Candace's face, Nutsbe's expression was rigid. He looked like he was going through his own personal hell. As bad as she should feel, it still twitched the corners of Olivia's mouth as she tried not to smile at him.

Candace moved into the witness box.

When the bailiff came forward to administer the oath, Candace placed her hand on the Bible, said, "I do," and sank into the chair.

Beowolf sat to her side, his head draped over her lap, his jowls spreading wide.

Nutsbe handed Candace a drool rag, then went to the seat

that Olivia's paralegal vacated when she saw who was coming through the door.

A movement from over at the defense table pulled Olivia's attention around.

"You told me this would work." Offsed was on his feet. He was using his barrel of a belly as a battering ram, bumping his lawyer's face. "You said, 'Watch this, you're about to walk out of here a free man.'"

The bailiff was talking into his radio; his hand rested on the butt of his gun.

"You said," Offsed spat out, "if that chick didn't show up, I'd walk out of here a free man. Free." He bounced his belly into the lawyer again, and the defense had to grab at the table to stop himself from tipping backward. As soon as the feet of the chair were back on the ground, the defense jumped up. "Judge, I seek permission to withdraw from this case immediately."

Was this planned? Were they going for a mistrial?

Kyle Offsed's skin had changed to a reddish-purple. He was an overripe plum of seething anger. Veins throbbed at his temples. He gripped his hair and pulled it until it stood out wildly.

This was what Candace had described to Olivia—a transformation from something recognizable into something demonic.

Offsed planted his foot on his chair and climbed onto the table. There he stood with legs wide.

Candace's wails of horror, accompanied by the judge's pounding gavel and insistent command, "The court will come to order!" became the soundtrack for this terrifying scene.

Olivia moved around her table, dragging her chair to get some physical impediment into the aisle, separating them from this devil.

She glanced around, focusing only long enough to find Candace curled on the ground of the witness box. Nutsbe stood at the judge's desk like a lineman, knees bent, arms ready for a tackle. He had visibly expanded himself. His gaze was razor sharp.

Nutsbe was intimidating as hell in his warrior mode.

Olivia blinked, then forced her attention back to Offsed, obviously in the throes of a psychotic break.

Spittle flew from his mouth as he screamed, "The little shit will say I committed a crime. I committed *no* crime!" He grabbed the front of his shirt and tore it open, ripped it down his arms, and off. He whipped the cloth, making cracking sounds as he smacked the table.

The bailiff had his gun in his hand and stood between the defendant and the jury box. The courtroom was full of crouching, horrified spectators. If the guard shot Offsed and missed, an innocent might take the bullet.

The jury was out of their chairs, huddling together against the wall, inching toward the door.

"I follow The Decree. If *he* desires blood, I will make it so! If *he* demands the screams of the sacrificial lambs, then I will make them scream into the night. Guilty? No!" Offsed balled his fists and shook them in the air. "I am righteous in my actions! And The Decree now says to destroy anything that will stop me from serving his majesty."

Offsed leaped.

Bending his knees like a swimmer at the starting block, throwing his arms out, he dove over the open space to the judge's bench, sliding across the surface to grab Judge Madison's robe in fat fists.

The judge screamed in surprised horror.

27

Nutsbe

When Offsed tore his shirt and jumped onto the table, Nutsbe leaped to his feet.

As he saw it at that moment, his job was to protect Candace and Olivia.

Swinging his head to ensure Beowolf guarded Candace, Nutsbe found she had slipped to the ground and curled between the chair and the balusters.

Nutsbe had hoped to just grab the women and hustle them out the back.

A quick glance told him there was no egress.

At the back of the room, the court guards tried to push through the doors. The trial spectators were trying to rush out of the courtroom. No one was making any progress. Angry shouts from both tides rose louder.

From the jury room door, the same scenario: humans at cross purposes meant no one met their goal.

Beowolf rumbled threateningly as he stood over Candace, his gaze pinned to Offsed.

Offsed's arms swung back, then he launched himself toward the judge. The bailiff, a man close to retirement with slight body and wavering hands, turned his gun toward the judge, then slid his weapon back in the holster as he rounded behind the bench to stop Offsed from pummeling Judge Madison.

Olivia hadn't hesitated.

With Offsed still in mid-leap, she lunged forward as if to catch and throw him off.

There was no way in hell that Nutsbe was going to allow Olivia to touch that lunatic. He grabbed the railing with one hand and snagged her by the elbow with the other. Her momentum swung her sideways. He slid his arm around her waist. She was trying to move forward, and he was trying to drag her back. They landed on the ground.

"Stop it, Olivia. Stay with Candace." He got back on his feet.

Stretching out a hand to help Olivia up, Nutsbe shouted, "Beowolf!" He wasn't sure what command needed to come next. In his mind, Beowolf would grab Olivia and drag her like yesterday out of the fray, pull her toward Candace, and guard them both so Nutsbe could do whatever came next.

Instead, Beowolf was around the bar, past Olivia, and, with a lunge, grabbed a mouth full of Offsed's pants between his teeth.

Just like yesterday, dragging Judge Greenway in the parking lot, Beowolf sat into his haunches and hauled Offsed backward.

Offsed maintained a grip on Judge Madison's robes and pulled the judge with him back over the bench toward Nutsbe.

Beowolf stepped back and back.

Nutsbe leaned in so he could grab Offsed's pinkies. Prying Offsed's little fingers backward forced him to release his hold. The judge draped across his bench, clinging to the lip.

Without the counterbalance to Beowolf's powerful pull, Offsed hit face down on the ground.

Instantly, Beowolf moved up the man's body, laying over Offsed's head and chest like a grappler on the mats, pinning the man with his sheer size and weight.

Offsed's feet kicked. Next, he tried to bend his knees to the sides as he tried to lizard crawl out from under the suffocating weight.

Any moves were futile.

The court police had finally fought themselves upstream, salmon-like into the room, guns drawn, instructions shouted. Nutsbe got to his feet, immediately shifting his gaze to Olivia.

By then, Olivia had rounded into the witness box, dragged the chair away, and was trying to revive Candace.

"Beowolf, good job. To me." Honestly, Nutsbe wasn't sure that was going to work.

Beowolf swung his head around. He looked like he was exerting zero energy, just lounging in the sun.

"Beowolf, to me." Nutsbe patted his thigh.

Beowolf lumbered to his feet and moved into the instructed position.

Enough time had gone by without a breath, Offsed was unconscious.

Nutsbe focused on Olivia. "Is Candace okay?" he asked, holding his place, not wanting to crowd her.

"I think she fainted. She's hit her head and needs an ambulance." She looked at Nutsbe as if he should act, then seemed to realize he didn't have a phone. She looked down at the phone in her hand and thrust it toward him.

But sirens could already be heard up the road.

Help was coming.

28

Nutsbe

"Again?" Titus had his hands posted on his hips, standing in the middle of Panther Force War Room.

"Right place, right time," Nutsbe said. "I have the best luck when it comes to being where I'm needed."

"Outstanding, brother." Titus extended his hand for a shake as Bob came through the door.

"Where's Olivia?" Bob asked with a sweep of the room that landed on Beowolf, resting between Nutsbe's feet.

"She went in the ambulance with Candace. Candace has a goose egg from hitting the edge of the bench when she fainted. Olivia doesn't want her to navigate the emergency room alone." Nutsbe put his hand on Beowolf's head. "I had Beowolf, so I came here for a debrief."

"And the case?" Bob found a seat and leaned forward, moving his hands over Beowolf's body, giving him a cursory check.

"Olivia says it will be a while before this comes up again.

Offsed is going to have to go through a psych eval to see if he's competent to stand trial."

"With Candace on the stand, is it possible he was faking?" Titus asked. "That he was going for an insanity plea?"

"He transformed in front of me. I'll be honest. It was unnerving. I've never seen anything like it. The waves of violence coming off this guy. Yeah, it was like a horror show. And having seen that shift, Candace is one heroic woman to show up at all."

"Olivia's at the hospital?" Bob asked. "How's she getting back to her car?"

"She'll take a taxi from the hospital. Her car is here in Automotive. When the paramedic was packaging Candace, Olivia showed me that a warning had popped up on her phone as she drove to the courthouse this morning, saying she had an unidentified device tracking her. She wondered if I had put something on her car since I had it last night when Iniquus drove it home from the sniper parking lot. So today, Automotive took it to do a sweep."

"And?" Bob rested his hands on Beowolf's back.

"A luggage tracking pod was attached under her bumper with duct tape. Automotive took it to forensics to see if they could get prints."

"Pod and duct tape?" Thorn drew his brows in.

"Odd, right?" Nutsbe asked. "I want to know who wants to track her."

"While that's going on," Bob said as he moved to the chair near Nutsbe. "We need to talk about Beowolf's actions in the courtroom. You gave me the rundown while you were driving back to Iniquus. Have you caught Titus and Thorn up?"

"I did. You look concerned," Nutsbe observed.

"I have to admit that this isn't something that has come up in the two years of service to the courts. We've chosen the court dogs on our roster because none of them plays a security role per se. They aren't guard dogs. Valor and Truffles are strictly search and rescue, Hairyman is a stability service dog, and then there's Beowolf."

"I think Beowolf served his function, psychological support," Nutsbe said.

"I agree. But today," Bob said, "he also intervened to protect the witness from the accused."

"He intervened to protect the judge from being pummeled by a madman," Nutsbe countered.

"I'm not saying what he did was the wrong choice." Bob leaned back in his chair and pulled an ankle over his knee. "From a dog handler's point of view, Iniquus K9s are trained to do jobs that complement their DNA. Our tactical dogs' favorite day is when they get to bite the bad guy. It's when they're best aligned with their genetic purpose. Beowolf's genetic purpose is to stop the poacher through submission. And that's what he did today for the first time in a real-world or a training situation. We avoided allowing that to happen, just like some people try to avoid letting their dogs get that first taste of blood."

"All right." Nutsbe rubbed his thumbs in circles on Beowolf's head.

"Today lit up his bullmastiff DNA. Now, if in the future Beowolf deems it necessary to protect the lawyer, the handler, the witness, or all three, I believe he could act of his own accord as he did today."

"You could train him not to, though," Nutsbe asserted.

"I have to get with Reaper Hamilton and have a talk about this. I'm not sure that Beowolf can go into courts anymore." Bob stood. "But it sounds like it was mayhem. I'm glad he was there today to give you an assist." Bob held out his hand to shake Nutsbe's. "I'll take Beowolf back to the kennels with me. The vet always likes to look the dogs over after a violent event. Thanks for stepping in and doing this, man. I know this wasn't in your comfort zone." Bob stooped to pick up the lead, patted his leg, and said, "With me."

It was a kick in the gut watching Beowolf walk out the door.

When the door closed behind Bob, Titus said, "Going back to what we were talking about. Olivia's car was tracked by a pod?"

"What do you make of that?" Nutsbe asked.

Titus pulled his vibrating phone from his pocket. "Titus here." After listening he ended the call looking at Nutsbe. "Thanks for the information. We'll do what we can." The phone went back in his pocket. "Sy Covington."

"I'm making his life hard these last couple of days," Nutsbe said.

"Our PR department is getting media calls. He suggests that you keep your head down. Let the news cycle turn to the next shiny object. This is twice in as many days, two judges."

"They have word on Judge Greenway?" Nutsbe asked. There wasn't anything in the news when he'd scrolled.

"He's in a second surgery, trying to keep his leg." He paused as Nutsbe took that hit. "Nutsbe, the man's alive because you risked your life. Another thirty seconds without that tourniquet, and he'd be gone. You should be lauded as a hero, but you need to keep your name and face out of the media."

"I would do that anyway. I don't need that kind of attention. I just did the thing that needed doing. It's hopeful for his leg?" Nutsbe asked.

"I don't have anything beyond that. Covington's office is

in contact with the family. I'm sure they'll fill us in when they have more."

"Good. Thanks."

"The pod?" Titus asked.

"My money," Thorn said, "is on hubby wanting to track Olivia's movements to get her out of her house for that talk you interrupted."

"Possibly." Nutsbe's gut said no. That didn't mean he would ignore the chance that it was right. It was on his list. "My concern is that someone might have seen me drive away in her vehicle and associate that car with me."

"Really? A blue sedan?" Thorn smirked.

"It's a stretch that I'd buy that car. The point is that I was in the car. And I wasn't always with the car. We took it to have the tire patched. For a time, it was parked at the far edge of the shop's parking lot, out of view, while the guy worked in his bay. Olivia told me that her phone flashed the warning for the first time this morning as she drove to the courthouse. The person tracking might be trying to find me. If they were, they'd be close to my house since Olivia lives right behind me. I don't want anyone to know where either of us lives. But, more importantly, I don't want some Albanian to have hired some hitman to target me and find her by mistake."

"That's what you think is happening?" Titus asked.

"I'm stuck on the American throwing those ineffective Molotov cocktails in Germany. They didn't hire the sharpest knife."

29

Nutsbe

Nutsbe felt bad in his body. Edgy, unable to settle.

All day at work, his mind churned the details from Kennedy and Finley.

The details that mentioned Olivia.

The details that focused on him.

What he was supposed to be doing was focusing on the details for the new Panther Force mission that was spooling up.

He needed his head in the game. The safety of his team and the Iniquus clients depended on his attention to details—*their* details.

Iniquus had parked Olivia's car in her garage but had brought Nutsbe the keys to return to her.

Moving through the backyard, Nutsbe walked up the sidewalk and rang her bell.

The house felt empty.

Henrietta barked a warning.

Nutsbe looked down at the keyring Olivia had handed over, house and car keys, and he doubted she had another set handy.

Surely, she'd be over as soon as she got home, and he'd know she was safe.

Walking back through her yard, Nutsbe noticed that cardboard still filled the empty window in her back door. He got that Olivia was full-up and that window glass served as only the scantest protection, but still, he didn't like that.

He'd offered to fix it. She'd said no, thank you, and—like it or not—he needed to respect those boundaries.

Still, selfishly, having a help-someone project would be good medicine. And it looked like Nutsbe saw one available to him.

Nutsbe rang his next-door neighbor's bell, and Clive shuffled to the door.

"Checking on you and Milly. I see your grass is getting high."

"I keep putting it off, Tad. All these motorcycles keeping Milly and me up nights. I haven't had the energy. I'll get to this."

"I'm not calling you out, Clive." Nutsbe smiled at his elderly neighbor. "I was looking for a little exercise and was wondering if you'd allow me the opportunity to push a mower around for a bit. That, and I'm making up a pot of my ziti and cheese and was hoping I could bring it over when it's out of the oven. It's been a while since I let you beat me at gin rummy."

"We'd enjoy the company," Clive said.

Nutsbe went home, dropped her keys on the table, washed his hands, and put a soup pot of water on the stove set on a medium temperature to slow the boil. By the time he finished the lawn, it would be ready for the pasta.

And maybe Olivia would be home.

Olivia might even like to join them, get her out of her head a bit, away from the pressing challenges of the day.

But when Olivia hadn't come over by the time Nutsbe put the mower away, showered and changed, and finished his ziti prep, Nutsbe was getting worried.

He looked out the window at the darkened sky, pulling his phone from his pocket. Just then, the motion sensor floodlights flashed on. And a moment later, his fence door was pushed wide.

Nutsbe repocketed his phone and went outside to meet Olivia on his back porch. She had Henrietta on a lead, and she'd changed her clothes to a pretty sundress and flip flops—must have gone in the back door with the cardboard.

"Hey, there. I came for my keys." She smiled and looked around. "No Beowolf?"

"He's at the kennel." Nutsbe leaned his shoulder into the post.

Olivia looked down at her pup. "Sorry to disappoint you, sweet girl. Your new boyfriend isn't here." She turned back, and Nutsbe held out her key ring. "Were they able to find anything on my car?" She slid the keys into her dress pocket.

Nutsbe pulled out his phone and showed her the picture. "Any office supply store in the country would have these tracking pods. Iniquus forensics is checking for fingerprints. I need to head back to work tonight. I have an overseas call coming in. I'll check then for any updates."

"Well, that's just unnerving as hell, isn't it? I mean … yeah, this feels scary. I definitely want to know who thought this up." She handed him back his phone. "Thanks for finding it. Thanks for telling me about it." She looked down at his uniform. "Are you going in now?"

Nutsbe thumbed toward the house next door. "I'm making

my neighbors, Clive and Milly, some of my famous ziti and cheese." As he turned back to Olivia, Nutsbe spotted a shooting star flying across the night sky. Pointing, he said, "Make a wish."

She closed her eyes and smiled.

He wanted to paint his finger down the soft curve of her neck. He wanted to trace kisses along her clavicle. To take her into his arms. Nutsbe took a physical step back and a mental one, too.

When she opened her eyes again, Nutsbe asked, "What did you wish for?"

"Isn't that the first rule of wish-making?" Olivia took Henrietta off her lead and laid the leash on the chair. "If you tell your wish, you've cancelled it out?"

He needed the bright lights of his kitchen to pull him away from the romance of this beautiful night sky.

Bad timing sucked, for sure.

"Do you believe in wishes? In fate? Like things are written in the stars?" He started through his back door with Olivia trailing behind.

She left Henrietta outside to enjoy. "The stars? I don't know. I think it's entertaining. I both quasi-believe and don't believe, you know? It's good fun. Like if my horoscope pops up in my email, I'll read it."

He rounded to the other side of the counter. "I was just on an assignment where I met a woman following her star chart to a specific place on a specific day."

"Close by?" Olivia shut the door behind her, then let her gaze wander around his kitchen, taking in her surroundings.

"She lives in Virginia. She flew to Tallinn, Estonia."

"Huh. That's pretty far away." Olivia pulled out a counter stool and sat down. "And was it worth it?"

"I'd say so."

She reached down to smooth the flowered skirt of her light blue dress—pretty, fresh, feminine. "Why's that?" Olivia asked, posting her elbows on the counter.

"Well, I'm just back from that assignment, so it's hard to say. It looks like she's going to marry one of the Cerberus K9 team, though. They made an intense connection fast."

"Interesting. She was sent by her chart all the way over to Estonia to meet him?" She wrinkled her brow. "You'd think the universe could conspire better."

Nutsbe pulled a salad bowl and one for scraps from the cupboard and set them beside his cutting board. "I think the universe did an excellent job of getting her where she needed to be when she needed to be there. Lives, many, many lives changed because she followed through. Made me a bit of a believer." Nutsbe wanted to move off this subject. He was veering into sappy territory, and he didn't want to share his thoughts about the why of his suddenly meeting Olivia after two years of her living directly behind him. So, as he wandered to the fridge, he went with, "Olivia, that grand jury case you have going, do you feel like it puts you in danger?"

"It's one of the reasons why I'm so glad that I moved here." She flicked her hand toward her house. "It would be all but impossible to trace me to that house. Anonymity gives me a layer of security. Work is pretty secure, too. Not today or yesterday, but generally."

He pulled salad ingredients from the fridge and washed them in the sink. "Except for Mickey." He looked up from his work to see her curl a derisive lip. "Is it out of bounds for me to ask why you're divorcing?

"Since you have been candid with me, I will do the same with you." She moved her hands to her lap, and her shoulders edged up toward her ears. "Usually, when people ask me that question, I shrug it off with a 'we grew apart,' but it's more complicated than that. My soon-to-be ex has some monsters in his head—I think they were there from day one. When Mickey got out of the military, he joined the police and trained as a sniper. I wonder now about the why of that. He seems to relish the taste of blood, and when he's out on patrol, he can get that legitimately. He likes the physical contact of a fight. It feels good to him. But outside of an innate brutality, he's generally an honest man. I didn't think he'd ever make a false report about you."

"I think he was high," Nutsbe observed.

"That's a given. Lots of pills. He would have gotten away with it at the police department because he has prescriptions. If it were anything else, I'd turn him in, and he knows it. Yeah, I really don't think it was the police department that made him who he is. I believe that being a cop gave him a path to express his nature. Turns out, he's cruel in small ways and in big. He's never broken the law around me, and that includes physical attacks against me. The mental and emotional ones, though, have been ramping up year after year. I'm done. My turning point wasn't precipitated by any specific ordeal. It came uneventfully, unexpectedly. I woke up one day, and I realized I'd severed our relationship in my sleep."

Olivia held up a finger and squeezed her eyes.

"I'm going to tell you. And like you, only one other person has heard this part of my story."

Nutsbe stilled.

"Your story about your grandmother … The night I severed my relationship with Mickey, I dreamed of my mom. She's still alive—this isn't like your experience." Olivia looked down to her lap, where she played with the ring on her finger. "Yeah, I dreamed about my mom and how much love she poured into me as a child. In my dream, she was lying on the bathroom floor, hugging a towel and sobbing because the person who had promised to gently care for me all the days of my life was tearing me down." Olivia opened her mouth, pulled in a breath, and blew it out. "I remember this dream very vividly. I remember saying, 'Mama, please, stop crying. It's over.' My best friend, Jaylen, says it was my subconscious talking to me, but I know for sure it was my mom. I could smell her—roses." She lifted her prayer hands to her face, spread them just wide enough to cover her nose and mouth, and audibly inhaled as if reenacting the dream. "She uses argan oil infused with roses on her face. And where I wiped her tears in my dreams, my hands smelled of roses when I woke up." She smiled over at Nutsbe. "To be clear, she shed *dream* tears, not real-life tears. But when I was awake, my hands smelled of roses for no explicable reason."

His lips drew tight, and they looked at each other for a long moment across the counter.

She blinked, lowered her gaze to her hands, and rubbed them as if they were sore.

"Do you think those motorcycles are associated with Mickey?" he asked softly.

"Could be." She looked up and tilted her head. "It's crossed my mind."

Nutsbe glanced out his kitchen window. "What kind of security have you got on that house?"

"It's a rental property, so none. Well, I have floodlights now." She smiled.

"Hey, I'm making ziti and cheese for Hank and Milly next door. I like to keep an eye out for them. They're having some health issues, and their kids live in other states. Why don't you have dinner with us so you don't have to call for delivery?"

"Thank you, but I'll eat at my desk. I'm behind on some things that need my attention."

Nutsbe was chopping celery and, without looking up, said, "I bet you're an only child."

"How would you come to that conclusion?" Olivia asked.

"Isolation in your own space is a balm." He let her have privacy to hear him say that by not glancing over to catch her gaze as he slid the vegetables into the bowl.

"What else do you think you've figured out about me?" She reached out a hand and grabbed a piece of the celery, popping it into her mouth.

"Was I right?" He picked up the tomato.

"Well, yes. So far." She smiled. "What else have you deduced?"

Again, he looked away as he sliced into the fruit. "You've got a toe on the ADHD spectrum."

"Wait, how?" She sat up straight.

"Just say I recognize it from other relationships. For example, you were very focused today." He sent her a smile.

"Of course."

He lifted his brows in a question. "Did you eat?" He handed her a slice of tomato.

Accepting it, she drew her lips in and looked at the ground as if looking for the answer.

"I'm going to guess, no. Did you drink anything beyond your first cup of coffee?" he asked, pulling a glass from the cupboard, filling it with filtered water, and setting it near her elbow.

Olivia focused on it. "Thank you." Then lifted it to drink. "I left my coffee on my table this morning, so I didn't even get that." She set the glass back on the counter.

"See? Very focused, and that's exhausting because you don't have the calories or the water to fuel you." He smiled and popped a bite of carrot in his mouth, then held out a piece to her, which she accepted.

"Knowing that about me," she crunched into the stick, "then you know why I don't cook. My mind is on a million things, and I lose track of time, which leads to kitchen disasters. Less smoke and fire alarms if I order in."

"So beyond your liking space without anyone's energy in it, you would also need space to just sit and do something mindless. What works for you? Doomscrolling in a hot bath? Cooking shows?" He peeled a cucumber into the scrap bowl.

"Not a complete mind reader. It's violence," Olivia said.

"How's that?"

"Violence where the good guy wins, and the bad guy gets destroyed. I'm not the chick you used to date who likes baking shows." There was the tiniest bit of scolding in her voice.

"That's not some chick. That's my mom and all three of my sisters. The only child part is from my observations in the military."

"Oh, okay, spot on then with your observations. I get that. It's your job to ensure your team is ready for the fight. Make sure you pay attention to even the smallest detail. You're like a safety overlord, then?"

"It's an aspect of my job, yes. The smallest factor is what makes or breaks a mission. As a company, that's a philosophy."

"Explains a lot." She slid from the stool and walked around to where the dishcloth fell on the floor. She picked it up and laid it on the sink. "Okay, thank you for inviting me to join you. Another day that would be cool."

"If you want to hang out while the ziti cooks, I can send a plate home with you to have while you work." The stove beeped to let him know it had preheated. He set the timer for forty minutes, then slid his green casserole dish in to bake.

Olivia reached out and pulled his cookbook over. She looked at the picture. "That's the same-colored casserole dish you used. And the plate has the same pattern as your bowl." Then she noticed his name. "You wrote this recipe?"

"I did." He tapped the book. "Wedding gift for dear friends. The wedding coordinator made copies for us. It's one of my favorite possessions."

"Amazing. This is amazing." Olivia flips through. "I love this idea." She leaned back against the counter while reading the printed letter he had written to go with his dish. "This is nice. It sounds like you. Nutsbe Crushed." She paused, staring at the name. "That's the first time I'm putting it together. Nutsbe is like a military name?"

"Call sign."

"Huh." She mouthed the names together and blushed bright pink, looking like she was trying hard to avert her eyes from his crotch.

And was unsuccessful.

"I lost my legs from the IED," Nutsbe said. "Everything above my knees is fine."

She lifted a single arched brow. "Fine?"

He offered her a slow, sexy grin. "Excellent if I'm not being modest." She could take that as she liked. It gave her a chance to move into his arms or farther out of them. He tried not to hold his breath. Tried to keep any tension out of his face and his body.

She changed the subject. "I was telling my friend Jaylen about your military nickname, Nutsbe."

"Call sign," he offered. "Yeah?"

"I wonder what they'd call me. Something like Olive Oil, I'd imagine."

"I'd probably go with something like Martini," he offered.

"That flowed right out, and I guess it makes sense—olives."

"Usually, it's more than that. In your case, I was putting your name together with some adjectives: classy, sophisticated, subtle cunning. I was thinking more about Bond and less about olives. I could see you perched on a bar stool in a cocktail dress, surveying the landscape and plotting the destruction of the bad guys."

"I sound a bit nefarious."

"You'd only use your powers to captivate for the greater good." He reached out to brushed her hair over her shoulder. "I hope."

"Let's do that." She smiled

"What?"

"Cocktails. Let's dress up and go somewhere for cocktails sometime after Tuesday." She took a step closer, closing the space between them, and he caught her under her elbows.

Resting her hands on his shoulders, she pressed up on her toes and kissed him. It was different this time—deeper. This was less exploration of the possibility and more about need.

Nutsbe was *not* down with this.

He moved his hands to her hips to hold her in place and took a step back. "Olivia, you set boundaries," he reminded her.

She was breathing heavily through pursed lips, and his cock stood at attention, *"Ready for duty, ma'am."*

Olivia stepped back too, reaching to either side of her, gripping the edge of the counter, her head tipped exposing the length of her neck. She was so *damned* beautiful.

"You can't have it both ways." His voice was gruff. "I'm

not a faucet that can get turned from hot to cold. You're playing with me."

"I'm sorry." She put a hand over her lips and held his gaze without blinking.

"Did you want to reconsider?" he asked gently with a questioning tip of his head.

"Yes," she whispered.

A slow smile slid into place. As Nutsbe stepped forward. He lifted her until she sat onto the counter. His body hummed with impatience.

She spread her legs so he could nestle between her thighs. He held her chin up with thumb and forefinger to read her eyes. "What is it you want from this?" In his imagination, he knew exactly what he wanted to do with her. "Be explicit and detailed."

She licked her lips then leaned to the side, reading the ziti timer.

"Right now, *explicitly*," she smiled the most wanton smile, "I'd like you to find a condom, and I'd like us to use the next forty minutes until the dinner buzzer sounds, getting to know each other intimately. And *explicitly*, I'd like you to do whatever it was that you imagined that put the lascivious glint in your eyes."

Nutsbe's dick throbbed behind his zipper.

"Your bed?" Leaning back, she painted her hand up the length of his cock. "Or maybe even right here in the kitchen?"

30

NUTSBE

NUTSBE WAS ON CLOUD NINE.

Time was too short. The ziti buzzer sounded too fast, but he had made the most of every second. *Savored* every second.

Everything about Olivia turned him on. The only thing that would have made this evening better was if neither of them had obligations, and he could just hold her to his heart. This was definitely new territory for him, and Nutsbe couldn't wait to explore.

But for now, they both had work to do.

After plating dinner for Olivia and watching her safely across the lawn, he'd boxed the food for next door.

Clive pushed the screen wide. "One of my favorite dinners, but that's between us. Milly thinks her mac and cheese is the best."

Nutsbe followed Clive to their kitchen.

"She'll be down in a minute. She's just finishing up something upstairs."

Nutsbe pulled the dinner components from the box and set them on the table.

"I appreciate your looking after the lawn. You did a good job. I like the neat lines. The boy down the street did it most of the summer. He's back at college now. He seemed to mow a patch over here and a patch over there. The grass looked crazy." Clive scowled to show his disapproval. "But getting it fixed up was on my list before you offered. I finally got a good night's sleep last night. First time in a couple weeks. No motorcycles."

Nutsbe stilled, empty box in hand. "I'm sorry, sir. What did you just say?"

"The motorcycles buzzing around for the last couple weeks has been keeping us up, not you?" Clive asked.

"I can sleep through it. Habit from Afghanistan. But what did you say about last night?"

"I slept. No motorcycles."

Fear traced its way out of Nutsbe's bowels and into his stomach, along his limbs. No motorcycles? "Hey, Clive, I'm going to leave you with dinner. You just gave me a thought—something at work. I need to go and figure it out. I hope you'll forgive me." He extended his hand for a shake. "I was looking forward to that game of gin rummy. But I'm going to have to take a rain check."

"Sure. Sure. Anytime. "

"Enjoy the dinner, okay?" And that was his goodbye. He hustled to his vehicle, slammed it into reverse, and jetted to Iniquus.

The pressing thought: Olivia discovered a tracker was on her car this morning. The motorcycles stopped last night.

Could the motorcycles possibly have an idea of the area she lived in but not the exact address? Were they roaming around at night after most people were home and in bed—so past the point of burning the midnight oil at work, as Olivia often did—looking for her car?

Olivia parked her car in her garage with the door shut. They wouldn't have found it in her drive.

If they knew that Olivia was at the courthouse, they could have placed the tracker on her car at any point from the morning when she parked until the night when he picked it up. They could have followed him from the courthouse, and when he took the car to the mechanic, they might have decided that they needed to put on the tracker. Heck, there was an office supply store in the same strip mall.

Could the stalker now know where she lived and no longer need to ride the streets?

And conversely, wasn't that the exact same scenario for someone trying to track him?

It might even make more sense.

Nutsbe also parked his car in the garage. And per Iniqqus regulations, he consistently traded his vehicle once a week. The motorcycles wouldn't have found his vehicle either.

Did that thought process even work?

Why would the motorcycles buzz the streets if they could figure out with a court docket search that Olivia would be at the federal courthouse for the last week?

Whose name was newly listed with the court? *His.*

Could an AI program, say from an enemy nation or a self-preserving counterintelligence chief, have searched him out? They didn't catch him at the police station but could have watched him leave the courthouse. And shot at him. Then tracked him when they failed.

Who put the pod in place, and who were they trying to track?

Data was what Nutsbe needed.

And data was what he was good at.

Sitting at his desk, his computer humming, Nutsbe searched backward along the route that ended in the ambush. The images at the last camera showed two riders and their motorcycles. He searched for Mickey Pauley in the Department of Motor Vehicles database. The make and model didn't line up. Neither did either of the silhouettes. He did another search for the Offsed brothers' names and images with the police department. Olivia said they were out on parole. He didn't think those men were the ones on the bikes behind them. He looked up their vehicle registrations anyway, and those bikes didn't line up either.

This looked like a dead end.

Still, their riding behavior wasn't normal. If they had thought Nutsbe's driving was erratic, it would have been easier and better to just buzz on around his vehicle and get ahead of him.

He worked backward. The first cameras that he crossed in his vehicle also showed those motorcycles.

But what happened to them *after* the ambush?

Nutsbe pulled up the cameras on the other side of the road at the correct time and located the two men riding side by side. Their license plates were covered over. Nutsbe followed the bikes along a route back to where he'd first picked them up. Out for a drive and called it a day after witnessing an ambush? He'd know soon enough.

They continued to the first camera that had registered Nutsbe's vehicle on his way to Iniquus. Instead of moving forward to where another camera would pick up their route, one of the men held out his arm, signaling a left turn.

That put them back at the parking lot where Olivia had left her car.

They would have had all the time they needed at that point if they wanted to place the tracker.

Nutsbe's phone wouldn't have received any kind of warning message because his phone wasn't associated with that car.

Were they trying to track him?

Track Olivia?

It didn't matter.

Connecting the dots trying to form a coherent picture, the bikers might have placed the tracker after the ambush when they could no longer follow Nutsbe or Olivia to their destination.

No matter whom they were trying to track, the pod had an end destination last night.

And the motorcycles weren't buzzing the neighborhood last night.

That was enough for Nutsbe to snatch his phone up to call Olivia.

But her phone was in sleep mode.

There was no option to push an alert.

Nutsbe sprang from his chair and raced from the building.

He had to get to Olivia. And warn her.

31

Olivia

With Henrietta on her lead, Olivia patted her pocket for the key, pulled the door shut, and checked the lock was in place. It was late, and the neighborhood lights were winking dark as the families curled into their beds.

There were just too many thoughts racing through her mind, and she was unproductive. Walking was always a good thing. Something about seeing nature and getting her body moving shuffled her thoughts into a polite line—well, less unruly, at least.

When the macaroni and cheese buzzer had pulled her from the post-coital bliss of Nutsbe's arms around her, she was loathe to leave that space of contentment and push herself back into a bleak world.

As she gathered her far-strewn clothes, Nutsbe hadn't pressed her to stay. He simply cleaned up in the bathroom and came out wearing his uniform. He was in the kitchen packaging her dinner when she moved down the stairs from his bedroom.

He handed her the bag.

"Thank you. To be clear, by going home, I'm not pushing you away. I haven't changed my mind about figuring this out—a way to make an *us* happen—as much as I'd like to step off the treadmill tonight, I can't."

"In my line of work, when we're in motion, lives are on the line. You'll understand where I'm coming from when I get pressed by my obligations."

And he kissed her nose.

Kissed. Her. Nose.

It was so endearing. Yeah, sweet. His eyes …

These were the thoughts that had kept her from accomplishing anything.

Olivia pulled out her phone and called Jaylen. She opened with, "It's been a day filled with wild swings of emotions. Please say something normal to me. What's happening in your world?"

Tilly was happily singing a nonsense song, and water splashes were in the background.

"Take your pick," Jaylen said. "First, I always thought those sweet gray doves that show up when I'm feeding Tilly her breakfast were *morning* doves. And I loved that."

"I've seen your pictures. That's right."

"Yeah, no. In my head, that's spelled m-o-r-n-i-n-g. As in, I've come to coo and welcome the day with my lovely soft gray dawn-colored feathers. But as it turns out, it's mourning dove like grief and weeping, which has now sapped a lot of happiness from my day."

"I'm sorry." Henrietta was baptizing the fire hydrant. It was her favorite place to stop.

"Then Tilly woke up with diarrhea this morning, probably

from licking that frog, I called the pediatrician. They said to keep an eye on her for rash or fever. If her butt isn't any better, in a couple days, I need to go in and get her stool tested. Olivia, this child stank so bad just now with whatever it was that exploded into her diaper that I vomited on her, which makes me feel like a human but also a very bad mommy. She's having her third bath for the day as we speak. And obviously, she's not asleep like she should be."

"Sorry again. You're not a bad mommy."

"Well, thank you," Jaylen said. "So why do you sound like that?"

"Just thinking that I had a word gone wrong thing too, like your mourning dove discovery. Thaddeus Crushed is called Tad by everyday folks. Our neighbors, for example, call him Tad. His Iniquus brothers, like Bob who introduced us, call him 'Nutsbe.'"

Jaylen affected an accent. "'You can call me whatever you want, just don't call me late for dinner.' Who said that?"

"No idea. Serious here. They call him *Nutsbe*."

"Right. I know. Nutsbe. That's cute, I guess." Jaylen paused. "I don't get it."

"Yeah, I didn't put it together myself until I saw it written out. His last name is Crushed. Nuts-be Crushed."

"Oh! Oh shit. Did it—did it happen when his legs were ... What's a polite phrase? Did it happen from the IED?"

"His junk is fine." Henrietta trotted down the road, and Olivia was quick-stepping behind her.

"'Cause you checked."

"Of course I did." Olivia scowled at her phone. "With a name like that, wouldn't you be curious?"

"Did you stop at a fact-finding mission?" Jaylen's voice brightened with interest. "Or did you jump his bones?"

"I did not necessarily jump his bones."

"You had sex, though?"

"We did." Olivia smiled.

"Are you thinking your usual serial killer thoughts?" Jaylen's voice was muted as she moved away from the phone.

"About the sex? Absolutely not. No."

There was a pause; a moment later, Jaylen's voice was back in range. "So he didn't get rough in bed, choke you, or insist you wear a matching bra and panty set?"

"I was very mismatched, so I felt safe." Olivia smiled wider, remembering. "Nothing kinky. Nothing violent. Lots of consensual questions. 'Is this okay?' 'Would you like it if I …?' I'm not used to that."

"What did you say no to?" Jaylen asked.

"Nothing. Everything he wanted to do was great by me. More than great. Best."

"Best?" Jaylen's voice was shocked.

"*Best*." Olivia let Henrietta run to the end of her retractable lead.

"He's ruined you for all other men."

"Shut up." Olivia laughed. "Stop teasing." She felt content, and that was so foreign to her. "Yeah. It was surprising."

"Mmm, that's not always a great sentence to say after a roll in the sack."

"He certainly has a lot of talent," Olivia said. "No details."

"But you were thinking serial killer around him?"

"You said that, not me. But also, with all my years in the prosecutor's office—"

"Will make you terrified of any human interaction." Jaylen finished her friend's thought. "I get it. Aw, look, you have a Crush on Crushed." Jaylen laughed. "You're Crushed."

"Maybe just a *tad*." Tilly screeched in the background. "And that's the signal to say good-bye."

"Hey, do you realize that both Nuts and Olives grow on trees?"

"Helpful information. Goodbye," Olivia sang, then added, "I hope Tilly feels better soon."

Amidst the splashing of Jaylen pulling Tilly from the tub, Olivia heard, "Nutsbe and Olivia sitting in a tree—"

Olivia swiped the phone to end their connection. Then let out an amused huff. Yeah, something about Jaylen's teasing felt happy.

Wasn't that interesting?

Olivia had been a stranger to that emotion for quite a long time. The best she had been lately was "head above water."

As she walked home, she wondered when she'd last thought about feeling good.

What reasonable person would even consider happiness with all the tumult tangling around her these last few days?

As she moved up her sidewalk, Henrietta ran excitedly for the porch, dragging Olivia.

Usually, Henrietta didn't like to go home from a walk. Olivia scowled at the pile in front of her door and realized a dead rat was lying on her doormat.

Olivia pulled at Henrietta's lead to get her away.

"All those years as a prosecutor can make you paranoid. It's Occam's razor," she said aloud. "The simplest solution is probably right." Two simple ideas: The rat died on her porch. The rat died elsewhere, but the stray cat she was feeding brought it to her and laid it in front of her door as a sign of appreciation. Mickey's cats had done that. One morning, Olivia woke to Goldy trying to drop a mouse into her mouth. After that, Olivia insisted on the cats being removed from the bedroom and the door shut each night.

Mickey had protested, but some things were not to be borne.

Mickey knew how much she hated the cat gifts—the dead birds, rodents, and snakes.

Was this Mickey?

That could also fit Occam's razor—Mickey was a simple explanation that made sense in her mind.

Olivia took a long moment, searching over the neighborhood.

There it was again, that sense she'd had when Mickey had been on the phone, insisting he needed to talk to her. Was it safe in her house? Was her car safe to drive? She looked down at Henrietta. Her pup had none of the posturing that Beowolf displayed before the violence ensued.

It had been a nerve-racking, emotion-jumbling day with lows. "But, my god, there were some spectacular highs."

Here she stood, feeling her nerves light up.

Were the last two days finally catching up to her? Was she overwrought?

With her hand on the doorknob, suddenly and inexplicably, home didn't feel safe.

32

Olivia

Olivia stood at her office window, pulling back the drape and looking over at Nutsbe's house. It was dark. So was the house next door, the house where Nutsbe said Clive and Milly lived. They must have gone to bed. Nutsbe said he had to go back to the office for an overseas call.

She felt better knowing he was just over the fence.

Olivia looked down at Henrietta. "We'll be okay, right?" She wandered through the house, checking the windows, checking the locks. She regretted that she hadn't fixed the back door yet. But if someone wanted to get in, what was breaking a pane of glass other than a bit of a warning sound?

Standing in the hall, her thoughts vacillated with indecision.

She had showered and was dressed in her nightshirt, ready for bed.

Olivia thought back to that fear-prickle and Mickey. Remembering her thoughts about the intuitive flashes people had before the moment of violence and that inconvenience pushed them forward into the path of the criminal, she examined her own decisions.

She had protected her aunt by sending her to a hotel.

Until her divorce, maybe she should do that for herself as well. "Tomorrow, I'll go to a hotel." She took a step toward her room, and her body convulsed. Her shoulders were up to her ears. She was frozen in place. "Henrietta, did you hear something?" she whispered.

Nope, tonight. Tonight, we'll go to a hotel. We won't take my car. I'll call a taxi.

Olivia hustled to her room and grabbed an overnight bag. "Ten minutes, and we're out of here, Henny. Five minutes." Her hands shook as she gathered her toothbrush and a comb. "Three. I can be out of here in three."

She stilled.

Were those footsteps on the stairs?

Olivia looked down to find Henrietta staring at the bathroom door and was startled to hear her dog rumble warning noises that Olivia had never heard her make before.

Grabbing up her phone, holding it impatiently to her face to open the screen, Olivia jabbed at the phone pad to call 9-1-1.

The door burst open.

A smack to her hand sent the phone flying. It hit the wall with a crack and fell silently onto the bathmat.

A gun at her temple had enormous power of persuasion.

Following instructions, Olivia walked slowly to her office.

Henrietta snarled and danced, trying to be brave and helpful when she, too, was so obviously terrified. The next lunge and the second man gave Henrietta a kick that sent her sailing back into the bathroom. And he shut the door.

Olivia listened hard.

Henrietta sounded freaked. But those weren't the sounds she made when she was in pain.

And with the cold metal pressing against her temple, there was nothing Olivia was willing to do right now except to try very hard to remember that if they wanted to pull that trigger —if they wanted her dead—it would be over.

Over might be the better outcome here, was the thought that whispered just under her breath.

Death might be their endgame. But there was at least a middle. And in that middle, she had an opportunity to survive, she reasoned. And that began with compliance.

Did she learn: Hide. Run. Fight?

Yes.

Was that going to work here?

No.

They didn't teach her in those shooter scenarios how her body would stop functioning, that she was basically an autonomic system—heart beating, eyelids blinking, the inhale and exhale of oxygen, though that was strangled and shallow.

No, Olivia couldn't get her body to fight or run, couldn't make her mouth open and scream.

She fell into the desk chair that had been dragged to the middle of her office.

She offered nothing by way of counter when her forearms were duct taped in place.

She watched them do it like she was an indifferent observer.

Somewhere in her mind, Olivia remembered that duct tape was an illusion. One could get out of it. But that would take privacy and time. And Olivia had neither. Nor did she have control of her limbs or thoughts in any meaningful way.

A gun to the head had magical powers, debilitating, enfeebling powers.

The man—in his jeans and biker boots, his heavy leather jacket, and wallet chains, with his shoulder-length gray hair slicked back into a ponytail, and the neck tattoo—sat at her desk behind her, opened the laptop, tapped the screen open, and walked over to show the security app her face. "Thank you." He sat at her desk and started looking through her files.

Olivia had tried a lot of cases. And she had learned about the depravity of humanity.

This was her midnight.

Things were dire.

The sniper and even the ambush, by comparison, felt benign.

Olivia knew that there was nothing she owned—no valuable in the physical world, no piece of intelligence in the factual world that she was willing to suffer for.

Take it.

What was she willing to protect with pain?

Those she loved.

And all she could think was that Mickey had done this. These were some bikers that owed him. He'd let them get away with some crime along the way, and he was pulling in his chit.

She was one day closer to her divorce.

He was one day closer to being locked out of his millions-of-dollars payday.

Olivia wished her aunt was poor. Olivia didn't need or even want the money. At this moment, Olivia wished Aunt Jo had never mentioned her will in passing. Mickey would have never guessed she was rich; Aunt Jo led a frugal life.

How long could she hold out against these men to protect her Aunt?

Her only hope was that somehow Nutsbe would look out his bedroom window and see too many shadows through the curtain and call her, and then …

Olivia mentally swiped at that thought, hoping to pocket it before it became a prayer—a wish—a self-fulfilling anything. No, she didn't want Nutsbe to come. Because he would try to protect her. And as brave and strong and wonderful as he was, he was one against two.

This guy had a *gun*.

And yes, seeing a problem—just like when Mickey was trying to dognap Henrietta—he'd swipe, calling into Iniquus, and Iniquus might well barrel full force their way—but could any reasonable person think they'd get here in time to make a difference?

Candace had called for help for her and her friends, but she alone survived.

Olivia hated that she lived behind Nutsbe. She honestly couldn't imagine he wouldn't come.

Mickey was a piece of shit. May he rot in hell.

Only one of what she'd counted as two intruders was sitting in front of her. Olivia could hear the other one downstairs emptying her drawers onto the floor.

Ponytail pushed a wheeled chair over in front of her. Looking at her with an easy smile. "Hello, Olivia,"

She pressed her lips together.

"I'm going to tape our little talk."

What is that accent?

He placed a micro recorder on the side table and pulled it closer to them.

Shit.

"Did you know that recently, the Middle East lost a top nuclear scientist?" he asked.

What?

"A machine gun was propped up in a parked car, and the man was killed by remote control." He reached out and swiped the piece of hair that had fallen across her eyes and tucked it neatly behind her ear. "Do you believe in tit-for-tat?"

"I'm not a scientist," Olivia said.

"That's not really how it happened. You can't remote-control an assassination like that. Assassinations are personal. They're the poetry of retribution. They should be performed with attention to nuance and detail."

Olivia blinked at the biker.

Nuance?

She'd never met a biker who would lace that word into a sentence. Was this guy in a costume, acting a part? She remembered the story of the motorcycles and the CIA. But the CIA's job was to gather foreign intelligence. In the U.S., it would be the FBI who worked domestically.

Who *was* this guy?

Why was he talking to her about the poetry of assassinations?

Did this have to do with the grand jury?

Did this have to do with the Offseds? What had Kyle been ranting about? Was Kyle having a psychotic break at court, or was it an act? Is it possible he was part of a cult?

Yes, maybe this man was a cult member.

Knowing what Olivia knew about Candace's story, she froze in space. The fear was a stranglehold.

"Do you know who did a good job with his attempted assassination?" He drew his finger across Olivia's lips.

Olivia forced herself to blink.

"There was the man in Brussels with the hostages on the train. Unfortunately, he went with only an ax. He wasn't able to kill anyone, let alone his required number, before the police shot him. He died beautifully, though. His body was elegant as it fell."

Elegant?

In court, Olivia looked at people's clothing and listened to their word choices. From those clues, she decided how best to question them. This man was an enigma. He confused her. Bird-like, her thoughts jumped from branch to branch as she tried to find a place to nest, the right tune to sing.

Henrietta was scratching furiously at the bathroom door. Her shrill bark sparked Olivia's high-voltage nerves.

"Sixty officers came. It's a lovely number, sixty. Round. I like the zero at the end. It feels complete." He put his hands on her knees. "And there was the man in Bern. And another one in Rome. These were accomplished by a string of asylum seekers who tried to leave their countries behind. It turns out that their families' pain weighed heavy on them, so they did as they were instructed. Failed, obviously, but the attempt was made."

Families? Aunt Jo? Jaylen? To whom was he referring to here?

"Do you know which country has not listened to a symphony of sadness for a while, or in decades, really? Here. In your United States. It would be good for America to throb with grief."

Throb?

He'd said, "Your United States." He wasn't from here. What was that accent? Canadian? But Canadians were known for being nice. This wasn't nice.

"Olivia," he whispered. "You know, don't you, that last year the FBI stopped a terrorist plot here in Washington."

Her case with the grand jury?

"The FBI spied on its own citizens with a digital spying authority. We waited until this year. Do you know what was happening this year? Congress is in disarray. The potential is that the foreign surveillance authority would be one of the many important pieces of US security that would fail to renew. And if that happened? We would have so much power to make so many vital changes in American infrastructure. Buildings would come down, subways taken offline, power grids could cease, and the beauty of a well-crafted assassination could be rendered." He squeezed her knees and looked into her eyes. "The House acted, thwarting our hopes. And alas," he shook his head, "our assassin was scraped up in the FBI's net."

Olivia swallowed.

Not Mickey. And not the Offseds. This *was* about her grand jury. *Shit.*

The FBI had done herculean work stopping domestic terror. And now it was on her team to put the would-be terrorists in jail.

"And so we need someone to take our assassin's place. And we feel that you would be the person to do this. But first," he smiled and tapped the recorder, "I was sent here to gather some understanding of who is talking to the grand jury, what they've said, and how we can find them."

33

Nutsbe

Nutsbe parked two doors down. He did want to warn Olivia. He did want her to sleep somewhere else. But if everything was okay right now, he wouldn't scare Olivia with lights pulling into her drive.

If he parked in his own drive, his motion-sensor lights would illuminate the backyard as he walked over her lawn.

And his gut was telling him to go in quietly.

As he moved up the street, he could see the steady glow through the corner window upstairs. Behind the drawn curtains, a human-shaped shadow shifted and bobbled on the right-hand side. Lights flashed on in other rooms downstairs in the front of the house.

Nutsbe moved up the walk and tried the front door.

Locked.

The light blinked on in the living room to his right. It went dark. It blinked on in her dining room to the left; it went dark. A softer glow shone, probably where the person had moved to the back of the house.

Olivia wasn't checking her rooms before she went to sleep. She couldn't be in two places at the same time.

"Iniquus Communications. Identification."

"Nutsbe, Panther Force. Possible home invasion. Track this phone's GPS. I'm in the yard now, making a circuit to investigate the exterior. Over."

"Copy. Possible home invasion. We have you on the board. Be advised that Alexandria P.D. is being routed to your GPS coordinates. Over."

Nutsbe moved to the empty driveway and up to Olivia's detached garage. Shining his phone's flashlight into the garage door window, Olivia's was the lone vehicle. Nutsbe extinguished the flashlight and scanned up and down the street. The neighborhood was dark. There were no extraneous cars parked along the roadway save his. This wasn't a late-night visit from her bestie.

Rounding to the back, Nutsbe flattened himself against the side of the house and sidestepped slowly, hoping to avoid illuminating the floodlights he had positioned to protect Olivia.

He made it to her back door. It was shut and locked, but the cardboard was missing from the pane with the broken glass.

Thick storm clouds had momentarily cleared a portion of the full moon, allowing Nutsbe to decipher the most obvious of shapes inside. This was a laundry-mudroom kind of space. The door into the kitchen was half open, and a light shone from somewhere toward the front of the house.

From this position, Nutsbe could now hear a wailing cry that sent a shiver down his spine. K9 or human, he couldn't tell.

He whispered into his comms, "Are you picking this up? Over."

"Our computer system has identified a distress vocalization at your location. Over."

And he wasn't waiting. That could be an angry or injured Henrietta, or someone could be doing something terrible to Olivia.

Nutsbe slowly reached his hand through the broken glass, grasped the door handle, and turned, letting it open just past the catch and then pulling his arm back.

There was the clatter of things hitting a wooden floor, someone dumping a drawer in the living room?

"I'm entering the house through the back door. Over."

"Be advised, Iniquus has rerouted closest available tactical force operator. ETA nine minutes. This line will remain open and recording. Over."

A hell of a lot could happen in nine minutes. "Nine minutes. Copy. Over."

Nutsbe stole through the kitchen, slid along the wall in the darkened hallway, and peeked to the right, where a biker was rifling through a stack of papers.

Above, on the second floor, was the droning, sleepy sound of a man's voice as if reading from a book and not engaged in a back-and-forth conversation.

Nutsbe didn't hear Olivia.

He rounded onto the stairs and dropped his hands to the risers. He bear-crawled, both to keep his profile below that banister and for stability and quiet.

The hall upstairs was dark.

His back to the wall, he slid toward the light in the next room and squinted through the crack by the hinges.

Olivia, dressed in a nightshirt, was duct-taped to a chair.

The man in front of her wore jeans and wallet chains,

spiked boots, and a heavy leather jacket. His neck muscles were massive. But his voice didn't work with the getup. His word choices made this man educated, even refined. The oddity of the two aspects confused Nutsbe's ability to process how to go forward. In a fight, you had to assess the background of the fighter—Chuck, the martial artist, was one kind of fight. Mickey Pauley and an alley brawl was another.

What was this?

Two against one.

An Iniquus brother was nine minutes out. Eight. Maybe seven.

Should he wait?

Olivia rolled her lips in and shook her head.

And when the biker stood, reached over his shoulder, and back-slapped her, Nutsbe's body was moving.

He flew through the door, grabbed the lamp, jerking it from the wall socket. In the sudden dark, the man spun to face Nutsbe.

With the moonlight streaming through the curtain, Nutsbe clocked the guy across the temple with the heavy lamp base.

The impact momentarily twisted and bent the man, dropping him to a knee.

The man grunted and sprang to his feet as Nutsbe loaded the lamp as if it were a bat and he was going to hit one out of the park. Aiming, Nutsbe swung.

Throwing up an arm to block, the intruder collapsed the lampshade. The house momentarily brightened with the glistening, tinkling sound of glass shards as the bulb broke.

Feet pounded up the stairs as the other man roared toward the scene. The upstairs man fell toward the door as, once again, he collapsed to one knee. Rising from the ground, he reached a hand toward his back belt.

The downstairs man shoved the door open, hitting Upstairs, making him stagger to catch his balance.

Nutsbe took advantage, pulling his knee to his chest; he aimed his boot toward Upstairs's hip and push-kicked him back to the door to block Downstairs from getting in.

One at a damned time.

Nutsbe, with the lamp base still in his hands, dropped his hips onto the small of Upstairs's back. The sheer weight and velocity collapsed Upstairs to the ground.

When Upstairs tried to rise, Nutsbe chambered his fist and pounded him in the back of the head and the base of his neck.

Every drop of adrenaline, every ounce of fear, every boiling degree of anger found its way into Nutsbe's fist, and he punched.

Nutsbe only stopped when Upstairs's body relaxed into unconsciousness.

Outside in the hall, there was a scramble and thuds.

A set of feet thundered down the stairs, followed by another.

The bang of the door being jerked open and hitting the wall.

Feet back on the stairs, a voice outside the office, "Iniquus. Iniquus. Iniquus."

34

Nutsbe

"I'm not answering questions, officer, while my adrenaline is rushing around," Olivia said. "I *will* go to the hospital for a check. And then, I *will* have at least one good night's sleep or two, *then* my lawyer, my boss at the prosecutor's office, and I will sit down with the correct person and answer your questions."

"Ma'am." The officer swirled the tip of his ballpoint pen over his pad. "We need a statement."

"If I'm under arrest, you can talk to my lawyer. If you're telling me, as a witness and victim, that I am required to say anything to you at all, you're wrong, and you know it."

Olivia had a swollen red patch on the side of her face. She had refused an ambulance, but she insisted they both needed to be seen at the hospital.

And Nutsbe agreed. In the small space, he'd manipulated his body in ways that he knew were problematic for his legs.

The upstairs man was being hauled out of the house cuffed to a gurney, seemingly concussive and out of it.

After Downstairs had bolted into the night, Gator—the responding operator from Strike Force—had turned his attention to the fight on the second floor, ensuring that Nutsbe and Olivia had the support they needed.

Now, Gator was outside, waiting for Bob to bring in Whiskey and Chaser, the Iniquus-trained bloodhounds. There was no visible escape vehicle, meaning a criminal roamed the sleeping neighborhood. Iniquus wanted to track him down before he did more harm.

Knowing that, Nutsbe had already pulled off Upstairs' boot and handed it over to Gator as a scent source.

"Okay, the emergency vehicles will pull out in a minute," Nutsbe said. "It's time to head to the hospital."

"I need shoes. And keys." She clenched her fists, trying to get her systems to function properly. "I've got this. Just need to pull on my big girl panties, and I'll be ready."

"Olivia?" *Man, this is a hard one.* He fought hard to keep his tone even.

"Yes?"

"Did you have panties on when they broke in?"

"No. I was in bed. I sleep in a nightshirt." She pulled the cloth out as if that gave him more information, then looked down. "Oh, I see what you're asking me." She popped her gaze back to meet his. "No. I wasn't sexually assaulted."

He nodded. It took him a minute to let that fear go. "Okay. Good." His voice was gruff.

"Yeah. Whew! Right?" She turned toward the stairs. "Okay, shoes and cellphone."

Nutsbe reached out and touched her arm to still her for a moment. "Olivia?"

She turned. "Yes?"

"When you go upstairs, sit with your phone and record everything you remember happening. Every little detail that comes to you before anyone else talks to you."

"Yes. I know that. I knew that. I didn't think of that. Thank you for that."

"Panties." He points up the stairs.

"Yes. Panties."

THEY HAD to wait until the last emergency vehicle left before they could get going.

They sat in Olivia's car with their seatbelts in place and the engine idling.

Olivia was on her phone, waking her best friend, and asking for help with Henrietta. Wheels were turning. Players were in play. Things were humming along.

Just who was it in her house? And what did they want?

He'd push that to the side until the wellness checks were complete. Everyone needed a minute to reach equilibrium, and brains could function alongside the rattle of nerves.

Olivia looked at her phone and found the number of times Nutsbe had tried to call.

She stopped on the text: **CALL ME NOW!**

Turning the phone to him so he could see.

Nustbe briefly explained his concern when Clive said the motorcycles hadn't run the night before and what he found when he tracked the ambush motorcycles back to the courthouse.

"That's how you got to me so fast."

"Not fast enough," he said, feeling the ache in his lower leg bones. That had him a bit worried. They had never hurt like that before. It didn't seem to affect his ability to walk, but he still needed someone to check him out.

The rain didn't start in earnest until they turned out of their neighborhood, onto the main road, and eased onto the highway.

The ambulance, with Upstairs in the back, was ahead of them on the way to the same hospital. Olivia eased off on the gas and let the flow of cars make a buffer. Nutsbe wasn't sure that going to the same hospital and being in the same emergency department was a good idea, but Alexandria was the hospital Iniquus instructed Nutsbe to use.

The traffic inched along. Some venue must have just let out.

Behind them, a single headlight wove in and out of the cars, sometimes coming up the middle between lanes. Horns blared, and Olivia turned.

"Get down," Nutsbe said, hoping this wasn't Downstairs coming after Olivia.

Olivia curled over the wheel. Her hands laced behind her neck.

The motorcycle buzzed right by them.

"He's gone. You can get up."

"What—"

Nutsbe pulled out his phone and pressed the quick dial.

"Iniquus Communications. Identification."

How many times had he patched through in the last seventy-two hours? This was ridiculous. "Nutsbe. Panther Force. Track GPS coordinates to this phone. Over."

"I have you on the board, traveling north on 395. Over."

"Patch me through to Titus Kane. Over." Opening communications with Titus in this way gave Titus real-time information and looped communications in so they could move players into place without disrupting the dissemination of information.

"Go for Titus."

"Titus, man, you're aware of the situation? Over."

"Strike Force has kept me abreast. You're heading to the hospital with Olivia. Over."

She depressed the brake, bringing them to a complete stop in the snarl of traffic.

"Affirmative." *What in that actual hell?*

Olivia's hand gripped Nutsbe's forearm, and she squeezed tight.

"New situation. We are at a standstill in a traffic jam on 395. The car ahead of ours buffers us from the ambulance with the injured assailant from Olivia's house. A motorcycle has stopped beside the passenger side of the ambulance and has pulled a gun. I will refer to him as Assailant One. Visual is limited by rain. The person from the ambulance passenger seat is getting out. The driver is also getting out of the right side. Assailant One is waving them to the back of the ambulance. A rescue worker is opening the back door. The injured man from Olivia's house, whom I will now identify as Assailant Two, is in the back, handcuffed to the Gurney. Assailant One is waving his gun, and all three have now climbed into the ambulance. There are now four people in the ambulance. I can't make out the activity from this vantage point. Over."

"What are they doing?" Olivia asked under her breath, leaning forward.

Nutsbe assumed that was rhetorical. He continued to describe the situation. "Both assailants are emerging from the back of the ambulance. Assailant Two has his arm over Assailant One's shoulder. They are moving together to the motorcycle. Over"

"Nutsbe, you are to stand down. You will not intervene," Titus commanded. "Let them go. Over."

"Wilco. Standing down. Over and out."

Olivia was sitting safely beside him. Nutsbe wasn't going to go try to knock a guy off his bike when a gun was in the mix.

Sirens could be heard. The cops were in play. But with the rain, the traffic, and the dexterity of a bike, Nutsbe thought it was a lost cause. They would escape.

After a moment, the traffic flowed again on either side. Their lane wasn't moving. Nutsbe wondered what had happened that the ambulance wasn't moving. "I'm going to check on them," Olivia said as she jumped from the car.

Nutsbe reached out his hand, but she was already out the door.

She jogged forward, and a moment later, she was back, saying they had been handcuffed to the gurney.

With the handcuff key in Nutsbe's EDC, they released the first responders, who pulled to the side of the road.

Olivia put their car in gear and started them back down the highway, turning onto 420. In a moment, they'd be at the hospital.

Nutsbe was glad the shitstorm was clearing.

Things should go easier from here.

But in the back of his head, Nutsbe heard a chuckle and *Murphy's Law, man. Murphy's Law.*

35

Nutsbe

Olivia walked in wearing her jeans and a blue t-shirt, looking steady and focused.

Her gaze locked on him lying on the bed with his residual limbs extending past the end of his hospital gown. She scanned the room. "Where are your legs? Did they get damaged in the fight?"

"Over there." He pointed toward the chair.

Olivia went over to pick one up and examine the design painted on the robotic's casing. A flamingo in Hawaiian shirt and sunglasses with a beer and a bong were rendered in neon colors. "Festive." She set it down. "When I saw these the other night I noticed they weren't what you normally choose. You usually have something more subtle, don't you?"

"Yeah. Glad that wasn't a sudden turn off."

"Might have been. Luckily, I didn't see them until after our playtime." She winked.

He sent her a grin. "But yeah, these aren't what I chose—

those are a research lab prototype. I'm waiting for my buddy Thorn to bring my chair. The doctors say things look fine, but I want to give my legs a break for a couple of days. Marvin—the engineer working on the robotics—will want to take those to his lab and check the data to see how his stabilizing invention did."

"How did it do?" She came to the bed, slid her feet out of her clogs, and threw a leg onto the mattress, signaling that she planned to climb on beside him.

Nutsbe budged over to make space for her. "Hard to say. I had other things that had my attention."

"So until they're back," she hitched her thumb toward the prostheses, "you'll be in the chair?"

"I have another set at home. Sometimes, I take a day or two off and use the chair, fight or no fight."

She reached up and combed his hair into place with her fingers. "Are you often in a fight?" She held his chin and pushed his face this way and that to see under the fluorescent light the damage he'd sustained. "This bruising needs a bag of peas."

"The nurse is getting me an ice pack. Purposefully, I fight several times a week for training. But going hand to hand with a bad guy? That's for my other team members."

Her thumb painted over his mouth, and she frowned at the cut on his lips. "You're always smiling," she said.

"I'm always smiling at *you*," he corrected.

They held each other's gaze for a long moment. "Thank you," Olivia said. There was a lot packed into those two words. He felt the importance of them moving into his body.

He wondered what she would have had him do other than what he did.

She was *his* to protect.

Anything that hurt her hurt him. No thanks necessary for self-preservation.

The bed was in an upright position, and she settled back, reaching for his hand, dusting her fingers over his bruised knuckles.

They were quiet. For a while, Nutsbe thought that Olivia might have fallen asleep. That wouldn't be unusual as adrenaline left her system, and she felt safe.

But after a moment, she said, "Your smile—do you ever get down about life? I get down about life," she whispered. "I get overwhelmed. Depressed. Sad." She didn't look at him and instead played with his fingers. "Today. This week. For too long now, to be honest."

"Of course you do. And I do, just like everyone else."

"You don't seem like it," she ventured, turning to lay a kiss on his chest before snuggling back down. "You're so even-keel except for around women's tears. I feel like I should present as sunnier. I mean, what have I got to be upset about? I have friends, a career I wanted, financial stability, and my health." She shook her head. "I felt mildly guilty when I said that last one out loud." She swiveled to look him in the eye, her forehead crinkled with a new thought. "And I shouldn't, should I?" She gestured toward his legs. "You're one of the healthiest people I've ever met."

"Are all my days blinking golden joy at my circumstances? No. Some days are darned hard. Painful. Sad. On other days, I'm gutted by the sheer amazement that I'm alive. Most days, it's a non-thing. I don't think about it anymore than I do the color of my hair." He took a moment, then added, "Olivia, you shouldn't worry about saying things like that around me. The sunnier part, yeah, don't do that." He scooted over a bit more so he could turn and really look at Olivia. "Nothing I dislike more than toxic positivity. You know, at Iniquus," he brushed his hand through her hair, "we're all a bunch of recalibrated special ops guys. Destroyed? Hell no. But our bodies have been through it. We've seen things, been involved in things. We're damaged from that life—physically—ears, backs, knees, repeated traumatic brain injuries. And mentally, that took a toll. Iniquus makes sure we have ongoing health support. There's a big emphasis on making sure everyone is properly cared for. Speaking of caring, did your friend's husband get Henrietta and take her to the vet?"

"I got a text. Hen's fine," Olivia said. "She's going to spend the rest of the week at Jaylen's property, playing with their dog and goat. Go back to what you were saying about toxic positivity, please. I need to hear this."

"Everyone seems to be looking for their happily ever after. And I just think that's not a thing."

"No?"

"Nope. You wake up and live that day. You're happy. You're sad. Angry. Frustrated. Tired. You're headachy or depressed. Would you really want a *happily* ever after? It would be a one-dimensional life. Where's the ecstasy of more than happy? Where's the surprise and the sense of relief? You have to go through a storm in order to feel awe in the brilliance of a silver lining."

"Okay, I get what you're saying. But if happily *ever after* shouldn't be the target. What's the goal?"

"Community. Purpose. Effort. Love, and—" He tangled his fingers into hers as she stopped him, finishing that sentence with a kiss.

Bob came in. "Sorry to interrupt." The door began to shut.

"Bob, come back," Olivia called. "It's okay."

Beowolf plodded in wearing a "service dog in training vest." He came over and thrust his head onto Nutsbe's lap.

"He missed you," Bob said, letting the lead drop.

"I missed him." Olivia bent and kissed Beowolf's head. "Hey, buddy. Looks like you're wearing a new uniform."

"Came to talk to you about that," Bob said, leaning a shoulder into the wall. "Reaper and Command made the call. Beowolf has been retired from the court program."

"What's going to happen to Beowolf then?" Olivia asked, her voice colored with worry.

"Well, that's what I want to talk to Nutsbe about. I explained to Reaper how Beowolf responds to you and how he gets mopey every time you bring him back to me. It occurred to us that you might be amenable to adopting Beowolf and having him work with you as a service dog. Reaper says that Beowolf needs little training to fill that role, mostly domestic commands."

"Like what?" Nutsbe asked.

"Bring me a beer." Bob shot him a grin.

"He can do that?" Olivia scooted her hips up the bed to sit upright.

"Open a fridge and get you a beer?" Bob asked. "That's easy."

"I could see how that might be a problematic skill for a dog to have. Especially if you've just gone to the store." Olivia smiled.

Nutsbe locked eyes with Beowolf. *His?*

"Brother, you totally held your own against two brawlers with weapons. This is in no way a sign of disrespect."

"I'm not reading it that way. I'm just not sure I qualify for using a service dog, is all."

"You absolutely do. I saw Thorn getting your chair out of his vehicle in the parking lot. There are days that, for whatever reason, you use your chair. And having Beowolf with you is just an added layer of protection and peace of mind, a little extra help. He can pick things up that you dropped, open doors, pull your chair."

"Go on beer runs." Nutsbe grinned.

"Exactly." Bob extended a drool rag to Olivia and another one to Nutsbe.

"Look, Noah performs your position with Cerberus. His stability service dog, Hairyman, is always by his side; if Hairy wasn't, a mother and her two small children would have drowned. Right? You never know when a K9 will make the difference."

"Besides," Olivia added. "Beowolf has been mopey and sad."

"He wants Henrietta's fine company." Nutsbe leaned over and put his forehead to Beowolf's.

"Would you deny him that?" Olivia asked.

"Of course not. Of course, I'll take Beowolf in as my dog. Grateful to have him, Bob. I guess I'm caught on the service dog part of that."

"Service dogs can go anywhere the public can."

"Not easily, and not his size," Nutsbe said. "How long does it take to train a service dog?"

"Not long. He has all of his public behaviors down. We can teach him to open doors. How to wear a stability harness if that's ever an issue."

"Which is all great. It means he can be in the office with me. But there are times I can't take on his care. I have to have one hundred percent focus on my team."

"We've got that covered. Bring Beowolf to the kennel or call us for a kennel hand to collect him. We'd like to keep his training up and use him for hospital outreach visits if you can work that into your schedule. He's a big hit with the kids. I think you'd get a kick out of it. And fewer sobbing women. Except tears of laughter—that's my experience."

"Are you leaving him with me now?" Nutsbe asked.

"I can. I gave him his breakfast before I brought him over." Bob looked around. "Are you going to be here long? I talked to Titus, and that's how I knew I would find you here. Beowolf was in the room when I had that conversation on speaker phone, and he got very upset when he heard hospital. He insisted we come. Titus said you were just getting a once-over. Nothing bad?"

"All's good. I just signed out and was about to dress."

"And I have my car," Olivia said. "I can get everyone home safe and sound." She grinned down at Beowolf. "You, too, slobber machine."

"Fine, I need to get back to the morning routine with the dogs." Bob stepped forward. "I'll have a kennel hand drop off supplies. He can put them on your back porch for when you get home." He bent to pick up the lead and made sure Beowolf was watching when he handed it over to Nutsbe. "Congratulations on the addition to your family." Bob waved a goodbye hand as he walked out.

Nutsbe looked at Olivia. "Look at that. I'm a dad!"

36

Nutsbe

"There he is." Thorn backed through the door, pulling the wheelchair through. "Looking good, brother. I'd shake your hand, but don't want to interrupt." Thorn swiveled the chair toward the bed.

"That's all right, Thorn. I'm going to put on my prostheses even if I'm wheeling out of here. It makes transferring to the car easier. Olivia, can you hand those to me?" He pointed to the side of the room, and she swiveled off the bed.

Beowolf came to sniff Thorn. "Hey buddy," Thorn squatted down to rub Beowolf. "I see you took on a new role at Iniquus. Really coming up in the world." Thorn looked up. "He's working with you now?"

"Yeah, after I got him kicked off his court gig. He needs a new job."

Thorn turned his back while Nutsbe got dressed and into the chair, then went to the back to push.

Beowolf trotted on one side, and Olivia walked on the other.

They were silent as they moved outside and across to the far edge of the parking lot, where Olivia had found an open space.

Olivia looked wrung out, and Nutsbe wondered if she had caught a cat nap at the hospital. She moved round to the driver's side, pressed the button to unlock her car, and climbed in. There, she was able to tap the button to open the trunk.

As Nutsbe stood, Beowolf sniffed curiously at the trunk.

The interior light made prisms in the pre-dawn misting rain as the lid yawned wide.

"Uh oh," the men said in unison.

Thorn and Nutsbe stepped forward, looked, and stepped back again.

"This your work? Kind of sloppy." Thorn's hands landed on his hips. "Do you know this guy?"

"Mickey Pauley, Olivia's soon-to-be-ex." Nutsbe wrinkled his nose and took another half-step back. "Though, that's, apparently, no longer an issue."

"No flies," Thorn observed. "This must be freshly moved. But he's been dead for a while. Using a tarp or something under him would have been polite. Rude to have just dumped him in like that. Looks like someone pinned a note to his shirt."

They stood there.

After a moment, Olivia climbed from under her steering wheel and came to the back of the car to see what they were doing.

She walked right up to the trunk and looked in at the bound, beat-to-hell body of her husband, bent in odd ways to get the corpse into her car.

"That's Mickey. What's he doing in my trunk?" she asked.

Thorn looked at Nutsbe. "Give it a minute."

Olivia took a step closer, and Nutsbe lifted his hands to stop her, then thought better of it. She needed to see. Olivia twisted her head so she looked Mickey in the face. One side of his head was purplish-pink, where the blood had pooled after there was no more circulation.

"Oh!" She wrapped her arms around her stomach and gagged.

Both Thorn and Nutsbe lunged forward, grabbed Olivia, and dragged her away from the trunk.

Hands on her knees, her whole body heaving, Nutsbe kept his hands on her hips to steady her. He looked at Thorn. "That beating? It happened on Tuesday before I was arrested. That's not new."

"The dead is new," Thorn said.

"He was alive when he left the police station. They had an arrest warrant and couldn't find him to lock him up."

"Monday was the last time you saw him around? He was alive longer than that." Thorn leaned in. "What does the note say?" He read it aloud, "Mrs. Pauley, Your deadbeat husband—now dead husband ran up a considerable debt to us. He said you were good for it. We came by your house tonight to have a chat. First time we left a present on your doorstep. You like rats? We don't like rats. You see what happens when we come upon a rat? Remember that. Second time we came by to see if you were back, you already had company, so we left this gift in your trunk. Here's what you need to know—Mickey's being dead don't mean his debt's paid. As his wife, it's now on you to pay up. You owe us 62 large and some change. We're playing nice here by letting you have the body for closure and a funeral. Might as well pocket this note before you call the cops because nice isn't usual for us. We'll be in touch, expect us."

"Expect us," Olivia whispered. Lurching forward, she vomited near Nutsbe's shoes. He ignored it, grabbing her hair back in one hand, and wrapping his arm around her to rest a steadying hand on her hip, ready to take her weight if she were to collapse from shock.

"He hasn't been in the trunk that long," Nutsbe said under his breath to Thorn. "Iniquus was looking for bugs—not flies, mind you—tracking devices. So, they did a thorough inspection of her vehicle. That was this morning. If the note is right, they were loading the body into the trunk as the bikers were in her house. I looked into the garage. I didn't see anyone there. They must have come and gone before I got to Olivia's."

"You drove from her house to the hospital with this guy in your trunk. That's some messed up shit," Thorn said as he dialed into Iniquus.

"Iniquus Communications. Identification."

"Thorn, Panther Force. I am at the Alexandria Hospital parking lot E. I am here with Nutsbe and US Prosecutor Olivia Gladstone. We are with her car. There is a dead body in the trunk. Over."

"Copy. Body in the trunk. Is it a known identification? Over."

Nutsbe leaned toward the phone. "Nutsbe. That's Mickey Pauley, legally separated husband of Olivia Gladstone. Over."

Another gush of Olivia's vomit came up after the dead body comment. So much for the nutritional value of the dinner he'd sent home with her. Nutsbe stepped closer and held Olivia against him.

"Don't." She coughed. "I'm getting it on your shoes."

"Puke, I can handle. It's tears that are the problem."

"Yup, better out than in," Thorn said. "Do you have any water in your car?"

"Yes." Olivia lifted a hand to point. "In the trunk." She quickly realized what she said, and she bent again as her body convulsed with dry heaves. Olivia tried to push Nutsbe away.

"Panther Force, be advised the Alexandria P.D. and their forensics lab have been notified. Are any of the Iniquus personnel involved in this situation? Do you need legal? Over."

Nutsbe leaned over again and said, "Nutsbe here. I am involved. I've been working with Sy Covington. Over."

"Copy. A message has been sent. Nutsbe will hear from Covington directly. If that call has not come through in the next fifteen minutes, apprise Communications. Over."

"Nutsbe. Wilco. Over." He adjusted his hand on Olivia's hair.

"Do you request continuous monitoring and taping? Over."

"Thorn. Thank you. We're good. Out." Thorn put the phone away. He turned to Nutsbe.

Nutsbe, using his hip to bump Beowolf away from both puke and dead body, said, "Strange idea of 'we're good,' brother."

37

Nutsbe

"This is Olivia Gladstone." Nutsbe introduced her to his counterpart Deep from Strike Force over the video feed on a big screen in the Panther Force War Room.

Olivia sat next to Nutsbe, her hand gripping his thigh.

"Deep, Strike Force TOC. Glad to meet you, ma'am. Sorry for your troubles."

"Thank you," she murmured.

"What have you got, Deep?" Nutsbe asked.

"Information from last night, when Gator was backing you up."

"Much appreciated," Nutsbe said.

"Glad to be there." Deep looked down as he shifted papers. "So here's what I have for you from our end."

Nutsbe looked over at Olivia. She was stoic.

Titus glanced at his phone. "Finley, FBI, is on his way up. Go on, Deep."

"About the home invasion. Whiskey and Chaser—"

Nutsbe turned to explain. "Those are the names of Iniquus bloodhounds who were tracking from your house last night."

She nodded. Her grip tightened.

"Whiskey and Chaser followed the scent from Olivia's house to the strip mall outside of your neighborhood. Cameras from the sandwich shop showed two bikes arriving together last night at twenty-three twenty hours. One bike was still in the parking lot when we got there. I had a look at the surveillance tapes. In the right time frame, a man ran into the parking lot, jumped on his motorcycle, and took off, leaving the second bike in place. That bike has fingerprints that our team picked up and put through our computer system without getting a name. More interestingly, the bike had a Canadian plate. The Canadian government is cooperating with the FBI on the case. We don't have any information from them. But the symbols on the motorcycle are affiliated with a group known for their paid intimidation efforts. The bikes' make and model are the same as the two motorcycles that Nutsbe traced from the courthouse, turned at the ambush, and drove back to the courthouse. Our AI system indicates that the body proportions of the rider who returned to his bike and the left-riding biker following you at the ambush conform. The traffic camera feed shows that the plates were covered on the road."

"Thanks for the assist, Deep," Titus said.

"Glad to help," Deep said. "That's it from me."

And they disconnected.

"So they ride their bikes to the shop, walk over, break into my house, and interrogate me," Olivia said.

"Do you mind sharing what he wanted from you, Olivia?" Titus asked.

Olivia shifted in her chair. "He wanted to know all the details of the case my team is bringing to a grand jury."

"The assassinations of Middle Eastern dissidents in America?" Nutsbe asked.

Olivia's head whipped toward Nutsbe. "How did you know that?" Olivia held up a hand. "Don't tell me, it's the magic of Iniquus." She cast her gaze around the men. "You all are a little intimidating, to be honest. At least we know the motorcycles weren't the Offseds."

"Any interference from Kyle's brothers is off the table," Nutsbe said, rubbing Olivia's hand so she'd relax her death grip. "They're in Maryland, held on armed robbery charges, and have been there since last weekend. They haven't been able to post bail."

Nutsbe hated this shit show, but it would be so much worse if he thought he'd directed his own Russia-FBI crap in Olivia's direction.

She said she understood how dangerous his job was. And now he knew they both lived in that world. He'd always be worried that he was adding to her dangers instead of providing her with his protection.

Thorn turned to Olivia with Beowolf sprawled at her feet. "According to the medical examiner's preliminary report, Mickey probably died late Tuesday night, the same night you encountered the sniper and ambush."

"Monday, Mickey Pauley attacks you," Thorn said to Nutsbe. "You both get arrested."

Thorn went to the whiteboard and wrote it out.

"He'd already been beaten," Nutsbe said. "Not enough for a tier one to worry about it. That's just another day at the office. But a civilian would think they'd been beaten within an inch of their life."

"Mickey liked the pain of a punch." Olivia shifted back and forth in her chair. "He said it woke up his mind, whatever that means."

Titus added. "Pauley was released. That was the last anyone saw of him until the trunk."

"Someone saw him before the trunk," Thorn countered. "They did something to put him in the trunk."

"Granted," Titus acknowledged.

"The thing about this week is that there are a lot of ducks, and they do not need to be in a row." Olivia sat quietly at the table.

Nutsbe thought she was pale.

"The bikes out of Canada, who saw that coming?" Olivia asked.

Nutsbe wheeled to the other side of the room, grabbed some waters and distributed them around, then moved a basket of coffee pastries onto the table within easy reach of Olivia.

The door opened, and Gage—a fellow Panther—escorted Finley into the war room.

Nutsbe lifted a hand. "There he is, the man we've been waiting for. Finley, I hope you have answers for us. Olivia, this is Special Agent Finley, FBI, Terror. Finley, Olivia Gladstone." Nutsbe wasn't sure that they'd been introduced, only that Finley knew of Olivia and her reputation.

Finley settled onto a seat right across from Olivia. "Seems like you had the golden key, Olivia," he said. "The police got Mickey's passwords from you?"

"They did." She put her hand on Beowolf's head.

"The passwords still worked. Very helpful. The investigators got into Pauley's computer and searched his history."

"And?" Nutsbe moved his chair to sit near Olivia. Beowolf shifted to lay between them and put a paw on Olivia's foot.

"They found a spreadsheet with his notes on sports games, bets, wins, and losses. His losses were up there in the sixty-thousand range. They also found a life insurance policy on his bedside table. Olivia, were you covered for a million dollars? And only you?"

Olivia's brows went to her hairline. "We took that out when we got married. If I were to die, we needed to replace my future income to pay for our marital home. He couldn't keep up the mortgage payment on a police officer's salary. And he got his insurance through work."

"Seeing the insurance papers, the detectives did a file search using the word 'Insurance,' which they located. MP3 and MP4 files contained video and audio recordings that would identify the people he was interacting with over the gambling debt. We have a trail to figure out who killed Pauley and who put him in your trunk. It's very good evidence. A lot of people are going to get rolled up in this case."

Nutsbe was tapping his fingers on his thigh.

"I'm going to cut to the chase here," Finley said. "Nutsbe's impatient." He focused on Nutsbe. "I don't know if you have a way to get this information, but Judge Greenway is stable. It looks like he'll keep his leg. I don't have details beyond that."

Nutsbe pursed his lips and nodded his acknowledgment. Stable. That was a load off his mind.

"All arrows are pointing to Mickey being the sniper at the courthouse."

Olivia crossed her arms over her chest and leaned forward. "The motive was paying off some people who were threatening him?"

"The FBI is working on it. What are your thoughts, Olivia?"

"Unpaid gambling debt makes sense. Gambling debts and a high-dollar life insurance plan—someone was threatening

Mickey; I wasn't helpful to him anymore except as a means for getting his hand on some cash. Yeah. I guess I could see that. Mickey wanted to talk to me the day before the sniper. And I told him I wouldn't do that. I could see him taking Henrietta, my dog, to force communication. He tried to break into my house, and he fought Nutsbe." She frowned. "Maybe it came down to him or me, and he decided he was going to prevail. I can see that, too." She was rocking back and forth as she spoke. "But, Finley, how did they land on Mickey being the sniper? What evidence do you have?"

"On camera, the only car that left the parking garage at the time when the sirens blared belonged to a guy. In his interview, he said that he hadn't driven the car all week. He said during the incident, he was down the street at work. And he had numerous witnesses backing him up. He walks to work. When asked who had access to his keys, he said no one. Next question. Did you ever lend your car to anyone? Answer? 'My friend Mickey Pauley.' But he said that was over a month ago. The FBI has camera footage of Pauley's car driving to the block behind the friend's house in the correct time window."

"Circumstantial," Olivia said.

"Pauley's weapon was recently fired."

"Damning, perhaps, but still circumstantial," Olivia said.

"Spoken like a federal prosecutor." Finley stood. "The case is still under investigation. We'll keep you up to date."

"Thank you," Titus said as Finley left.

Olivia looked at the clock. She needed to call the office and let them know she wouldn't be in today. Though, the police had already gone over to check on Steph and make sure she was safe. So Olivia wouldn't need to explain why she was taking a personal day. "The detectives wondered if I knew Mickey's passwords. I remembered them. He wasn't great with cyber security, so it's possible he didn't think to change everything from two years ago. That's the last I know. Other than that, I'm exhausted, and I need to get some sleep."

"Do you have friends or family you could stay with for a while?" Titus asked.

"No, of course not." Olivia scowled. "I wouldn't put a target on them; that's absurd."

"Stay at my place," Nutsbe said.

She blinked at him.

"I have two master suites, one upstairs for when I'm walking and one downstairs for when I'm in my chair. You can stay upstairs and have your own floor."

"Okay." She nodded. "Yes, thank you. For a bit anyway, until things settle down and we have some answers."

Nutsbe drove them home in complete silence. It felt good to be encapsulated and moving. Nutsbe released some stress along their route by just breathing and listening to classical music on the radio. It seemed to work for Olivia, too.

When he pulled into his drive, they sat in the car, holding hands. "Is this too much for you?" she asked. "All this violence I seem to be dragging you into?"

"Your job is dangerous." Nutsbe unfastened his seat belt and turned to her. "My job is dangerous. Your job puts you in international crosshairs and so does mine. We are not the kind of people with a low tolerance for danger. It isn't naivete. Someone has to do it—why not me? That's how I think about it anyway."

"A calling for me," she agreed. "I am risk-aware but not risk-averse." She cleared her throat. "Is that only our jobs, Nutsbe? Or is that private lives too?" She put her free hand to her heart. "I care for you deeply—what I know about you in a few days is all about character and not much about the details. But still, I feel deeply connected. One could, I guess, even call it falling in love."

"One could?" He grinned, his eyes alight with teasing.

"Yeah, that was cautious. Sorry. Here's me bravely saying that I'm most definitely falling in love."

"I bravely return your feelings." He chuckled. "Oh what a few days can do to the trajectory of a life, right?" He painted his thumb over the back of her hand. "Though I'm not in the process of falling. I love you, Olivia. Simple as that."

"Okay, so we agree then? We're going to be brave enough to start a new relationship, but we need to do it knowing that we will always be a danger to ourselves and each other."

"I don't know," Nutsbe said. "Do I want to be around when you're hangry because you always forget to eat?" He winked. "Look, Olivia, we're past the shiny expectations of youth, right? We get that there will be rough patches. I want your lows so I can take care of you. And I want the highs so I can rejoice with you. And I want the calm of sharing a bowl of ziti and cheese and hang out with Beowolf and Henrietta on the couch."

"We haven't done that yet," Olivia whispered.

"A guy can dream. I want to fully live and fully love *all* of you."

She leaned in to kiss him, pulling back just enough to whisper. "Just no tears."

"Yeah, that's my deal breaker." His eyes warm with emotion. "Other than that? Bring it."

EPILOGUE

Panther Force had the bar to themselves.

They'd gathered around the table. "Mac! Drinks all around. And turn up that news station," Thorn called to the bartender.

Cheers went up amongst the operators when Olivia's image flashed onto the screen. She stood in front of the outdoor podium in a plum suit with her hair whipped by the wind.

"Shh," Nutsbe said. "Let's hear this."

"It took years of effort to get here. But it feels so good to have the conviction. We're anxious to hear how the judge will rule regarding prison time."

The image changed to a newscaster sitting rigidly in her brightly colored set across from New York's Representative Alejandro Sanchez. "Break it down for us, Representative. What happened with this verdict in the federal courts today, and how will it affect our international relations going forward?"

"Canada and America are firm friends. We work in collaboration to solve crimes across our borders. Here in

D.C., the DOJ brought a case against two Canadian nationals in a conspiracy scheme to intimidate federal prosecutors. The convicted Canadian nationals have an affiliation with a group that earns money through narco-trafficking and other illicit money-making ventures. In this instance, they were working not only to bring in drugs from the Middle East, but they were also invested in finding and assassinating dissidents. The terrorists involved in this scheme were concerned that names and practices were being revealed to a secret Eastern District grand jury being run by Stephany Abner and Olivia Gladstone."

Panther Force whooped.

"Shut it," Nutsbe yelled over them.

The reporter said, "From court documents, we learned the Canadians came to America to intimidate and harass Abner and Gladstone into—what would you call it—like taking a dive in a boxing match?"

"That's right," Sanchez responded. "Their intended goal was to intimidate the prosecutors into hiding evidence and shifting the questioning of the witnesses in such a way that the grand jury would fail to bring charges."

"That did not happen. Even when there was a home invasion and a physical assault, our federal prosecutor, Olivia Gladstone, stood strong and continued to bring the case. She's an American hero."

Panther Force cheered. And Nutsbe shushed.

"That targeting is a lucrative job to many. The Canadians were offered two hundred thousand dollars to discover the details of the Eastern Virginia case and their list of witnesses so that those witnesses could be targeted for assassination. A half-million if they got all the information and then killed the prosecution's case and it failed to move through the grand jury."

Nutsbe reached out for Olivia's hand and squeezed it hard.

She smiled thinly to let him know she was all right.

He wasn't all right. He'd never be all right thinking of that night or this case.

Knowing what might have happened was still a dragon roaring in his psyche.

It was hard as hell shutting up and watching her go off and do her job when Nutsbe knew the dangers.

He was sure it was the same for her.

Olivia knew about the Russo-Albanian case and that the DOJ was working to extradite McMahan back to the States to face trial where Nutsbe would be the star witness. And until that case resolved, he would remain a target.

Sanchez tapped his finger onto the desk. "Now, there are some controversial means by which our intelligence communities gather information. But this is an example of how the system was put into use to take down a cell of dangerous actors who wished to commit terrorism on American soil."

"Thank you for your perspective, Representative Sanchez. Up next, the latest on the massive storm heading for Florida's east coast."

Panther Force gave a last round of whoops. Nutsbe looked down at Beowolf, who lay at Olivia's side.

Right now, Olivia was safe. And Nutsbe wasn't going to lose this moment of celebration for fear of tomorrow.

Holding Olivia's hand, he stood with a broad grin. "As we're celebrating tonight, we want to tell you all that Olivia and I have decided to get married."

Olivia's face was bright with excitement as she lifted her left hand, flashing her engagement ring. Standing beside Nutsbe, she said, "And we've decided not to wait. So this weekend, we'll be quasi-eloping. Our maid of honor and the best man," she nodded toward Thorn, "will be in tow. When Nutsbe returns Monday morning, we will be husband and wife."

"Here's to your happily ever after," Margot said, raising her glass.

Nutsbe leaned over and whispered to Olivia, "Not for us."

"No," she leaned in to him, her eyes filled with love. "We want to ride all the waves and experience everything this crazy life has to offer."

The kiss she gave Nutsbe was everything he could ever want.

Olivia Gladstone was Nutsbe's third precious miracle.

I hope you enjoyed getting to know Nutsbe, Beowolf, and Olivia. If you had fun reading Beowolf, I'd appreciate it if you'd help others enjoy it too.

Recommend it: A few words to your friends, book groups, and social networks would be fantastic.

Review it: Please tell your fellow readers what you liked about my book by reviewing **BEOWOLF**.

Discuss it! – I have a SPOILERS group on Facebook.

COMING SOON!

Better Red than dead.

THE WORLD of INIQUUS
Chronological Order

Ubicumque, Quoties. Quidquid

Weakest Lynx (Lynx Series)

Missing Lynx (Lynx Series)

Chain Lynx (Lynx Series)

Cuff Lynx (Lynx Series)

WASP (Uncommon Enemies)

In Too DEEP (Strike Force)

Relic (Uncommon Enemies)

Mine (Kate Hamilton Mystery)

Jack Be Quick (Strike Force)

Deadlock (Uncommon Enemies)

Instigator (Strike Force)

Yours (Kate Hamilton Mystery)

Gulf Lynx (Lynx Series)

Open Secret (FBI Joint Task Force)

Thorn (Uncommon Enemies)

Ours (Kate Hamilton Mysteries)

Cold Red (FBI Joint Task Force)

Even Odds (FBI Joint Task Force)

Survival Instinct - (Cerberus Tactical K9 Team Alpha)

Protective Instinct - (Cerberus Tactical K9 Team Alpha)

Defender's Instinct - (Cerberus Tactical K9 Team Alpha)

Danger Signs - (Delta Force Echo)

Hyper Lynx - (Lynx Series)

Danger Zone - (Delta Force Echo)

Danger Close - (Delta Force Echo)

Fear the REAPER – (Strike Force)

Warrior's Instinct - (Cerberus Tactical K9 Team Bravo)

Rescue Instinct - (Cerberus Tactical K9 Team Bravo)

Heroes Instinct - (Cerberus Tactical K9 Team Bravo)

Striker (Striker Force)

Marriage Lynx (Lynx Series)

A Family of the Heart Cookbook

Guardian's Instinct - (Cerberus Tactical K9 Team Charlie)

Beowulf - (Certified Cerberus Tactical K9)

This list was created in 2024.

For an up-to-date list, please visit www.FionaQuinnBooks.com

Acknowledgments

My great appreciation:

To my publicist, **Margaret Daly**

To my cover artist, **Melody Simmons**

To my editor, **Rossana Tarantini**

To my editor, **Kathleen Payne**

To my Street Force, who support me and my writing with such enthusiasm and kindness.

To all the professionals I worked with when we had our service dog. And all those whom I've met who have shared their stories about the specialized K9 services they provide in support of those in need, I am so very grateful for what you do.

My thanks to all the wonderful professionals whom I called on to get the details right as I conducted my research, especially —
 M. Carlon for her medical expertise and sounding board talent extraordinaire.

Tina Glasneck for her legal expertise (see note below). Readers, you can find Tina's writing HERE. She writes fabulous urban fantasy!

Peter Culpepper for his expertise in grappling. Peter, thank you for helping Nutsbe get a lock on Chuck to win the fight.

Isaac Kramer for introducing me to the fascinating sport of sumo wrestling, which I find very satisfying, like my character Olivia.

Wei Chu, Wei was part of a group I lived alongside in Marrakesh, Morocco. We had fun with all the plays on words we came up with based on his first name. He was such a good sport, listening to jokes he'd probably heard a thousand times. While writing the "Tad bit" jokes, I thought warmly of Wei and his lovely sense of humor. Wei holds a special place in my heart. He is the kind of friend who will go out of his way to assist when he knows how and who, like the hero in this story, stands beside you when things go crazily awry—even when it's out of his comfort zone—and I am grateful to him.

Katie Mettner — I first met Katie when I read her book Liberty Belle many years ago. At that time, I reached out to her to discuss writing disability stories, and I took so much away from that conversation. As I wrote Nutsbe's story, I am grateful for her feedback. I highly suggest you read her books. You can follow the link HERE. I'm sure you will enjoy her authentic voice as much as I.

Please note: This is a work of fiction, and while I always try my best to get all the details correct, there are times when it serves the story to go slightly to the left or right of perfection. For example, placing a parking lot and parking deck near Virginia's Eastern District Federal Courthouse and some trial details, including using a facility dog in a federal court—though, in Virginia, certified facility dogs are allowed by law. Please understand that any mistakes or discrepancies are my authorial decision-making alone and sit squarely on my shoulders.

Thank you to my family for your love and support.

I send my love to my husband. T, you were very patient when I went into my writing cave, and I appreciate you so much.

And, of course, thank *YOU* for reading my stories. I always smile joyfully as I type this sentence. I so appreciate you!

ABOUT THE AUTHOR

Fiona Quinn is a USA Today bestselling author, a Kindle Scout winner, and an Amazon Top 40 author.

Quinn writes smart suspense with a psychic twist in her Iniquus World of action-adventure stories, including Lynx, Strike Force, Uncommon Enemies, Kate Hamilton Mysteries, FBI Joint Taskforce, Cerberus Tactical K9, and Delta Force Echo Series.

She writes urban fantasy as Fiona Angelica Quinn for her Elemental Witches Series.

And, just for fun, she writes the Badge Bunny Booze Mystery Collection with her dear friend, Tina Glasneck, under the name Quinn Glasneck.

Quinn is rooted in the Old Dominion, where she lives with her husband. There, she pops chocolates, devours books, and taps continuously on her laptop.

Visit www.FionaQuinnBooks.com

- facebook.com/FionaQuinnBooks
- x.com/fionaquinnbooks
- instagram.com/fionaquinnbooks
- bookbub.com/authors/fiona-quinn
- goodreads.com/fionaquinnbooks

COPYRIGHT

Beowolf is a work of fiction. Names, characters, places, and incidents either are the product of the author's imagination or are used fictitiously, and any resemblance to actual persons, living or dead, business establishments, events, or locales is entirely coincidental.

©2024 Fiona Quinn, LLC
hello@fionaquinnbooks.com
All Rights Reserved
Kindle eBook ISBN-13: 978-1-946661-87-6
Print Paperback ISBN-13: 978-1-946661-88-3
Print Hardback ISBN-13: 978-1-946661-89-0
Library of Congress Control Number: 2024907369

Cover Design by Melody Simmons from eBookindlecovers
Fonts used with permission from Microsoft

Publisher's Note:

Neither the publisher nor the author has any control over and does not assume any responsibility for third-party websites and their content.

No part of this book may be scanned, reproduced, or distributed in any printed, or in any electronic form, nor can it be used to educate AI or used in conjunction with AI in any form or for any reason, without the express written permission from the publisher or author. Doing any of these actions via the Internet or in any other way without express written permission from the author is illegal and punishable by law. *It is considered piracy.* Please purchase only authorized editions. In accordance with the US Copyright Act of 1976, the scanning, uploading, and electronic sharing of any part of this book without the permission of the publisher constitute unlawful piracy and theft of the author's intellectual property. If you would like to use material from the book (other than for review purposes), prior written permission must be obtained by contacting the publisher at Hello@FionaQuinnBooks.com

Thank you for your support of the author's rights.

Made in the USA
Las Vegas, NV
27 February 2025